"What's wrong, Emily?"

Salem laid her on the sofa in his office. When he tried to let her go, she grasped his shirt.

Even through her clothing, her skin burned. Just like Emily to come here like this, to bring mayhem into his well-ordered existence. She liked drama. He liked peace. She liked chaos. He needed order.

"Emily," he said, keeping his voice low to soothe her as he would a skittish animal. "I need to get water."

She nodded. "Yes. Water."

Even so, she didn't ease her grip.

"Let go." He became stern. "I'll come back."

"Promise?" Her insecurity tore at him. Trouble roiled in her witchy blue-hazel eyes.

Where was his confident, brash Emily? *What happened to you?*

"I'm always here for you, Emily. You know that."

She smiled so sweetly it broke his heart. Yes, Salem was always here for her, but she wasn't always there for him.

Dear Reader,

Always Emily is my tenth Harlequin Superromance book. I can't tell you how much I enjoy writing them and living my dream job!

In this story, I deal with two large issues—the first of finding trust again once it's been broken, and the second of rebuilding ourselves after the choices we've made backfire.

In every life, there will be issues and hardships. I called up difficult circumstances in my past, when I learned I was strong enough to not only survive, but also thrive. At the time, it required a lot of flexibility and adaptability. To give my characters depth in this novel, I delved into the emotions I felt back then.

When I write, I look for tidbits of insight or wisdom to pass along through my characters' journeys and often look at what others around me are dealing with. Ultimately, though, I come back to my own journey and the lessons I've learned. These inform my stories.

I hope you enjoy reading *Always Emily* as much as I did writing it.

Mary Sullivan

MARY SULLIVAN

—

Always Emily

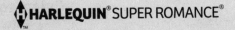

H HARLEQUIN® SUPER ROMANCE®

Recycling programs
for this product may
not exist in your area.

ISBN-13: 978-0-373-60847-8

ALWAYS EMILY

Copyright © 2014 by Mary Sullivan

Printed in U.S.A.

ABOUT THE AUTHOR

Mary grew up a daydreamer amid the pop and fizz of Toronto's multicultural community, wondering why those around her didn't have stories rattling around in their brains, too. This novel involves an archeologist and a museum curator, dovetailing with her enjoyment of all of history's lively stories. New ideas continue to pop into her head, often at the strangest moments. Snatches of conversations or newspaper articles or song lyrics—everything is fodder for her imagination. Be careful what you say around her. It might end up in a novel! She loves to hear from readers. To learn more about Mary or to contact her, please visit her at www.marysullivanbooks.com

Books by Mary Sullivan

HARLEQUIN SUPERROMANCE

1570—NO ORDINARY COWBOY
1631—A COWBOY'S PLAN
1653—THIS COWBOY'S SON
1717—BEYOND ORDINARY
1743—THESE TIES THAT BIND
1780—NO ORDINARY SHERIFF
1831—IN FROM THE COLD
1837—HOME TO LAURA
1883—BECAUSE OF AUDREY

Other titles by this author available in ebook format.

For eleven years, I was a member of an amazing critique group. It ran its course and is over now, but I will be grateful to these wonderful women for the rest of my days. We learned to write together, laughed a lot and inspired each other to be better writers, to do our best always.

My utmost respect and admiration go out to Ann Lethbridge, Maureen McGowan, Molly O'Keefe and Sinead Murphy.

Simply put, I am in awe of your talent.

CHAPTER ONE

One year ago

"YOU COULD ALWAYS STAY here with me," Salem Pearce whispered into the velvety night, his butter-soft voice a contrast to the chirrups of crickets in the tall grasses lining the road.

G. veletis. Spring crickets. Only the males sing. Like crickets, men had their calling, courtship and rivalry songs. Emily Jordan had heard them all. In her experience, men were full of bluster.

But not Salem. Not her friend of few words.

These words shocked her. Even more, they frustrated her because his timing couldn't be worse.

"I've waited years for you to ask me that," she said fiercely. "How could you do this to me now? The night before my flight out?"

"You're always catching a flight." The bitterness in his voice might have been justified if not for their history. She wasn't the only one who had turned away in the past. "You're always leaving."

The pale moon shone on hair as black as a cricket's back and sent his deep-set eyes, as dark as the night weaving through the woods beside them, into shadow. His Native American skin, honey-gold in sunlight, glowed darker in the moonlight. An intensity she hadn't seen before hardened his features.

"Of course I'm always leaving," she answered. "Because I don't work here. My livelihood takes me everywhere but here."

"You set a record this time." His voice hardened and cut through her defenses like an acetylene torch, the steel of the armor she'd spent years shaping useless against him when he used that harsh tone. She'd loved him for years, and then she'd learned to turn it off when he'd married someone else. "You didn't last even a weekend."

That set up her dander. "I'm returning to work."

"Work? Is that what you call it?"

"Yes," Emily shouted. Ooh, the man could make her so mad. "I'm a good archeologist. I do great work."

"Archeology. Yes. You're great." He touched her arm, sending a zing of pleasure through her. "But we both know that isn't why you go back, over and over again." His tension swirled around them like fog, separating them as much as age and distance ever had.

"I'm returning to my *work*," Emily insisted.

Salem stepped close so quickly, his long jet-black braid fell forward over his shoulder. "You're returning to *him*." The heat from his body chased away the late April chill.

"No." She was involved with Jean-Marc, but her work called to her.

"He'll be there."

"Of course he will. He's working on the same dig. He's my boss. That doesn't mean anything, Salem. There are a lot of people there."

"You're going back to him," he repeated.

Relenting, she forced herself to answer honestly. "Yes." Jean-Marc drew her as relentlessly as her work did. As equally.

A car on its way into Accord cast its headlights across the Colorado night and the glare turned the landscape to black and white.

She and Salem had been driving past each other on the small highway and had pulled over to talk. She'd wanted to tell him she was leaving in the morning. How could she have expected his beautiful, terrible bombshell? *Stay with me.*

In the wash of the car's lights, Salem did his imitation of a sphinx, Native American-style. He closed up and set his beautiful lips into a thin line beneath his broad Ute cheekbones. Stone man. Lord, she hated when he did that.

This was so unfair. "You abandoned me first. Why?" Salem didn't answer. She knew he understood the question, the one he'd never answered years ago. "Why?" she pressed. "You could have waited for me. You wanted me."

"Not when we first met. You were so young. Like a kid sister. We had a bond, yeah. You were my little buddy. I couldn't believe a twelve-year-old actually *got* me, understood my love of nature and my heritage, of history."

He tapped his fist against his chin, a measured action, maybe judging how much to tell her? "I felt less alone because you were there. Why else would an eighteen-year-old hang out with a twelve-year-old? Why else would I pour my dreams out to you? I'd never known a kid who was so good at listening. I—I wished you were part of my family." He angled away, as though embarrassed to admit to the very thing she had felt when she first met him—an unprecedented affinity with another person. Her heart soared. He had felt the same way as her!

"Then you were fourteen, almost fifteen, and beginning to look like a woman, and things changed. I fell in love with you."

Her heart rate kicked up, did a song-and-dance routine in her chest.

"I found you attractive." He grasped her upper arms, expression intense. "Don't you get how young you still were? I respected both you and your dad too much to touch you. And myself, when it comes down to it. For God's sake, it wouldn't even have been legal. I tried waiting, but I kept on thinking about you, dreaming about you. I had to change how I dealt with you, to cut off the friendship, because it was becoming something it shouldn't have been until you got older."

All that time when she'd been dreaming about him, and he had started to turn away from her, he'd been doing the same with her. She'd had no idea. He'd hidden it well.

When he said, "I *hated* that attraction. It drove me

nuts," he shattered her blossoming happiness. "I *had* to distract myself with other women. Waiting was hard for a guy that age. What was I supposed to do? Wait four or five years?"

"Yes." It came out a sibilant plea. "Why didn't you?"

"You were a girl. I was a young man. I needed companionship."

"You needed sex," Emily said, still bitter sixteen years later.

"What was so wrong with that?" The sphinx was gone and Salem's anger slipped through. "I was a guy. That's what men do. They have sex with willing women. Annie was willing."

"You didn't have to get her pregnant." *And break my fourteen-year-old heart.*

"That was an accident. Failed birth control."

"You didn't have to marry her."

"Seriously, Emily? Leave Annie to raise the baby alone? Maybe let some other man step in? Don't you know *me* at all?"

Yes, she did. Through and through. Proud, ethical Salem would do the right thing. She expected no less. It had been only her vulnerable young heart that had been unreasonable. It had hurt to lose him.

To lose something you never had, Emily?

But we did have something, a connection. Everyone thought so, not just me. Salem just told you he felt it, too.

"Why were you distant after you got married?

We still saw each other all the time, but you treated me differently."

"Of course I did." The statement exploded out of him. "I was married and committed to making it work. I would have been a fool not to. I had children and was trying to create a strong family. My children had to believe I cared for their mother. Annie tried hard, too."

It all made perfect sense. Her own naïveté had wounded her, not Salem.

"Stay," Salem said again. "With me and the girls. Annie's been dead for four years. We could make it work now."

The age gap that had mattered when they were teenagers no longer did at thirty-six and thirty.

One big, big thing besides her career did separate them, though. Jean-Marc. She couldn't dump him, long distance, just because Salem asked her to. Out of the blue, she might add. Where on earth had this come from?

"Don't go back, Emily."

"I have to."

"Then this is goodbye."

Her heart chilled. "What do you mean?"

"No more hanging together. No more contact. It's too hard on me. I need to walk away. I need a clean break."

The ice in his voice stripped her skin raw and opened a yawning pit where his presence had always been, dependable and *there*. She might see him only three or four times a year, but he was always present in her mind, like a beacon lighting a path through her dark times.

The thought of losing Salem, her rock, sent her into a panic. "You don't mean that."

"I do, Emily," he said, the sphinx back and unyielding. "The next time you come home, stay away from me. Leave me alone."

Bewildered, she said, "But—but you're my best friend."

"For the love of God, Emily, *friend?* Is that how you see me?" Before she realized he'd moved, he gripped her wrists, his shoulders blocking the spill of moonlight from overhead. He swore and pulled her against him. His lips hovered above hers.

He'd never— She'd always wanted— At last.

But he didn't kiss her. He moved his mouth to her temple but didn't touch her, simply breathed on her skin, raising goose bumps across her flesh.

Time stilled while his soapy aftershave wove ribbons of scent around her.

Lick me. Lick my temple, my cheek, my lips. Make love to me.

His breath swept her cheek, lingered on her ear and then trailed down her neck. He made no contact, but shivers followed in his wake. Her mind knew she couldn't give in, but her body, oh, her body wanted *nothing* to do with common sense. Her heart wanted to own his.

Fingers of cool air caressed her shoulders, but

Salem's palms on her back were hot, drawing her closer to his hard chest and flat belly.

She'd always loved his height, his muscle. She touched him now, her hands flat against his chest and roaming his lean frame, measuring his dimensions for those nights when she would need memories, *something,* to hold close in the Sudan. *Salem.* Words, thought, fled. Only *Salem.* Only *this* and *now.*

Too soon, he set her away from him, his hands hard on her shoulders. "I'm not your *friend,* Emily. The next time that jackass hurts you, the next time he screws around on you, don't come crying to me. If you leave tomorrow, this will be our last time together."

She struggled to catch her breath. She wasn't this kind of woman. She didn't keep two men at one time. When Salem had been married, and since her relationship with Jean-Marc started, she'd been careful to not give Salem any sign he might construe as encouragement. She had put aside her youthful infatuation, had buried it deeper than the most elusive artifact, opting instead for only friendship and a shoulder to cry on. By the time Annie died, Emily had already become deeply involved with Jean-Marc.

Shaken that she'd almost lost reason, she stepped away.

Salem wreaked havoc with her good intentions. And he hadn't even kissed her. Lordy, Lordy, what if he had?

She swiped beads of sweat from her upper lip and

pulled herself together. Her hand shook. *Salem, what you do to me should be against the law.*

"I have to go back," she whispered. "There are things—"

"Fine. It's over."

She saw red. She didn't know that could be real, but holy relics, it was. "Over?" she asked, her voice dangerously quiet. "How can something be over when it never began?"

"Get on that plane tomorrow morning and consider us done. The next time you visit your family, stay the hell away from me."

He strode to his beat-up old Jeep, slammed the door and spewed gravel, leaving ruts in the side of the road.

Her best friend, her onetime crush, meant it. He never wanted to see her again.

The air around Emily became thin, leaving her dizzy. For too long, she had taken Salem for granted, had assumed he would always be here waiting for her. Now he was gone, as far away from her emotionally as Jean-Marc was physically, and it cut a dent into her heart, hacked out a hunk of it and left it bleeding on the road.

Exhausted, she got into her car to drive home to her father's house, in the opposite direction Salem had gone, and wasn't that freaking symbolic?

Hadn't they always been heading different ways?

Stay here with me.

Oh, Salem, and what would I do about my work? About my...my what? My boyfriend? What a pale description for her relationship with Jean-Marc. And too simple. *My lover?* Yes, that, but more.

The following morning, although it made her sick in both heart and body, she boarded the plane to return to work and Jean-Marc.

Present day

"STAY WITH ME," Jean-Marc said, bringing back memories of one year ago, when the words came from a better man. She'd made the wrong choice, and now it was too late. Too late to get Salem at any rate.

She could certainly dump Jean-Marc, though, and gladly.

"We can work everything out," he said, ramping up the charm with his too-easy grin and continental good looks—long tawny hair and ghostly pale blue eyes above high cheekbones in a rugged face. Over time, the elements roughened his skin and made him look even better, as though the sun's sole purpose was to serve this man. She'd grown tired of his looks and his arrogance. Other women hadn't. They flew to him like moths to a flame, but like a flame, Jean-Marc burned brightly but only briefly for any given woman.

Women envied her. *Don't,* she should tell them. *He'll only tear you to pieces, too, just as he has me.*

Brilliant at getting governments and countries to open their borders and doors to him even in tumultuous times, when others couldn't, Jean-Marc had an enviable reputation in the world of archeology. He knew how to work the press, how to make digging in the dirt sound sexy and how to promote himself as much as any of the ancient ruins on which he worked. He brought glamor to archeology. With his daily tweets and constant Facebook presence, added to his raging good looks, he'd become a star.

Humans were a great lot for mythmaking. She got that. In her line of work, how could she not? But her job was to separate fact from fiction. It should have been Jean-Marc's, too, but somewhere along the way, he'd begun to believe his own press. He thought he was God, all-powerful and above reproach.

"We can work this out," he repeated.

"Stuff it, Jean-Marc." Yeah, she was being rude. Dad's wife, Laura, would be appalled. Dad, on the other hand, would applaud. He was a fighter like Emily. A scrapper. She'd held her tongue for too long, the result of being involved with one's boss. Foolish girl.

Two nights ago, she'd caught Jean-Marc in bed with the latest PhD groupie, another one drawn in by his charisma. Until now, she'd been able to deny these things happened. In a weird and wonderful way, she was relieved that it was all out in the open. She could end it cleanly. If only she didn't feel so lousy. If only her breakfast would stop playing hopscotch in her stomach.

Over the years, she'd endured whispered rumors about his affairs and pitying glances. She'd ignored it all. No longer. "I'm sick of it."

She lifted her backpack onto the bed to fill with her carry-on items. She had a flight to catch. Yesterday, she'd boxed up her tools and had arranged to have them sent home. She'd said goodbye to dear friends and colleagues.

A hot breeze blew the dust of the desert in through her open window. Local merchants hawked their wares four stories below. Inside, Jean-Marc tried to sell her damaged goods. "Come on," he said. "Be reasonable."

God, what an asinine phrase. Jean-Marc meant, *Agree with me.*

"Save your smiles for the young women you chase." She packed her cosmetic bag. "They no longer work on me."

Emily shoved a sweater into her backpack, ready to walk out of this man's life for good. It had taken her a year to come to her senses.

"You're running away." If one more man told her that, she would scream.

Disillusioned with him, she'd also come to the end of her love affair with the past. Somewhere along the way, archeology had lost its magical allure, had changed from the excitement of revealing ancient treasures and had become…digging in the dirt.

Relics, the secrets of ancient worlds, still commanded her respect and awe, but she was tired of it. She needed a firmer attachment to the present. She needed to get a life that worked. Past time to go home, she was determined to get out of here in one piece, with her sanity intact.

Too late, kid. That's long gone.

She swiped a hand across her brow, skimming sweat from her forehead. She was used to the heat of the desert, but today's heat was way too high for May. Even her brain felt foggy. She'd lost track of their argument. What had Jean-Marc said? Oh, yeah.

"I'm not running away," she stated. "I'm leaving. There's a difference."

"Explain it to me." She already had, but Jean-Marc was a notoriously bad listener, especially when he disagreed with a point.

She'd given the man too much, because that's what she did as a matter of course. When she committed, she gave her all. It had been her downfall with Jean-Marc.

Time for self-preservation.

She stuffed all of her socks beside her one sweater. Why did she bother? They were ragged. It might be hot as hell in the desert in the daytime, but nights were cold. She'd worn the daylights out of her clothes. They'd become as ragged as some of the relics she'd unearthed in her career, and a sad metaphor for her life.

Time for a new me. It starts with a clean break.

"We can work things out," Jean-Marc insisted.

"Really? By me being a doormat while you sleep your way through all of the young beauties of the Sudan?"

"You're exaggerating. I made only one or two mistakes."

Emily sent him a repressive look. "You're beginning to believe your own lies."

"You are a prude," he snapped. "This is how modern people conduct affairs."

Emily slammed her alarm clock into her backpack and snapped the buckles together, then tossed it toward the bedroom door. "I'm tired of your lies and your vanity. My God, is there another archeologist on earth, another *man,* with a bigger ego?"

Jean-Marc became a mini–Mount Etna, ready to blow. If she weren't so angry, she'd laugh. He didn't look much like the suave playboy now, did he? "I have an ego because I'm good. The best."

"Yeah, yeah, I've heard it all before." Her anger whooshed out of her on a giant exhalation. Her shoulders slumped. "Why me? If you wanted to sleep around, fine, but why keep me dangling? Why not just let me go?"

In a split second of honesty, his smile a ray of sunshine, he said, "I love you, chère. Don't you know that?"

She wouldn't give in to that smile, as she'd done so many times in the past, because it was too small, and she wanted, *deserved,* more. Love should be huge. Grand. She'd been sucked in by his larger-than-life personality and brilliance, but it hadn't translated into a big love. Only a troubled one.

She gestured between them. "I can't keep doing this. I need peace and quiet. I'm going home."

"Yes, to your small town where people do nothing magnificent, nothing lasting, where they never become world citizens working to enlighten all of humanity." She'd rejected his moment of sweetness, and his spiteful side took over.

She thought of Salem, with his light hidden under layers of modesty, and the way everyone with whom he came into contact respected him. How hard he worked to teach the community about his culture, with quiet humility. With Jean-Marc, she'd chosen flash over substance.

"Some people don't need the whole world held up to them as a mirror. Some people do great things even while they are humble."

"I don't need to be humble. Nor should I be."

"Please, Jean-Marc." Her head pounded. "Be a better man than this. Leave while I finish packing. I don't want to do this anymore."

"I will ruin you." There was something smug about his disgusting little smile, all sunshine gone now, proving as he often had that his ego was stronger than his love. He left the bedroom and, a moment later, the apartment door slammed shut behind him.

She double-checked that she hadn't left anything behind then carried everything to the front door, but decided to use the washroom one last time before going. She wished her stomach would settle down. Those airport lineups could be brutally long and slow. Khartoum was a small airport by international standards, but busy. She was washing her hands when she thought she heard something in the living room.

"Hello?" She stepped out. No one. Just her imagination.

She reached for the doorknob to leave. The door stood open a fraction of an inch. It should have been shut tightly, especially because Jean-Marc had slammed it on his way out. Had it been closed when she put her bag here? She rubbed her forehead. She couldn't remember.

She studied the small rooms. Nothing was amiss. She glanced at her knapsack and violin case. They looked fine. A thread of doubt ran up her spine and she opened her case. Jean-Marc would know where to hurt her most, by damaging her precious violin.

She checked every square inch of the instrument and found it sound, then packed it back into its case.

Her headache set off fireworks behind her eyes and she just wanted out—of the country and the relationship—so she shrugged off all thoughts of what that open door might mean. A shuffle in the building hallway alerted her. Someone was there. She threw open the door then let out a breath. Not Jean-Marc come back to wreak vengeance, thank goodness.

Instead, seven-year-old Maria Farouk, in all of her cosmopolitan beauty, compliments of an Egyptian father and an Italian mother, stared up at her with liquid brown eyes in an olive-skinned face. Her thick hair had been brushed to glossy perfection.

"Maria," Emily said. "What are you doing in the hallway alone?"

"I came to say goodbye." The child sounded too solemn. Of all of the farewells Emily had made in the past two days, this would be the most difficult.

Emily glanced toward Maria's apartment. Her mother, Daniela, stood in her doorway making sure her child was safe alone in the corridor. When she saw Emily, she waved.

Emily leaned forward and cupped Maria's face with her palms. "We became good friends, didn't we?"

Maria nodded. "Can you send me postcards?"

It had become a game with them, that Emily would find the funniest cards in her travels and mail them to Maria. Also, because she'd loved the child so much, she had bought her a child-size violin and had taught her to play.

"Yes, lots of postcards," she promised. "Will you practice your violin?" Maria had great talent, more than Emily would ever possess.

"Every single minute," Maria shouted. Emily laughed and kissed her forehead.

"Not that much, little one. Make time for fun." She made sure she had eye contact before saying from her heart, "I promise you this. When you grow up and become a famous violinist, I will come to your concerts."

"You will come backstage," Maria ordered. "I will give you a pass. You come say hello to me."

"I will. I promise." Emily had to leave right away because if she stayed, she would cry, and that would sadden Maria. "In the meantime, I'll send you a postcard of a bear from Colorado." From home. Her longing overcame the sadness of leaving. She wanted home. Her family. Peace and quiet.

Maria returned to her apartment. Emily watched until she was safely inside. Despite the clean break, bits of Emily would linger behind, with Maria, with her friends Penelope Chadwick and Les Reed, and with her impassioned colleagues. She had enjoyed her time with them all.

But Jean-Marc? That connection was gone for good, severed as cleanly as though she'd taken an amazon's sword to it. If not for the sweat seething from her pores, she would be on top of the world. Free at last.

Only one more goodbye left. She went down to the second floor of the apartment building in which all of the archeologists lived. Penny answered the door when she knocked.

Jean-Marc used to call Penelope Chadwick the Horse. Yes, she had a long face and those endless legs, but also a bosom most women envied.

Her smile eased some of Emily's apprehension. Penny, in her oversize T-shirts and baggy trousers, with her manly tramping about the toughest terrain on her muscled athletic legs, had been a dear friend, and Emily loved her every capable, unfeminine, not-too-attractive molecule.

Penny was one of the good people.

Behind Penny, Les Reed, her compatriot and lover, touched Penny's elbow, the movement a subtle sign of possession and pride.

Where Penny was tall, Les was short and rotund. When Penny held Les, her ample breasts would flank his face. Emily wondered if he ever felt smothered. Judging by his satisfied grin, he would die a happy man.

She loved these people. She loved their honesty, loyalty and boundless integrity. Why couldn't everyone in the world be like them?

She fell into Penny's enveloping embrace. "I will miss you so much." Her sinuses ached. Why wasn't life easier? Why couldn't she carry her friends with her in her pockets, wherever she went, and take them out when she needed them? "I'll write often."

"You'll visit us in England when we're at home." From Penny, it came out as order rather than an invitation.

"Yes," Emily promised. "I will."

After copious hugs and kisses with both Penny and Les, and a too-brief goodbye, Emily was on her way to her new life.

Fifty minutes later, she stood at the airport in a lineup that moved with glacial slowness toward security.

At last second in line, she put her violin case onto the conveyor belt that would carry it through the X-ray machine.

Sweat poured from her face and a pair of Japanese Kodo drummers hammered her temples in unrelenting waves. This had nothing to do with the heat of the desert. She was sick. Some kind of flu. Rotten timing. *Suck it up, kid.* Nothing would hold her back from getting on that plane.

Unsnapping the buckles on her knapsack, she reached inside for her cosmetic bag, where she kept cotton hankies. Her hand touched something unexpected, something she hadn't packed, and she froze.

Whatever the object was, *she* hadn't put it there. She peeked inside, keeping her actions unobtrusive. In her palm, she held a tiny ancient prayer book. She'd seen it before. On their dig. It was supposed to be under lock and key at the National Museum of Sudan, where every artifact they unearthed eventually found a home. So what was it doing in her bag?

She dropped it back into the knapsack, but a tiny gasp betrayed her. Despite how insignificant that intake of breath, it drew the guard's attention. He approached.

Damn, damn, damn.

Her mouth dried up like the Sahara. Too late to turn and leave. If she took her bag and violin from the belt, he would know something was up and would detain her. One way or another, her bag would be searched today.

The penalty for smuggling artifacts out of the country was jail time. No questions asked. No leniency. No compassion. Too much had been stolen from these civilizations over the centuries. They'd been robbed blind.

If she denied ownership, they would think she was lying. If she tried to tell them she'd been set up, they would think she was lying.

There was no good outcome here. She was the most screwed piece of metaphorical toast on the face of the planet, and she knew whom to blame.

Jean-Marc. Her open apartment door. He'd retrieved the relic from his apartment down the hall and then had slipped back into her place long enough to stash it in her things so she would be caught with it as she left the country. Vindictive piece of decrepit crap.

I will ruin you. Yes, he had.

Rage filled her, and not just because of what he was doing to her, but because this precious article shouldn't have been in *his* possession. Why was it, damn him?

The day she let Jean-Marc win was the day she rolled over and died. She had to get out of this airport and get the relic back where it belonged, with the people of the Sudan.

Think. Think!

What could she do?

Sweat dripping from her forehead burned her eyes. She grasped the hankie in her hand and ran it over her face. The man in front of her in the lineup hadn't bathed recently, and the smell made her ill.

"Is something wrong, miss?" the guard asked, tone solicitous but eyes hard. "Are you nervous about your flight?"

She shook her head. "Sick."

His brow furrowed. "If you are sick, you cannot fly."

"Have to. Need to get home." She wasn't thinking clearly. The fever was messing with her brain. She had to get *out* of the airport, not onto a plane.

Her violin case and bag crept along the belt closer to the X-ray machine. They would question the prayer book. It wasn't shaped like a paperback novel. It was flat and small—and oh so ancient and precious. She reached to take it back. The guard stopped her.

They would find the relic and send her to the closest prison, where she would rot for years. Nothing and no one would be able to help her. The thought turned her stomach.

And wasn't that fortunate? She was desperate enough to try anything.

She glanced at the guard's immaculate uniform and her reflection in the glossy surface of his spit-shined brown shoes. *Vanity, you just might be my saving grace.*

This past winter, she'd had a cold that had left her with a cough that wouldn't quit. One day, it had been so bad she'd coughed so hard, she had ended up losing her breakfast.

The bag slid closer to the machine. The belt stopped abruptly. They questioned the man in front of her about an item in his carry-on luggage.

She took advantage of the lull and started to cough, covering her mouth with the hankie. She coughed harder, contracting her muscles to get them to obey.

Given the heat of the day, the unnatural fever and the sour scent of the man in front of her, it didn't take much to get her stomach to cooperate.

Her breakfast rose into her mouth and—oops— her hankie slipped away from her lips. She vomited on the floor, leaning forward enough that she also hit the guard's shoes.

"Hey!" he yelled and swore in Arabic.

Another guard joined them. "What's wrong here?"

"She's sick," the first guard spat. "Disgusting."

Good. Maybe they would let her turn around and walk out of here. She could get the relic back to where it belonged.

Her mouth tasted like hell. "Maybe I should return to my apartment and take a later flight." She held her breath, willing the man to agree. He ignored her as though she were a gnat.

"Clean this up," the second guard called to a janitor. Pointing at her, he said, "You come with us."

Oh crap, oh crap. He took her past security to the offices. Scrap that thought. They were headed to a private interrogation room. She was in deep trouble.

The first guard had retrieved her knapsack and her violin case from the belt and carried them into the room. He dropped them onto the table and she reacted before she could think, yelling, "Hey, be careful. That violin is old."

He paid no heed while the second guard took his time checking her passport and documents. "Why did you think you would be able to fly while you are so ill? Did you not consider the other passengers? They would not want to get sick."

She wouldn't lose her cool. There had to be a way out of this. "I didn't feel this ill when I left my apartment. It came on suddenly."

A firm knock sounded on the door.

"Come," one of the men said.

A man Emily recognized stepped into the room— tall, handsome Dr. Damiri. Everyone on the dig used his services when they were ill. "Doctor! What are you doing here?"

"More to the point," he said in his soft, sensible voice, "what are you doing here? I was in another lineup and saw you get ill."

He turned to the guards and handed them his identification. "I am her doctor. May I check her out?"

The first guard scowled, but the second returned Damiri's ID. "It's okay. I know him. He is my sister's doctor."

Dr. Damiri felt Emily's forehead. "High fever," he murmured. He examined her throat, pressed on her stomach and asked endless questions, at the end of which, he pronounced, "Malaria."

"What?" She hiccupped a tiny sob, playing the pity card, willing to do whatever it took to save her skin. Maybe they would let her go through without checking her bag. "But I just want to go home."

To the guards, the doctor said, "It isn't infectious. She can fly."

To Emily, he instructed, "It won't be a comfortable trip home, but you can make it. You will have fever. Chills. Great fatigue." He smiled gently. "Maybe more vomiting."

"My brain wants to pound out of my skull."

"Yes, headache, too." He wrote on a pad of paper he pulled from his briefcase. "In my estimation, you have uncomplicated malaria. There's nothing you can do but ride it out. In America, go to your doctor and get a prescription for this medication and take it to prevent a reoccurrence."

"That's it?"

"Yes. That's all you can do." He handed her a small vial of pills. "Take these."

"What are they?"

"Anti-nausea tablets. I always carry them when I fly, but you need them today more than I do."

With a wink, he was gone and she was alone with two unhappy guards and a stolen artifact in her luggage.

Emily stood, her brain so foggy she didn't know whether to come or go. "I can return to my apartment and get better, and then take a different flight another day."

For the second time, the guards ignored her suggestion.

"The doctor has cleared you to fly. You will go today." He reached for her bag. No!

She retrieved her cosmetic bag, leaning close to breathe in his face. "I vomited. I have to brush my teeth before I get on the flight."

Screwing up his nose, he waved her away.

In the washroom, she entered a stall and locked the door. The washroom might have cameras, but the stalls wouldn't. After she pulled the prayer book out of the bag, she took a moment to examine it, a little beauty in good condition. The papyrus had yellowed with age and the tiny paintings had faded, but it had obviously been cared for and well-loved by its owner.

She dumped her small toiletry bottles out of the zipped plastic bag she'd stored them in, put the book into it, secured the edges together and stuffed it into her bra, protecting it from the sweat of her fever.

After using the toilet, she washed her hands and made a show of brushing her teeth carefully, because she needed to, but also in case they watched her. She chewed a mint from her makeup kit.

Back in the room, the guards had emptied her bags and were searching every object, every item of clothing. Shivering, she picked up a pashmina she'd bought on her travels and wrapped it around her throat, dropping the ends to cover the slight bulge in her bra.

Thanks to Dr. Damiri's list of symptoms, they wouldn't find her behavior suspicious. She hoped.

One of the guards took her makeup bag and searched it. The other left the room, presumably to search the bathroom. When he came back, he gave the guard a surreptitious shake of his head.

She was allowed to repack her belongings, while feeling an inexorable sense of losing control. Not for long. She would fix this. Somehow.

They led her to the departure lounge and left her there. This was too wrong. Taking an artifact out of its native country, out of its home, went against every ethic, every part of her moral code.

Nausea rose into her throat, and she took one of Dr. Damiri's pills.

She had no choice but to leave. At the moment, self-preservation was more important than ethics. And didn't that suck? The prayer book belonged *here,* not thousands of miles away in Colorado.

Jean-Marc had known exactly what he was doing. Her rat of an ex-boyfriend had ruined her plan for a clean break. The prayer book tied her to him.

An hour later, she was on the first of many flights that would take her home, curled under a blanket with chills that had nothing to do with inflight air-conditioning, and everything to do with a smuggled artifact burning a hole in her chest wall, so far up shit creek without a paddle she wasn't sure how she would recover.

CHAPTER TWO

EMILY CAME HOME to Accord angry, railing against men and their perfidy, and scared.

She'd returned to answer the toughest questions of her life—who was Emily Jordan? Who had she allowed herself to become? And how did she find her way back to being a better person?

And what on earth was she going to do with the rest of her life?

The hand she ran across her forehead came away damp. She'd been sweating for three days. The fever had to break soon.

She stood in front of her father's house. Another year come and gone and nothing to show for it. She didn't even have her own home.

She wrapped her arms around her violin, pressing the case hard against her breastbone, anything to stop the shudders that wracked her body.

Cars lined the long driveway to her dad's house, a white sanctuary in a sea of green conifers, lit up like a birthday cake. As it should be. Today was his birthday—the big five-O—and she didn't even have a birthday present for him. *Was I always this self-*

centered? Then again, she was sick and had other things on her mind.

Where were the years going? How did her father get to be fifty already? How could Emily herself possibly be thirty-one, and what did she have to show for it?

At her age, her dad had been a parent for twelve years, had already made his first few million and had owned a big house in Seattle.

Emily had the knapsack on her back, the violin she clutched to her chest like a treasured doll and a career as an archaeologist she would never pursue again.

She'd left the dry, dusty heat of the Sudan behind as though she were a mummy shedding her wrappings, one difficult twist at a time.

Too bad it felt as if those wrappings still clung to her, like a ribbon stretching between Colorado and the Middle East, sticking to her pores like the sand of the desert during a windstorm.

She imagined one long thread of decaying but tough fabric winding its way across the earth from her to Jean-Marc. With that one artifact he'd hidden in her bag, he'd bound her to him.

"Get lost," she whispered to the mummy wrapping. It didn't listen. Resigned to that tug toward a man and a part of the world she had rejected, she opened the front door and stepped into a wall of sound, light and warmth, of conviviality and happiness—the most beautiful, welcoming homecoming she could imagine. And it felt all wrong.

Oh, the things she'd done. She didn't deserve these people.

"Emily!" The voice belonged to Laura, who rushed down the hall toward her with arms spread wide. If Dad was fifty, that made Laura fifty-three. Wasn't it a crime for a woman her age to look so good when Emily felt like crap?

Laura had a body men drooled over, albeit a little thicker around the middle than it used to be. Her chestnut hair, threaded now with silver but still thick, fell past her shoulders and framed a face with a few more wrinkles.

A crocheted sweater fell off one shoulder, revealing freckles that dotted pale skin, and a filmy flowered skirt floated around her ankles. Earth mother.

"Nick!" Laura called toward the kitchen. "Our girl is home!"

Enveloping Emily in a hug, she cloaked her in a cloud of patchouli and incense, the scent so familiar and dear it brought Emily to the edge of control.

She'd been awful to Laura when she'd first met her, a twelve-year-old witch who'd wanted her father all to herself, but Laura had persevered in creating a lasting friendship. Thank God.

Emily didn't think of Laura as a *step*-mom. More like a second mom. Emily's first mom lived outside Paris, and Emily visited when she could. Laura pulled back from Emily, puzzlement wrinkling her brow. "Are you all right? You feel—"

A fine-boned hand touched Emily's elbow. Pearl.

Her baby sister had grown up. Last time Emily had been home—one year, one month and three days ago, but who was counting?—Pearl had been eighteen. Now, at nineteen, adulthood showed on her face in quiet, elegant bones that spoke of blossoming maturity and dainty beauty.

She had her mother's striking thick chestnut hair rather than Emily's tawny richness, almost overwhelming her delicate features, and striking blue eyes with the odd ring of hazel that she'd inherited from her Grandpa Mort, as Emily had. *Oh, you beauty. The guys at college must be falling like dominoes.*

Emily's features and body were sturdier than Pearl's. Or usually were. At the moment, Emily was as weak as a kitten.

Her little Pearl had grown up. Hard to believe Emily had ever resented Laura's pregnancy all those years ago when it had produced such a devoted sister, and a too-perceptive friend. Pearl watched her with a knowing gaze. "What is it, Emily? What's wrong?"

"What? No greeting?" Emily said, voice brittle and too bright. "Aren't you glad to see me?"

"Emily," Pearl admonished. She valued honestly.

Emily deflated and said quietly, "Malaria."

Laura gasped and Emily touched her arm. "It's okay. It's uncomplicated."

"What does that mean?" Laura frowned. "Isn't malaria bad? We need to get you to the doctor."

"I stopped at the hospital in Denver when the flight landed." She dropped her knapsack and violin at the bottom of the stairs. She'd take them upstairs later, when her legs stopped feeling as heavy as stone sarcophagi. "I picked up medication, but it's just to prevent further attacks in the future."

"What can we do this evening?" Pearl brushed hair back from Emily's forehead.

"Nothing. It has to run its course."

Laura placed a cool hand against her cheek. "What do you need?"

"Water. Lots of cold water." She'd returned to the land of plenty, where reaching for a glass of water was as natural as breathing. There were no shortages here, no rationing.

Laura took her hand and dragged her to the kitchen, threading their way through the crowd of friends and family saying hello. Her father looked up from slicing something at the counter, saw Emily, grinned and dropped what he was doing.

Scooping her into his arms, he spun her around.

"When did you get here? Why didn't you call? I would have driven into Denver to get you."

She held on to her father, breathing in his familiar scent and taking in his strength. *Oh, Daddy.* She was a girl again, protected and cherished. Nothing bad could happen to her here.

She was safe.

The tug of that mummy wrap tying her to the past, to dusty old digs and dried relics, to pain and betrayal, tugged her to the past, but she resisted. She'd stayed in the land of the dead too long.

These people were vital. Alive.

Laura handed her a glass of cold water and she downed it in two gulps, giving it back for a refill. Only after she drank three glasses could she answer questions.

Yes, this time she was home for good. No, she wasn't going back. Yes, she was ecstatic to be here. Yes, she had missed everyone. No, she was no longer with…him. Silence fell over the group that surrounded her.

Laura broke it. "You need food."

Ah, yes, the answer to everything. A plate of food. A bowl of soup. As though any of that were going to fix what was so badly broken in Emily's life.

"We started early and a lot of the buffet food is eaten, but I've got one of your favorites here," Laura chattered. Nerves. Laura was so seldom affected by them; Emily must look really bad.

Laura handed her a cup of tea and one of her bakery's cinnamon buns. Emily's first bite buried her cynicism, and she sighed. Yes, maybe food *was* the answer.

She ate half the bun, but she'd put so little into her stomach in the past few days it had shrunk. She handed the rest to her little brother, Cody, though *little* was a misnomer. At eighteen and six feet tall, he might better be described more accurately as simply *younger*.

Cody finished the bun in two mouthfuls. Where Pearl's features were delicate, Cody's were strong, his jaw square, his trademark Jordan dark brown eyes beneath dark eyebrows and hair a replica of their father's. Cody was well on his way to being a good-looking man, like their dad, and Uncle Gabe, and Uncle Tyler, all of whom converged on Emily for hugs. So did their wives. And their children.

Oh, those Jordan men could hug, could administer love and support and affection like no one else on earth.

It suffocated her, the bosom of her family too accepting of her at a time when she knew she shouldn't take it.

Perceptive Pearl saw through her shaky smile, took Emily's hand and led her down the hallway toward the stairs. She picked up Emily's knapsack from the bottom step.

Emily retrieved her violin case and followed Pearl up two flights of stairs, to her small, private apartment under the eaves on the third floor. Dad had designed it for Emily when he'd built the house nineteen years ago just after Pearl's birth.

It ran the full length, with the roof's slanting edges cutting off height on the two long sides, and white wainscoting running under soft mauve walls.

Emily set her violin on a chair and glanced around. In the sitting area overlooking the garden, sketchpads and pencils were strewn over the sofa and coffee table and chintz armchair.

She picked up one of Pearl's sketchbooks and thumbed through it. Her sister was good—very good—the scenes of small-town life accurate, unsentimental, and yet attractive. Pearl had also sketched life around Accord, the forests, farms and ranches of Colorado.

Emily turned the page…and there it was. The Cathedral. Her name for the Native American Heritage Center, because it seemed beautiful and holy to her. *Salem's* Cathedral. Emily had first named it the Cathedral after it was built, and the name had stuck with everyone. Most people in town called it either the Cathedral or the Heritage Center.

Pearl had captured perfectly the lighting of a dying sunset as it glinted from glass walls. Longing expanded Emily's chest, but Salem had told her to stay away, and so sadness replaced her yearning.

"I'm sorry. I spend too much time up here." Pearl started to gather up her work, but Emily stopped her.

"This should be your room now. You're old enough to have your own space."

"Where would you stay when you come home?" Pearl dropped what she'd gathered onto the table.

Emily shrugged. Her head hurt too much for thinking right now. She took a tissue from a box on the bedside table and wiped sweat from her forehead. "How's school?"

"Good. You know me. I'm keen. I like school. I like learning. I'm a nerd."

A pretty nerd who the boys liked, no doubt.

"How's the art going?"

Pearl's face lit up. Even as the tiniest child, art had made her happy. "Great. I've had interest from a couple of advertising firms."

"Finish school first," Emily warned.

"I will."

Dreams shone in Pearl's eyes. Emily used to have dreams, too.

Pearl placed one of the pillows on the bed up against the headboard and leaned against it, curling her legs into the half-lotus yoga pose and laying another pillow across her knees.

She smiled and patted the pillow. Emily couldn't help but return that serene smile. As a child, Pearl had spent many hours up here visiting Emily with her head in her sister's lap.

Laura would come upstairs to find Pearl asleep and Emily reading a book while she stroked her baby sister's hair.

Emily laid her head into the dip in the center of the pillow, where it rested on Pearl's calves. The pupil had become the teacher.

Pearl touched her cheek. "Your skin is clammy. Are you cold?"

"Cold and hot."

"You're pale, but your cheeks are bright red."

"I have fever and chills."

"How long will it last?"

"Another day or so."

"Tell me what's wrong, Emily."

Pearl didn't mean the malaria. She was right. That was a surface thing. What was wrong with Emily went bone deep. Somewhere along the way, she'd lost herself.

"Everything." She sighed.

Pearl stroked her hair. "You should sleep."

"I wish I could."

"Do you want me to leave?"

Emily thought about it. Solitude? Was that what she needed? She'd give it a try. "Yes."

Pearl struggled out from beneath Emily, stood and kissed her forehead. "Love you, sis. See you in the morning."

But Pearl had only just closed the door at the bottom of the stairs when Emily missed her already. So... solitude wasn't the answer.

Neither was rest. As exhausted as she was, she knew she wouldn't sleep, not with the problem of the prayer book turning her inside out. She retrieved her laptop from its pocket in her backpack and set it up on her desk.

A moment later, she had her email open. It exploded with messages from the past two days, the tone of all of them, from friends and colleagues, frantic.

Where are you?

What have you done?

You stole an artifact??? That is so not *you!*

No one believes what Jean-Marc is saying.

What was Jean-Marc saying? She could only imagine.

She opened her Twitter account, and that's when it sank in—how much Jean-Marc wanted to hurt her and exactly how much he'd succeeded.

The whole archeological world thought she had been stealing artifacts from the dig. He hinted that there had been a series of objects that had gone missing. There had? Whether or not it was true, Jean-Marc had succeeded in implicating her, in tarnishing her reputation. He'd done it with just the right amount of innuendo, with no real accusation she could take as slander and use against him in court.

Furious that she hadn't been caught at the airport, he'd pulled out all of the stops in social media. Bully. Traitor.

The wash of shame that heated her chest was old, familiar, an enemy she'd fought before in a battle she had never wanted to revisit. She had thought she'd gotten over those old demons. Hadn't she worked her butt off to leave all of that behind, including leaving her home literally to travel the world? Now this. Jean-Marc brought it back to the surface with a few strokes of a keyboard and an enter key. She'd traded one set of bullies for another.

No. She wouldn't let him destroy her. People had tried in the past. She'd been too young to know how to fight back then, but now she did. With maturity came perspective and strength. Maybe not enough, though. This bloody malaria was killing her.

She, and only she, knew who the real culprit was. The question was, would they come after her? And who would *they* be? Her own government? Would they come here and search her father's home?

No way was she going to wait to get caught. She'd done nothing wrong. She wouldn't give Jean-Marc the satisfaction of seeing her hurt. But how could she protect herself? And her family?

Where could she go? What could she do? She shouldn't have come here. She would only bring them pain.

Her panicked glance fell on Pearl's sketchbook, on the exquisite drawing of the Cathedral. She wanted to be there, in that place that brought her peace.

She had to get there, but she couldn't leave through the front or back doors. Too many people downstairs. They wouldn't let her go. They would worry, and rightly so.

Catching a glimpse of herself in the mirror, she worried, too. She looked like hell, her hair a mass of tangled curls. Pearl was right. In spite of her deathly pallor, two red spots rode her cheekbones like clown's paint, the look unnatural. Unhealthy.

Even so, now that she'd thought of the Cathedral, she couldn't, wouldn't, stop herself.

She had rejected Jean-Marc's ultimatum. *Stay or I'll ruin you.* And she had accepted Salem's. *Don't contact me. Leave me alone.* That didn't mean she couldn't visit the Cathedral.

She took the prayer book out of the baggy and wrapped it tightly in plastic she found in the wastebasket. It looked as if it came from Pearl's sketchbook. She put the wrapped artifact back into the baggy and made sure it was zipped firmly against moisture, and then tucked the whole thing into her bra.

Grabbing her jacket, she buttoned it to protect the

book before opening the door to the tiny back balcony. She closed it behind her and peered over the railing. Her father had never trimmed the maple tree she used to climb down to sneak out during high school.

She slung a leg over the railing to reach the nearest limb. Dizziness swamped her. She hung over the gap, robbed of breath, the ground far below wavering in her vision. She gripped the slippery wood until the nausea passed. Heights. She hated heights. But she could do this.

When her head felt steady enough, and her pulse had calmed, she grasped the branch and pulled herself into the tree. She climbed down, branch by branch, a trip that should have taken five minutes taking ten in her weakened state.

Or maybe it was age. She felt old these days when she should feel young and vibrant. She worked hard on the digs. She was in good shape.

On the ground, she rummaged through the garden shed until she found what she needed. A trowel. She crept around the side of the house and out onto the road.

A brisk wind gusted. A Roman legion of rain clouds advanced on the horizon, heavy with menace.

Maybe a heavier jacket would have been a good idea.

Fifteen minutes later, she arrived at the Accord Golf and Cross-Country Ski Resort. Her father's pride and joy.

The hotel, sleek in glass and wood and shining like

a Christmas tree, held no interest for her. Through the windows, guests lounged around a huge stone fireplace. Looked as if the place was fully booked, even in May. Good for Dad. A drop of rain plopped onto her forehead.

As though wading through mud, she trudged to the clearing in the woods behind the resort, leaf mold and pine needles crunching underfoot and kicking up a damp, mossy scent that reminded her of childhood.

She plodded through the darkening woods, aware that there wasn't a dry bone or sand dune in sight, nothing beige or desiccated here. Only vibrant, green life. Her spirits lifted, even if her body couldn't. More drops of rain hit her face, anointing her spirit with hope, but also chilling her body.

The Cathedral stood in the middle of tall Rocky Mountain Douglas firs. When her father had wanted to build the resort twenty years ago, construction had been held up by Salem and his fellow band members. They'd staged a demonstration and had refused to move until her father had given in to their demands to research the land. Despite being so young, Salem had been chosen as their spokesperson. Emily remembered him being quiet, but articulate and passionate about the land and its history. Parts of these lands used to be migratory routes for their ancestors. A nomadic tribe, Utes had buried their dead where they fell, so Emily's father couldn't build without going through the proper channels first, even though his family had owned the land for a few generations.

With the help of local elders, and professors who taught and studied Native American affairs, they had determined that the routes ran through another portion of land, so the construction wasn't likely to disturb any burial sites.

To appease the elders, and to thank them, her father had given Salem this piece of land and had paid to build the Native American Heritage Center, which had become a tourist attraction for the resort. Her father, recognizing Salem's passion and uncommon maturity, had asked Salem to set up the exhibits and to care for the collections. It hadn't taken long for her dad to stop supervising Salem and give him free rein. Salem had proven her father's trust in him to be well deserved.

As curator, Salem had helped to design the building and had turned it into one of the best museums in the state, and as beautiful as Emily remembered.

A crystal in a sea of green, three stories of glass and brushed steel with a polished wooden column running up the center that housed the elevator and washrooms, it shone like an oasis in the desert of her life.

The hallowed beauty of both the woods and the building had given her peace over the years.

Small spotlights on the first floor highlighted the artwork on a full-size teepee in the foyer. The architect had created a twenty-foot ceiling to accommodate it. Her breath caught in her throat. Lord, the place was gorgeous, glowing from within.

Since it was Saturday and the museum was closed for the evening, the public areas were dark.

On the third floor, a single yellow light shone in Salem's office. Why was he here on a Saturday night? He should be home with his family. Or maybe a better question was why he wasn't at her father's birthday party. He was a friend of the family. He and her father had buckets of respect for each other. She should have noticed that he wasn't at the house when she'd arrived.

Salem is here. The hell with his order to stay away. She needed him.

So close and yet so far away. She needed Salem, his calming energy and his quiet efficiency. Salem could handle anything thrown at him, and Emily was running on empty. She needed a friend.

She had to get up there, to him, if only her shaky legs would cooperate. He might be upset with her, but could he really turn a sick person away? She planned to take advantage of his innate decency.

First, though, she had to hide the prayer book.

A good forty yards from the back door of the Heritage Center, she dug a hole at the edge of the woods then placed the plastic-wrapped relic reverently in its new burial site.

"Just for now," she whispered as though it were alive. "Until I figure out what to do with you. I'll get you home somehow."

She covered the package with soil and leaves and branches, and lastly, a large rock she pushed and pulled into place until her arms burned. Glancing around, she tried to memorize her position so she would know where to dig when she came back to retrieve it, but

the rain, dusk and her fever messed with her eyesight.
What if she made a mistake and wasn't able to find
it again? She would never forgive herself. She hung
the trowel from the remainder of a broken tree branch
where it sat against the trunk of the tree, above the new
grave to mark the spot. No one would notice it here.

There. She'd done as much as she could tonight.

Her breath whooshing in and out of her, she leaned
against the tree for a moment to regain enough strength
to get into the Cathedral and up those stairs to Salem.

She managed to make it to the building and stepped
out of the rain that was coming down harder now. If
nothing had changed in the years she'd been gone, she
should be able to avoid banging into display cases and
follow that sole yellow lamp shining on the third floor.

Beside the door, she found the felt slippers that all
visitors donned to protect the glass floors and stairs
from grit and dirt. She slid her old hiking boots into
the oversize slippers.

When she pressed the elevator button, nothing happened. Shut down for the night, she guessed.

She climbed the stairs gingerly, but her headache
still worsened with every step.

The second floor, she knew, housed displays of gorgeous beaded and quilled moccasins as well as artifacts the Jordan land had yielded to both professional
and student archaeologists.

At the moment she didn't care. She'd spent too much
time in the past and not enough paying attention to the
present, to her *self* slipping away from her so slowly

and subtly she'd been stripped bare without knowing it, left skinned and vulnerable with nowhere to turn but here.

So dizzy her stomach roiled, she clung to the banister. Her hands shook again, this time more from greed than illness.

I want...

She wasn't sure what.

She knew only that she was exhausted with the struggle to keep herself in one piece.

She forced one foot in front of the other. On the second-floor landing, she stopped to catch her breath, like an old woman on her last legs, so close to finally achieving...what?

On the landing on the third floor, she stopped and stared at Salem through glass walls.

He bent over his desk, over a book, his attention focused and disciplined, as was his way. His dark straight hair hung in a braid down the center of his back.

This close to him, peace enveloped her. It settled over her with the softness of a flannel blanket. She watched him. This, *he,* was exactly who she needed. She wanted to lay her head and her troubles on his broad chest.

When she swayed, it alerted him to her presence.

His jaw fell, his expression equal parts shock and anger. She knew she'd flitted into and out of his life too many times. *Oh, Salem, I'm home. For good.*

He stood, dropping the book onto the desk.

His simple male beauty stunned her. Why had she stayed away when perfection had been here all along?

He came to the door. "Emily?" His deepening frown reminded her of their argument.

When are you going to stop running, Emily?

Now, she thought. *I'm not going anywhere anymore. Honest.*

She felt herself slipping, falling.

"Emily!" He caught her before she hit the floor, his arms strong and dependable and oh so welcome.

"Salem," she whispered. "I'm sick."

Salem lifted her and carried her off. Her head fell against his solid shoulder. She didn't know where he took her. It didn't matter.

She'd made it home.

EMILY. LIKE FIREWORKS, or shooting stars, Emily was here one moment, but gone the next. What was she doing here now?

God or the devil or both had a wicked sense of humor. Why did they keep sending her back to him? It messed with the balance he strived so hard for in his life.

He'd told her to stay away. *After first asking her to stay here with you. After nearly asking her to marry you.*

A moment of temporary insanity, of wanting life to go my way, even briefly. Of needing an end to the loneliness.

That night in the moonlight, Emily had looked like heaven.

He loved his daughters and respected the daylights out of his father, but missed having a woman around. Worse, he missed Emily. He'd married one woman while he'd wanted another, and had spent his married life suppressing his desire and trying to be a good husband. He had paid a price, and the currency had been longing, yearning and too much time spent alone.

He'd spent his married years tamping his emotions into a hard brick of denial, constantly controlling everything he said to his wife, and everything he did with Emily.

Then Annie had died.

That night last year, he'd gotten this crazy thought. There had been a long period of mourning, out of respect for the mother of his children. That time had passed. Now he and Emily could be together.

He had thought she would return his feelings and want to be with him, but despite telling her how he felt, she'd left anyway.

He'd blurted his heart's desire. Thank the Lord, she'd said no. He'd dodged a bullet.

In his smarter moments, he knew it would never work between them. Emily loved adventure.

Salem glanced longingly at the book he'd been studying. Reason, intellect and learned discussion were his gods.

But now here she was, despite him telling her to never return, and everything inside him rebelled against turning her away sick. Em was smart. She would have known that when she came here. He disliked being used. But he couldn't let her go.

He tamped down the emotions twisting in his belly like warring snakes, because she looked like hell. He didn't want to worry about this woman who weighed next to nothing, but he did. She angered and frustrated him, but he couldn't turn her away.

He laid her on the sofa in his office, where she had spent so many hours over the years when she came home from her digs sitting and pouring out her heart about Jean-Marc and his latest escapades. He'd heard her anger and pain, but he'd never interfered. Back then, he could never say, *Leave him and come to me.*

On all of her visits, he'd held a chunk of himself back—to protect both his peace of mind and his marriage. He might not have been in love with his wife, but he had been committed to her.

And so, *restraint* had become his middle name, and the act a habit, but sometimes these days, the restraints chafed and he wanted to bust out so badly.

When he finally did ask Emily to be with him, she'd said no. End of story.

"What's wrong, Emily?"

When he tried to let her go, she grasped his shirt.

Even through her clothing, her skin burned. Just like Emily to come here like this, to bring mayhem into his well-ordered existence. She liked drama. He liked peace. She liked chaos. He needed order.

"Emily," he said, keeping his voice low to soothe her as he would a skittish animal. "I need to get water."

She nodded. "Yes. Water."

Even so, she didn't ease her grip.

"Let go." He became stern. "I'll come back."

"Promise?" Her insecurity tore at him. Trouble roiled in her witchy blue-hazel eyes.

Where was his confident, brash Emily? *What happened to you?*

"I'm always here for you, Emily. You know that." Even when it was hard, and even when he had vowed to break away from her, to sever all ties. She called to a part of him he had trouble denying.

She smiled so sweetly it broke his heart. Yes, he was always here for her, but she wasn't always available for him.

He cut off the anger and bitterness. Now wasn't the time.

At this moment, she needed him, and that was all that mattered. He would get rid of her when she was well.

She released him and he retrieved water and damp towels from the washroom. Just before he left the room, he noticed muddy handprints on his shirt where Emily had gripped it. Strange.

When he returned, he asked, "What is it? The flu?"

She shook her head. "Malaria."

"Malaria?" He stilled his panic long enough to swab her face. "Isn't that bad?"

She lifted a shaky finger to smooth the frown from

his forehead, the smattering of freckles across her nose stark against her sickly white skin. "It's okay. I've seen a doctor."

"And?"

"And there's nothing to do but wait. I felt a bit better for a while, but I shouldn't have walked over here in the rain."

"You walked here? Sick? From your dad's?"

She nodded.

A flush of violence coursed through his blood. "So help me, Emily," he muttered, swabbing her face too hard, "you are infuriating."

She smiled, and it was weak, but sweet. "Wanted to see you." He fought the urge to wrap his arms around her and never let go. No one could make him feel warm and fuzzy as Emily could, even while he wanted to shake her.

Why didn't she take care of herself? Why hadn't she learned to control her impulses?

"When did you get home?"

"About an hour ago."

"And you rushed over here? Why not wait until morning?"

When his glance fell on her hands, the warm fuzzies came to a screeching halt. He grasped one. Mud caked her fingers. "What have you been up to?" Her nails were crammed with dirt. Digging? In the rain? Where? On this land?

Wanted to see me, my ass.

She pulled her hand out of his grasp.

"What did you do?" he asked, recrimination riding his tone like acid.

Her gaze slid away from his and she stared at the wall. "Nothing," she said, voice small but defiant nonetheless.

"Tell me," he insisted.

"I can't. It's better if you don't know." He recognized the stubborn set of her jaw, so particular to Emily. There was no fighting her when she dug in her heels.

"I'm not getting any more out of you, am I?"

She shook her head.

"So I'm good enough to come to when you need your forehead wiped, but not good enough to trust. Is that it?"

She didn't answer.

There'd been times when they'd been close, when there had been a connection he'd cherished, when he'd hoped…

Aw, forget about it.

"Let's get you home."

"Okay."

"Have you had malaria before?"

"No. I won't again. The medication will take care of that."

"You're taking medicine?"

"To prevent it from coming back."

"Can you walk?"

"Sure. Help me up."

He lifted her into his arms.

"Put me down. You can't carry me that far."

"Want to bet? What have you been eating? Feathers?" It angered him that she'd changed, that she wasn't the woman he knew, a go-getter, determined and sharp. Hale and healthy. "Don't you take care of yourself?"

"Not lately." For the first time, Salem understood what a sardonic laugh sounded like. He didn't like hearing this self-mockery from Emily.

At the elevator, he stood her on her feet for a minute while he used his key to start it up again. When the door opened and he moved to pick her up, she protested. "Love you holding me, but I can walk. Just let me lean on you."

Love you holding me. Did she know what she was saying?

They made it to the car with Emily leaning on him heavily, with Salem rushing them through the rain to his Jeep, parked behind the resort. He put her into the passenger seat then climbed behind the wheel and swiped rainwater from his face.

"You picked a great night to come home."

Emily laughed, but it sounded hollow, as though more than her body was ailing.

"What happened to you in Egypt?" He sounded as disgusted as he felt.

"The Sudan."

"What?"

"Not Egypt this time. Too much political turmoil right now. Country's torn apart. I was in the Sudan."

"What happened?"

She didn't answer and he glanced at her, but the country road was too dark. "Are you crying?"

"Nope," she said, but the thickness in her voice betrayed her.

"Was it that boyfriend of yours? What did he do?"

"Screwed me over." A bitter laugh barked out of her, but she said nothing else.

He didn't want to know more, didn't want to hear another word about the guy.

Out of the silence, Emily's voice floated like a disembodied ghost. "I hit rock bottom."

CHAPTER THREE

AIYANA PEARCE CREPT past the living room where her grandfather dozed in the flowered armchair.

Dad would hit the roof if he knew she was going out without his permission, but what Dad wanted didn't matter. He wasn't home, was he?

She couldn't help being bitter. Dad used to be home in the evenings with her and Mika, but now he was usually at the Heritage Center, and then when he finally came home all he did was study for his college courses. He wanted to be an architect.

Dad said a person should have ambitions.

Gramps snored and Aiyana glanced at him. Gramps didn't have ambitions, hadn't even finished high school, but people still loved him anyway, didn't they?

Having justified her defiance, Aiyana stepped outside and closed the door slowly. She was careful. There was no way Grandpa would hear the click of the lock catching.

Bypassing the creaky third step, she ran down the walkway to the street. The cool breeze took her by surprise and she zipped up her jacket. The air smelled like rain.

A sharp whistle from a couple of houses down

caught her attention. Justin! Her heart rattled in her chest like a baby bird flapping its wings.

She raced toward the sound but squealed when he jumped out from behind a tree and wrapped his arms around her. "Did I scare you?"

"Yes." She gasped and caught her breath. She smacked her boyfriend's arm, but couldn't be mad at him for long. *Boyfriend*. She liked the sound of that. Yesterday, he'd said he was hers and had invited her out tonight for the first time. Hers, he'd said, forever and ever.

Justin White, the most popular boy in school, wanted *her* for his girlfriend. How cool was that?

He wanted to keep it a secret, even though she wanted to shout it to the whole world. He said it felt good that it was their special news, only theirs, and they should hang on to it for a while.

Under the streetlight, his hair shone like gold. His blue eyes filled with humor. Grandpa would call it the devil's mischief, but Aiyana knew Justin wasn't like that. He was a good guy. Everyone at school liked him. And he belonged to her!

He threaded his fingers through hers, his palm warm and callused from shooting hoops for a couple of hours every day after school. Holding hands felt good.

She glanced over her shoulder, but no one was following her. Good. Grandpa was still asleep.

Dad thought she was too young to see boys, maybe because Mom got pregnant with Aiyana when she was a teenager. Mom and Dad *had* to get married.

But Aiyana was too smart for that to happen to her. Dad should learn to trust her. For Pete's sake, in a few days, she would turn sixteen. Of course she was old enough to date. All the kids at school did.

Justin urged her toward the end of Marshall Avenue. "Come on."

"Where to?"

When he smiled, one side of his mouth hiked up higher than the other. She liked his lips. "You'll see."

He led her to the path that went down into the ravine. She never went down there this close to nightfall. The wind had picked up and the sky was getting dark. She shivered and Justin wrapped his arm around her. "Cold, babe?"

Her heart hammered. "Why are we going down here?" Even to her own ears, even trying as hard as she could to sound sixteen already, her giggle sounded shaky.

"Someplace private," Justin said, and the word both thrilled and scared her.

"I thought we were going for ice cream."

"We are. After."

"After what?"

"I made something special for you." Special. Just for her.

They stumbled to the bottom of the ravine, where he stopped and pointed. "Look."

In a hollow created by a boulder at the back and large old trees on either side, Justin had fashioned a makeshift tent of sorts. She wasn't sure exactly what it was. A cubbyhole? Just a private spot? He'd stretched a piece of canvas five feet above the ground between the two trees. On the ground he'd covered a plastic sheet with a blanket with a vaguely Native American pattern. It didn't look like Dad's blankets at home.

An overturned milk crate had a bunch of stuff on top of it.

"I made this for us," he said. "No one else knows about it."

She would rather have gone out for ice cream than sit in the woods when it was getting dark, but Justin looked so proud of himself, she smiled.

Crawling in on her hands and knees, she noticed that he had everything—candles, a flashlight, potato chips—and beer. She didn't drink. She'd already told him that yesterday.

The place smelled like dead leaves and damp earth, but at least the tarp overhead cut the wind.

He crawled in behind her and pulled the tab on a can of beer then sipped the foam that bubbled out. "It's warm." He shrugged. "Sorry," he said, handing her the can.

"I don't drink, Justin."

"I know, but it's only one beer. No biggie."

She sipped it but hated the taste. That put it mildly. He was right. It was warm and tasted like crap. When she handed the can back to him, he guzzled half the contents then belched.

She sat on the blanket not really knowing what to

do with her hands or where to put her legs. The space was cozy and her knees kept bumping Justin's thigh.

Every time they did, it felt as if electricity shot through her. She fidgeted.

"Relax," he said, reclining onto the pillows at the back of the tent. They looked as if they belonged on somebody's sofa.

He took her arm and urged her down beside him. She resisted, but his grip was strong. "Easy. I'm not going to hurt you. I just want to keep you warm."

She settled her head on his shoulder. It was solid and warm and felt nice.

He unzipped her jacket. When she tensed, he said, "I want see that necklace you always wear. What is the design? Does it have significance in your culture?" he asked, taking it between two fingers.

She was having trouble breathing. His heavy arm rested between her breasts. No boy had ever touched her there. He was strong. An athlete. A basketball player. He said Coach made them lift weights to keep fit.

"It was my mother's necklace," she finally answered when she thought her voice might be steady. "She did the beadwork herself. She's dead now."

"I know. The beading's pretty." He dropped the necklace. "Your name's pretty, too. Aiyana. Does it mean something in English?"

"Eternal Blossom."

Justin nodded. "Cool. Maybe I should call you Pretty Flower or Princess Blossom."

No. She wanted a white name, like Tiffany or Brittany or Madison. Dad had chosen stupid Native American names for her and her sister.

"I'm not a princess. My dad isn't a chief. I'm nothing."

Justin smiled and popped the tab on another beer. After drinking a bunch, he set the can aside and wrapped his arm across her shoulders then curled his fingers around the back of her neck, gently urging her head forward. "You're not nothing. You're my girlfriend. You're pretty."

She knew that wasn't true, but oh, it felt good that Justin thought she was.

He kissed her and his lips were gentle and sweet even if they did taste like beer. She liked his kiss, but wished he didn't make it so hard so fast. When he put his tongue in her mouth, the taste of yeasty alcohol overpowered her and it was awful. He pushed his tongue in farther.

His hand touched her breast. It was nice. Sort of. He squeezed and moved his fingers over her nipple. She felt a pull in her belly and lower, excitement and itchiness.

Following the path of that itch, his hand rested on her *there,* the heel of his palm rubbing her and his fingers pressing the seam of her jeans into her.

He was moving too fast, not giving her time to catch up. Her pulse pounded inside her head. His fingers were at the button of her jeans and pulling down her zipper.

How? What? Wait!

His hand was on her belly inside her underwear. She grasped his wrist, but he kept moving.

His fingers were in her curls, touching her dampness. Stop.

She yanked her head away from his beery kiss.

"Justin, no." She sounded breathless. Her chest heaved up and down and her breasts kept hitting his body. She put her hands between them and pushed, but he was strong.

Fear became a real thing bouncing around the tent.

"Hey, babe," Justin said. "We're just having fun." He kissed the side of her face, and his hot breath whooshed past her ear.

She grabbed his wrist again, tried to pull his hand out of her pants, but his fingers were inside her.

"Stop!" she cried, her heartbeat as loud as a train engine in her ears.

"What?" Justin sounded frustrated.

"I don't want to do this."

"Can't you feel what you do to me, Princess?" Something hard jutted against her thigh.

"Don't call me princess." Her voice shook. "I don't want you touching me there."

"You said you wanted to be my girlfriend."

"I do."

"This is what girlfriends *do,* Aiyana."

"It's too soon."

"Grow up." He pulled his hand out of her pants with a hard flick. It hurt and she winced.

"I can't believe how ungrateful you are." He downed

the rest of the beer. How many beers made a boy drunk? She didn't know. She wanted to get out of here, away from him.

"I went to a lot of trouble to make this place for us." Justin adjusted himself inside his pants. His place didn't feel safe, not to her, but more like a black hole in the dark woods.

"I want to go home." Her fingers trembled when she pulled up her zipper, but they shook too much to do up her button. She yanked her jacket down over it. "Don't tell anyone about this," she begged. "I don't want people to think I'm easy."

He thrust his fingers through his hair. Even messed up it looked good. What she could see of it. There was hardly any light left in the tent.

"Easy," he scoffed. "That's a laugh. Find your own damn way home." With that, he bolted.

Aiyana sat stunned. How could Justin do this? He'd seemed so nice. As though waking from a bad dream, she crawled out. The woods were almost completely dark and foreign. Hostile. Every rattling tree branch, every bush, was a monster coming to get her. Justin must have run up the hill because she couldn't see or hear him. He'd left her alone in the ravine at night-time. What kind of person did that? Terrified, she ran up the hill.

The rain started when she was only halfway up, scrambling in the darkness toward the patches of light from the streetlamps flickering through the trees. Something rustled the bushes beside her and she cried out, scrabbling to catch branches to help her up the steep incline.

Her feet slipped and slid in the muck.

Rain streamed down her face, ruining the makeup she'd put on to look good for Justin. At least the rain hid her tears.

She ran home, past their meeting place, and rushed into the house, careful to close the door quietly, even though she ached to throw and break things.

Grandpa was still sleeping. Thank goodness. If he'd woken up and seen her, all hell would have broken loose. She needed to get to her room, where she wanted to hide forever.

She was only halfway up the stairs when Gramps let out his "wakeup" snort and said, "What?" She stopped and tried to calm her runaway heart. He smacked his lips, part of his waking-up routine. She knew he'd be stretching his skinny body every which way to come awake. His spine would make popping sounds.

The sound of the TV turning on followed her up the rest of the stairs. She tiptoed along the hallway and into her room. Closing her bedroom door, she leaned against it and let her tears flow.

Justin hadn't really wanted *her*. He'd just wanted an easy lay.

What made him think she would be? She didn't go out with boys. She was quiet at school. Was it because of her heritage?

In her mirror, she saw the reflection of a girl with

dark raccoon eyes because of her ruined mascara. She swiped it with tissues until it was all gone.

Her hair, usually shiny and straight, hung in wet strings. With the broad cheekbones she'd inherited from her dad, there was no mistaking her heritage.

Native American. Ute.

She hated her face and she hated her name.

Would Justin have attacked her if her name had been Brittany? Or Madison? If she were white, would he have tried to make her drink beer and have sex?

She grasped the corners of the heavy blankets decorated with the symbols of her heritage and hauled them from the bed, wadding them into a ball and tossing them into the corner.

It took forever to get out of her wet clothes, to tug the wet denim down her legs and to put on her long nightshirt. She crammed her jeans into her laundry basket. Dad would be mad that she hadn't hung them to dry. So what? It didn't matter. *Nothing* mattered.

She curled into a ball on her plain white bedsheets and shivered.

"WHAT DID YOU SAY?" Salem asked, slowing the Jeep because they were near the turn onto her father's property.

"I've hit rock bottom. I'm as low as I can go. I need a place to rest."

He didn't know what to say. He'd told her to leave him alone, but she hadn't. She'd come to him sick. While he felt used, he also felt an odd sort of honor.

In her father's house, there would have been a dozen people willing to take care of her. She'd chosen him.

Or had she? He thought of her muddy hands.

"I'm dropping you off at your dad's, right?"

He felt her roll her head on the headrest and watch him.

He glanced at her. "What?"

"I need a friend, Salem. I can't go home tonight. Too many people there."

No, he didn't want her in his home. "There's no room at my house. You know that, Emily."

"I'll take anything."

Salem struggled to hold back his objections. This push-pull of love and anger was a struggle he'd lived with for too many years.

"Hey," Emily said quietly. "Why aren't you at Dad's party? You two are good friends."

"I meant to go after work, but started reading and lost track of time."

Emily's soft chuckle filled the interior of the car. He'd missed her laugh, and how it could lighten his darkest moments. "You've always been one for getting lost in a book. Remember when I used to sit in your office and say outrageous things about you and you would be so immersed in a book you wouldn't hear a thing?"

He remembered, with enough pleasure that he drove right past the turnoff to her dad's house to take her home with him.

Crazy fool, letting her use you like this.

Yes, I'm a fool, but I like having her close. This is just for tonight.

It had better be. You know how she breaks your heart when she leaves. Every time.

"What happened to you?" he asked.

"I left him. For good. Just like you said I should."

"What about work?"

"I left that, too."

"For how long? A couple of weeks?"

"For good."

She was leaving her career? The light from the dashboard wasn't strong enough to tell much more than that she had her eyes closed.

The nature of the silence in the car changed, became laden with censure, as though Emily were holding up a giant No Trespassing sign, making it clear that she'd said as much as she was going to.

Salem didn't know how he knew this when she hadn't said a word, but he knew, and held his tongue. Did he believe she'd left Jean-Marc for good? Not a chance. Had she left archeology for good? Never.

On the far side of town, he turned down his street and pulled into his driveway, where he helped her into the house. He led her to the kitchen. She plopped onto a chair and rested her head on her folded hands on top of the table.

His father wandered in. "Emily, hello."

She raised her head. "Hello, Mr. Pearce."

"You don't look good, girl."

"Feel awful," she said with a wan smile. Here in

the brightly lit room she looked even worse than she had in the dim Heritage Center office. Her skin was as ghostly as her voice had sounded in the car. Fever painted round red spots like old-fashioned rouge on cheekbones that didn't use to be so sharp. She put her head back down on fragile-looking wrists.

Salem should go to the Sudan and kill the bastard who did this to her, and that puzzled him. Emily had always been able to take care of herself. She'd never needed him to fight her battles for her.

"She has malaria, Dad."

"You need fattening, girl," Dad said. To Salem, he directed, "Warm her some of that soup I made yesterday."

Salem took a container of chicken soup out of the refrigerator and heated a bowl in the microwave. Old wives' tale or not, his father figured it was good for anything that ailed a body. He made a fresh pot every week.

Emily lifted a spoonful of soup, but the effort cost her. She needed to be in bed.

"Give me," he said. He took the utensil from her and raised soup to her mouth.

"Not a child."

"I know, but if I leave it to you, we'll be here all night." He got most of it into her before she batted his hand away.

"So tired," she whispered.

"Okay, let's get you to bed." He carried the bowl to the sink to wash it, but his dad took it from him.

"Take care of her," he said with a jut of his jaw toward Emily.

Salem led her upstairs to his bedroom and left her there while he went to the closet in the hallway to get fresh sheets. When he returned to his bedroom, Emily had stripped to her underwear—plain white cotton panties and bra.

He could probably wrap his fingers around her waist. There was a time when he'd craved her tight little body, but not tonight. Every part of Emily had been stripped down to bare essentials.

"Do you have a spare T-shirt?" She pulled back the covers.

"Of course." He took one out of his dresser then turned his back while she finished undressing. He heard her climb into bed.

"Wait."

She stopped with her knee on the mattress and watched him warily, her strange blue eyes with the odd hazel rings huge in her drawn face.

"I need to change the sheets."

She made a sound—a cross between a raspberry and an old-fashioned pshaw—and finished scrambling under the blankets.

The second her head hit the pillow, she closed her eyes.

By the time Salem returned the clean sheets to the closet and came back to the bedroom, Emily was asleep.

He grabbed a T-shirt and flannel pants, and washed

up and changed in the bathroom. When he finished, he laid a fresh towel and facecloth on the counter beside the sink and hoped neither of the girls used them in the morning before Emily got up, or before he could warn them he had a visitor.

From his supply of spare toiletries he kept under the counter—toothpaste, deodorant, tissues—he grabbed a toothbrush, unwrapped it and did a double-take. He held a child's toothbrush in his hand. With a sick sensation, he realized he was still buying his girls small toothbrushes when they were no longer children. They were adolescents.

He placed the foolishly small brush onto the facecloth. He also needed a fresh bar of soap, but couldn't find any under the counter. They were all out. He headed toward his younger daughter's room. She owned a collection of small soaps.

The light bleeding around the partially closed door of his older daughter's bedroom caught his attention. He pushed it open and said, "Hey, kid, time for lights-out."

Aiyana slept in a tight fetal ball on top of her bedsheets, her fingers curled over her shoulders—an egg with hands and feet. Where were her blankets?

"What the heck?" They were a tangled mass in the corner. He picked them up, straightened them and covered her, tucking them close around her body until they cocooned her, as he used to do when she was little.

She used to giggle and say, "Make me a mummy, Daddy."

She didn't laugh with him these days. She no longer called him Daddy, but he still thought of her as his little baby, a child who was growing up too fast.

He stared down at his daughter. No, she wasn't a child. She was becoming a woman, too quickly. He thought of those children's toothbrushes he'd been buying. He knew Aiyana went to the store and bought her own feminine products. Yes, she was becoming a young woman.

He'd missed turning points in his daughters' lives, and that made his chest ache.

When had he gotten so out of touch with them? With life around him?

Salem's ambition to be an architect, and his part-time school studies, were admirable, but his children had grown up while he'd had his head buried in one book after another, studying for tests and writing papers. Had his ambition harmed his children?

When he finished tucking her in, he kissed her forehead and said softly, "Good night, Eternal Blossom."

"Night, Daddy," she whispered, but as asleep as she was, probably had no idea that she had. She would certainly forget by morning when she'd be prickly as a porcupine again, as she'd been for the past year.

He had no idea how to deal with her. All he could do was give her the creature comforts—food, clothing, a roof over her head—and hope it was enough.

Satisfied that she was warm and safe for the night,

he left the room, turning out the light and closing the door behind him.

He checked in on Mika, who slept as though she hadn't a care in the world. A turtle-shaped lamp on her bedside table sent a soft glow around the room, highlighting her collection of raccoon statues that friends and family had given her every birthday and Christmas since she was old enough to talk, to express her desires, which had been early.

There was nothing shy about his Mika. Intelligent Raccoon.

On her dresser, she kept a bowl of tiny soaps and bubble bath capsules in different shapes and sizes. Mika wouldn't mind if he gave one to Emily. She'd inherited a generous spirit from her mother. Annie had been screwed up in many ways and her drug use was out of control at the end, but her generosity had been amazing.

For a split second, to his astonishment, he missed Annie, especially the good parts. Sure, she'd been neurotic at times, but she'd had a heart of gold. They hadn't loved each other, but they had tried hard for respect.

For Emily, he chose a pink heart-shaped soap, because he was just that foolish. In case she might want a bath instead of a shower, he also took a gold bubble bath bead in the shape of a star.

Emily Jordan. His shooting star, here today and gone tomorrow.

He leaned forward and kissed Mika's forehead.

She still smelled like a kid, not like the perfume he'd detected on Aiyana.

He turned off the light before he left. She liked to fall asleep with it on, but she was a heavy sleeper. She wouldn't need it for the rest of the night.

Salem smiled. No trouble with Mika yet, but then, she was only thirteen. Maybe adolescent hormones hadn't kicked in yet.

Back in the bathroom, he placed the soap and bath bead beside the ridiculous toothbrush. Was it enough? It had been years since there'd been a grown woman in the house—four years since Annie's death, and many more years since they'd had a guest. This wasn't really a guest, though. It was only Emily.

That thought brought him up short. There wasn't, never had been, and never would be anything *only* about Emily.

With one finger, he touched the pink heart soap that smelled like roses, and imagined her using it. He shook himself out of his foolish, romantic reverie, turned out the light and stepped into the hallway. *Romance* and *Emily* in the same thought? Dangerous.

"You sleeping downstairs?" His dad stood on the landing.

"Yep."

"Good night, then." His father entered the bedroom next to Salem's.

Salem nodded and went downstairs, turning off the remaining lights as he went. In the living room, he gathered afghans and blankets from the backs of the two armchairs and made himself a bed on the sofa.

He stretched out, but his six-foot frame was too long for the furniture, so his feet hung over the arm.

Not the least bit comfortable, he eventually fell asleep, but was awakened by a hand shaking his shoulder.

"Go take care of Emily." His father stood over him, illuminated by the streetlamp shining through sheer curtains. "She's making noise."

Salem threw off his covers and took the stairs two at a time. Emily thrashed on the bed.

"Hey, hey," he crooned, lifting her into a sitting position, but she sagged against his chest.

"Here," he said, reaching for the glass of water he'd left beside the bed. She gulped it down, with him holding her head to still her shuddering. He laid her back against the pillow and got fresh water from the bathroom.

Leaving it on the bedside table, he stared down at her. He couldn't leave her like this, too small and fragile. Too alone.

His Emily didn't *do* fragile. What did he mean *his* Emily? She wasn't his and never had been. She'd left too many times, dashing his hopes, for him to ever trust her again, the anger she inspired in him a constant throughout their relationship.

What relationship? You don't have one.

Damn right.

Remember that, Salem.

But she was his friend; or rather, he was hers. Sort of. Maybe. Reluctantly.

She shivered. He crawled in under the covers and nestled her against his chest. Gradually, the shaking stopped and she settled into an easier sleep.

He, however, did not sleep, not while he held Emily Jordan in his arms.

"I'M NOT GOING to school tomorrow." Aiyana stood in the doorway of the kitchen, scowling. Her eyes were red. She'd been crying. Dread hollowed out his gut. He couldn't take tears. He could handle—*had* handled—a lot in life, but crying made him feel useless.

"Are you sick?" Salem hoped this was physical, something the magic of chicken soup could fix. "What is it? The flu?"

She shrugged. Her hair stood out in all directions. She must have washed it before bed and fallen asleep while it was still wet.

"Dad, how about heating some of your soup?" Salem finished doctoring his coffee and caught his two slices of toast as they popped out of the toaster.

"You got it." His father retrieved the Tupperware.

"I don't want soup." Aiyana sounded like an odd mix of little-girl sulkiness and teenaged defiance.

Mika sat at the table eating her cereal, her brown eyes darting between him and Aiyana.

"How about toast?" Salem asked Aiyana. "You can have these and I'll make more for myself."

"No."

"But…"

"I don't want anything, okay?" she cried. "I just want to go back to bed. Just leave me alone today, okay?" She ran from the kitchen without waiting for anyone to respond.

Salem stared at her retreating back and what he could see of her feet running up the stairs.

His dad grunted. "I don't think it's the flu."

"Pardon?" Salem asked.

"It ain't the flu. It ain't physical."

That's what he was afraid of. "Crap."

"Why crap?"

"The flu or a cold would be easy. Soup, medication, hot tea. Boy or girlfriend or school trouble? Not so much. I don't know how to talk to her anymore."

Mika stood and picked up the present she'd wrapped yesterday. The social daughter, she was attending a friend's birthday party for the day. Aiyana, the quiet studious one, was more like him than Salem suspected she wanted to be.

"Boys," Mika said, with a nod of wisdom and a shrug that said, isn't it obvious? "See you after the party, Grandpa. Bye, Daddy." Then she was out the door and off to meet her friends down the street, so blessedly uncomplicated Salem thanked his lucky stars.

"What do I do about Aiyana?" Salem buttered his toast.

"Get your woman to talk to her."

His knife clattered to the counter. Clumsy fingers. "She's not my woman."

"Ask her to talk to your daughter."

"No." He might have let Emily sleep here last night, and he might have held her while she slept, but he'd be damned if he would expose his daughter to Emily's brand of heartache.

"She has been good to Aiyana since that girl was born."

True. She had showered Aiyana, and later Mika, with gifts and stuffed animals and postcards from abroad. "I know, but—"

"And Aiyana loves her."

Yes, he knew that, too, but maybe not so much lately. Anger at Emily had grown in Aiyana since her mother's death. Perhaps she'd hoped Emily might replace her mom, but that hope had been dashed every time Emily left.

Aiyana used to adore Emily, used to trail around behind her imitating her every move, and singing all of the silly songs Emily taught her.

When Emily would leave at the end of her visits, it was okay because Aiyana had her mother. Once Annie started using, though, she became less and less available to her daughter. Aiyana looked forward to Emily's visits too much after that, and was more devastated when she left.

Then, after Annie died, the questions started.

"Why is Emily going away? Doesn't she want to be with me? When is she coming back?"

Salem explained about her career, but it was hard to be convincing, because he'd always suspected there was more to it than there appeared to be.

"Aiyana is angry with her," his dad said, "but still loves her."

"Yeah, but—"

"Who else is there?"

No one now that her mother was dead. They didn't have an extended family.

"*Ask* her." Dad could be as persistent as a bear in the mood for dinner.

"*No.*"

"Stubborn." His father sniffed. "Like your mother."

He was *not*. "Emily is trouble."

"You need a little trouble."

Salem rounded on his father. "How can you say that? *You* of all people? After everything Mom did to you? To us?"

"I loved your mother, warts and all." His dad leaned back in his chair, crossed his feet and cupped the back of his head with his hands, as though they discussed nothing more serious than the weather. "Emily isn't like your mother."

Salem turned away and stared out the window.

"She isn't Annie, either," his dad said. "She is a different kind of lively. Not *trouble* trouble. *Fun* trouble."

"So what?"

"Aiyana is unhappy," Dad said. "Has been for a while."

"This is the first I've heard of it."

"You would know more if you spent more time at home."

"I work hard—"

His father cut him off with a shake of his head. "So what? Listen to what is important here. Something is wrong with Aiyana. I'm no good for her. You're no good. She needs a woman to talk to."

There wasn't one—Annie was dead and Salem's mother long dead—but damned if he would ask Emily to step in.

His mind cast about. "I'll phone Laura, Nick Jordan's wife."

"Uh-huh. Sure, you can. She's probably at the bakery right now serving customers, but you can call her and ask her to leave them and come right over."

Of course he couldn't. Weekend mornings were crazy busy at the café, Laura's busiest time. "How about Emily's sister, Pearl?"

"She won't think that's odd? You calling her while Emily is here in the house? And her knowing Aiyana idolizes Emily? That won't look strange?"

It would look ridiculous, and Salem knew it.

Emily was here. Still…he couldn't ask. He couldn't open Aiyana to heartbreak. But Aiyana was unhappy about something, and wouldn't confide in him.

His dad's white eyebrows rose in an exaggerated circumflex, low on the sides and high in the middle, almost meeting at the midpoint, compelling Salem to set aside his fears and seek help for his daughter.

It stuck in his craw. He didn't want Emily's help.

He could do this on his own. He wanted Emily out of his house and back in her own. Away from him. Away from his daughters.

"She won't hurt them," Dad said as though reading his mind. "She won't lead them astray."

His confusion with Aiyana, his utter...helplessness, had him swaying toward Dad's point of view. He needed *someone's* help. Emily was the only one available right now.

He'd made the decision to not see her again, to not think about her, to pretend she didn't exist, and yet here she was in his house. And Aiyana needed someone at this moment. Salem could deal with the consequences later.

"Okay," he said and trudged upstairs, footsteps heavy and slow like his thoughts.

At his closed bedroom door, he halted and glanced down the hallway toward Aiyana's door, also closed.

So many doors were closed to him these days. About the only thing that wasn't was school. No wonder he spent so much time buried in books. They opened pathways for him he couldn't breach elsewhere in his life.

He knocked and Emily called for him to come in.

She stood beside the bed, her skin pale and gray like ash, using his brush to calm her hair. He loved its thickness and color, a medium brown warmed by glints of blond and red tones. Natural highlights. Or, he assumed they were natural since they'd already been there when she was twelve.

He still remembered the first time he ever saw her and thinking he'd gone crazy because he'd felt such an immediate kinship with a stranger, and her only twelve while he was a strapping eighteen.

For a while, he'd wondered if he was some kind of pervert before realizing his attraction wasn't sexual. That had come later, when she was still too young at fifteen. It had driven him into the arms of another woman. Just his rotten luck their birth control had failed. No, that wasn't true. He might have regretted his marriage, but never his daughters, even now when they were teenagers and he didn't have a clue what to do with them.

"Are you okay?" he asked Emily.

"I'm fine," she replied, but wasn't.

He knew when Emily lied. She was lying now.

"What's up?" she asked shyly. Emily, who could go anywhere, do anything, was never shy. "You look upset."

"And you look a little better than last night. More like yourself. How do you feel?"

"Tired, but the fever broke during the night, thank goodness. The attack's almost run its course." She placed his hairbrush onto his dresser. "I've known others with this. I've seen the symptoms and how they progress. I'll be better soon."

"Do you need to be anywhere this morning? I have a problem."

"What kind of problem?"

"Aiyana's upset."

Her head shot up. "Aiyana? What's wrong?"

The request backed up in his throat, but the bottom line was that Aiyana needed help and Emily was here. Even with his father's help, Salem had been coping as both parents for so long, and he was out of his depth. "I think maybe she needs to talk to a woman."

Emily looked uncertain, another sign she wasn't herself. In all the years he'd known her, Salem had admired her generosity of spirit and her self-confidence.

He stepped back. "If you don't want to that's okay."

"No. I don't mind. It's just…"

"Just what?"

"What kind of help does she need? I mean, I don't know if I *can* help."

If she didn't help him figure out the puzzle that was his daughter, who would?

"What exactly is the problem?"

Salem shook his head like a bewildered old man, so far out of his element. "Mika says it's boys. She's at that age, right?"

Emily tilted her head, thinking. "Aiyana's what? Fourteen?"

"Fifteen. Almost sixteen."

"Yeah." Emily's mouth twisted wryly. "It's probably a boy."

"So, you'll talk to her?"

A wash of emotion that might have been sadness painted Emily's features.

"Okay." She seemed to rouse herself. "Where is she? In her bedroom?"

Salem nodded and went back downstairs, hoping he could deal with the repercussions of Emily leaving—again—later. Maybe. He hoped.

EMILY LEANED HER forehead against Aiyana's door to summon her strength before entering. She had to help the girl however she could, even though her resources were depleted. She just didn't know what she had to give. Damn this illness.

Aiyana, the girl who used to follow Emily around like a perky kitten, needed her. While Emily had completed high school, she'd spent time with Aiyana on the weekends, bringing her gifts—stuffed bunny rabbits, books and toys.

The child might have been born to another woman, and Emily might have resented Annie for marrying Salem, but Aiyana had been Salem's daughter, and a darling. And Emily had loved her from the first moment she met her.

Funny that Annie hadn't minded, but then, Annie had been a proud mother, and happy to show off her baby. She had even let Emily babysit.

When Emily had gone to college, she had sent Aiyana birthday cards and sweet little notes at Christmas, and more presents.

As an archeologist, she had mailed Aiyana postcards from all the exotic countries she had visited. So, Emily had enjoyed a correspondence both ways, with Maria in the Sudan when she was at home, and with Aiyana when she'd been away.

And now Aiyana was hurting.

Aware of how hypocritical it was to offer *boy* advice when her own love life was a mess, she knocked anyway, because Salem had asked her to. How could she say no?

"Go away, Dad." The voice sounded sullen, as only a teenager could, but Emily heard more. Desolation.

"It's Emily."

"Emily?" Emily heard a nose being blown. "Oh, um, just a sec."

Emily waited.

"Okay. Come in." It sounded thick with tears.

Emily opened the door cautiously. Aiyana sat on her bed with her arms wrapped around an oversize teddy bear, looking so much like a female version of a teenaged Salem that it brought back memories, both warm and tough. Aiyana was too old for stuffed animals, but Emily remembered the misery of unrequited love. Salem came to mind. She approached the bed.

"Hi," she said and smiled.

Aiyana didn't respond. Strange.

"Your dad says something's going on. Do you want to talk?"

Aiyana shrugged. "I don't know." Her nose was stuffed up, and her eyes bloodshot. "What are you doing here so early in the morning?"

Emily was taken aback by Aiyana's vaguely belligerent tone. It used to be that the girl would run into Emily's arms when she returned for her visits. But the past couple of years, Aiyana been a bit cool, and now this. Was it normal adolescence, or something deeper?

"I slept over last night."

"Did you sleep with Dad?"

Whoa. Did Aiyana mean *sleep* sleep or *have sex* sleep? Emily was pretty sure she meant sex. Where had this come from?

Before Emily could react, Aiyana asked, "So, like, did you guys kiss and make up?"

Ohhhh. Was this about Emily and Salem fighting before she left last year? Aiyana must have picked up on the change in Salem's attitude toward her.

Why did adults never think that kids understood what was happening around them?

"I *slept* here because I was sick last night. I fainted at the Cathedral and your dad brought me home and took care of me."

"How long are you staying *this* time?"

Emily finally got what was going on. The daughter had the same issues as the father.

"I'm staying for good this time."

Skeptical, Aiyana shrugged.

"You look really pale," Aiyana said, begrudgingly, as though she cared, but didn't want to. "Are you okay?" A glimmer of compassion softened the blunt edges of Aiyana's teenaged pique. Maybe they would get through this after all.

"It's the tail end of an attack of malaria."

"Isn't that really bad?"

"I'll be okay in a few days."

Emily tucked her hands into her pockets. She felt as lost as Aiyana looked miserable, and just as uncomfortable. She didn't know what to say or do.

This kind of thing had been easier when Aiyana's problems had been as simple as scraped knees and broken toys.

On the wall on the other side of the bed, Emily spotted a corkboard filled with all the postcards Emily had sent over the years. *Oh.* Aiyana had kept them, every last one.

Aiyana might as well have reached into Emily's chest and petted her heart as she was doing with the teddy bear's head. Emily *had* to find a way to help her. She wanted to regain what they used to have.

"You know, when your dad and I fought last year, it had nothing to do with you. I love you as much now as I ever have."

At the word *love,* Aiyana's expression softened even more.

Emily took advantage. "Maybe I can help you through this." It sounded like a question instead of an offer of help because, honestly, she had no idea what to *do.* She knew how to be a good listener. Maybe that's all it would take. "Do you want to talk about it?"

"I don't *know,*" Aiyana wailed. Oh, she must be hurting badly if she would consider confiding in Emily even though she was still so angry with her. "It's embarrassing."

"Did something happen to you?"

Aiyana buried her face in the bear's head. "Sort of."

Sort of? Oh, dear. "Can you explain what you mean?" Emily sat on the edge of the bed, but made sure she didn't touch Aiyana. She didn't want to invade the girl's space if things weren't fully right between them.

Aiyana covered her face with her hands. "I don't know if I can. You wouldn't understand."

"You'd be surprised."

Aiyana's head jerked up at the depth of emotion in Emily's voice.

Maybe in this situation, Emily would have to give before she would receive. "I broke up with my boyfriend three days ago when I left the Sudan to come home."

"Oh, that's so sad."

"It was long overdue. We'd been together for six years, but he didn't treat me well. I tolerated his behavior way longer than I should have. It was time for me to smarten up."

Something about the phrase *smarten up* must have resonated with Aiyana, because she opened her mouth to speak, and the dam broke.

Through tears, haltingly, she told her story, about how she'd thought the boy had cared for her, about how she was honored and happy he'd asked her to be his girlfriend, about how last night he'd taken her into the ravine and had tried to pressure her to have sex.

He'd pushed her too hard too fast, but Aiyana hadn't given in. Wow, strong girl for holding her own.

Emily was proud of her young friend. "That took

guts. You have to feel the time and the boy are right before taking that big step. You'll get over him."

"I already have, as soon as I realized what a jerk he is. That's not the problem. Look!" She jumped up from the bed. Anger vibrated in her slim frame. Good. Anger was a hell of a lot better than despair. Aiyana hit a few keys and her Twitter account came up. "Look what he did."

Emily joined her, pressing her hand onto Aiyana's shoulder. Oh, she had a bad feeling about this.

There, on the computer screen, tweets bounced around from the boy and his friends, and girls too, stating that she'd gone all the way with him last night... and that it hadn't been the first time, and he hadn't been the first boy, tweets like a hail of bullets cutting Aiyana down, too similar to Jean-Marc's assault, but much, much worse.

Aiyana was too young, her defenses too undeveloped, to repel an attack like this. No wonder she needed help.

Damn the internet for making bullying so painfully public.

"It's all lies," Aiyana wailed. "I'm still a virgin."

In Aiyana's pain, Emily heard echoes of her own.

She fell back to sit on the bed, her past rushing toward her from a long dark tunnel, whooshing full speed ahead, the memories she'd worked so hard to submerge surfacing here where she had thought she would be safe.

She could handle Jean-Marc and his ugly innuendo

miles and miles away, because she knew she could find a way to repair the damage, *somehow,* but this was here at home in Accord, and it was happening to a girl she loved, and it was happening in Emily's old school. And that easily, the woman Emily had matured into was gone, and she was back to the lost and lonely girl she used to be.

CHAPTER FOUR

I HAVE NOTHING TO GIVE.

Emily had left too much of herself with all of the relics she'd resurrected and studied, and with a man who'd only wanted to control her. Any resilience she'd once possessed had deserted her. Her life was in shambles. How on earth was she supposed to help this girl?

Emily stared into Aiyana's dark eyes, identical to Salem's, but filled with panic and fear. Emily couldn't turn away from the pain of being a young adolescent, of being unjustly accused, of experiencing the unfairness of life.

Aiyana needed a friend, and unless Emily wanted to disappoint herself and Salem, she had to try to help her.

Jean-Marc's unfair accusations had brought up her painful past. Aiyana's pain cemented her in it. All of those things she'd thought she had dealt with came brimming to the surface. She didn't want to be in this place. She wanted to escape.

How naive to have thought that by leaving Accord time and again she had left the past behind. It sat inside her gut like a hard ball, blocking growth because she had never dealt with it. She hadn't even *begun* to deal with it.

Salem had been right—she *had* been running—a lowering thought, that she'd based her life's major decision on denial.

Rather than facing the problems she'd had in school head-on, she'd hidden from them, had believed herself to have risen above them, but all she had done was to find herself another bully to live with. Rather than deal with the lack of self-esteem with which the bullying and isolation had left her, she had created a pattern.

And it made her sick with disappointment in herself.

Memories of her own helplessness in high school, and the unjust accusations of mean girls, brought to flaming life the shame she'd felt back then. It had scalded then and did again now.

Her dad had married Laura and it had looked as if Emily's life was turning away from the solitude she'd lived with for too many years since her parents' divorce. Her mother had moved to France with her new husband, and her father had been a workaholic. Emily spent too many evenings alone in their big Seattle home. Then they'd moved to Accord, a town Emily had fallen in love with on first sight. She'd been happy for a few years, until her body matured and a clique of the most popular girls hadn't liked that boys found her attractive.

By then, her dad and Laura had been busy with Pearl and then Cody. Emily's cousin and best friend, Ruby, had gone to live with her mother and new stepfather for a year. Salem started dating Annie. Emily had been devastated. Soon after, Annie was pregnant and Salem married. Emily had never felt so alone.

She had survived the mean girls, eventually, but had spent subsequent years burying those memories as though they'd never existed. She didn't want the old pain resurrected, she didn't want Jean-Marc repeating that behavior, not now at another low point in her life, not on top of everything else.

But this girl needs you. Dredge up something. Anything.

"We'll figure out how to handle this." She meant it, even if only intellectually.

Give what you can.

An hour later, she left Aiyana's bedroom and went downstairs. They had come up with a plan. Aiyana had to be proactive. Tomorrow morning, she would go to school as usual and pretend nothing had happened. She would be a better person than Justin and his friends. She wouldn't check social media for the rest of the day. Emily had convinced Aiyana to brazen it out, the only way to get through this kind of thing, advice she needed to take herself. Today, she had to deal with the prayer book.

She entered the kitchen and found Salem and Mr. Pearce sipping coffee and making desultory conversation.

When he saw her, Salem's expression became alert, and he stood so quickly his dad had to catch his chair before it toppled. "What is it? What's wrong?"

"It's boy trouble, and not good at all."

She told him about Aiyana going out with a boy the night before. Salem reacted as a father.

"I'm going to talk to her right now," he said, his stern-parent voice new to Emily. "This isn't acceptable."

Emily stepped in front of him before he could leave the room. "That's not important right now."

When he opened his mouth to object, she cut in, "It really isn't. You have a much bigger problem."

Salem became wary. She explained about Justin White trying to force Aiyana, about her resisting and him leaving her in the ravine alone.

Shadows roiled in Salem's eyes, dark things she'd never seen before expanding inside her quiet, stoic friend, like magma, hot and explosive just below the surface. Emily hesitated to tell him more, but he deserved the full truth about his daughter's troubles.

"The bigger problem is what the guy did this morning."

She explained about the tweets and emails.

"I'm going to kill the kid." Salem stormed from the kitchen. Emily followed him.

"Oh, Salem, no," she objected. "She already regrets going out with him."

"Not her. Him. Justin."

"I don't blame you, but—" She was talking to thin air. Salem had already stalked out of the house, slamming the front door behind him. The windows rattled.

"What's happening?" she asked his father.

Mr. Pearce, the laid-back man as worked up as she'd ever seen him, tried to run for the front door but hobbled. "Damn knees! Go after him."

"What's he doing?"

"He's going to find Justin."

Emily rushed outside too late to catch Salem. Mr. Pearce reached the front door just as Emily turned back.

"Will he hurt Justin?" She had no idea what he would do. She'd never seen him lift a finger to hurt another person or creature, but this angry Salem, Salem *this* angry, was a man she didn't know.

"I've never seen him this worked up. The boy's got powerful self-control, but this is about his daughter. He'll be wanting to protect her from that boy." Mr. Pearce worried his bottom lip with his teeth and watched Salem's taillights until they rounded the corner at the end of the street. "He loves those girls fierce."

He limped back inside. "You want breakfast?"

"No. I'd better go home." She couldn't eat a thing, not with worrying about Salem confronting Justin, and not while her stomach still churned with malaria. Her heart had always been attracted to Salem's still waters, but she had also known there was a deep undercurrent he'd never shared with her.

She needed to crawl back into bed, her own bed, to pull the covers over her head and sleep for a week. She called Pearl to pick her up.

WARNING SIGNALS CUT through the red haze clouding Salem's mind.

He didn't want this, hated to *be* like this, hotheaded and on the edge of control, but someone had hurt his Aiyana. He'd kept his cool, his control, time and again over the years, but when it came to the people he cared about, he protected them. This was about his baby girl. He had to warn the guy away from her because, so help him God, if Justin hurt her again, Salem wouldn't be responsible for his actions.

Be careful. Be smart.

He knew Justin and disliked him. The thought of Aiyana with him...

Imagining what had happened, or what could have happened if his daughter hadn't been able to get away...Salem couldn't go there. When he got home, he would discuss her taste in boys.

Cool it. She's young. She's still learning.

Too young for the likes of Justin White. The kid gave Salem the creeps. He didn't want to talk to Aiyana until he'd cooled down first, and the only way to do that was to have it out with Justin.

He knew where to find him on a Sunday—at the high school, practicing basketball. Same thing Salem used to do all day Sunday when he was that age.

As soon as he parked, he flew out of the vehicle and into the school, the hallways as familiar to him as the layout of his home.

Down the corridor, the shouts of boys and the squeak of sneakers on the gym floor lured him on.

Silently, Salem shoved open the door to the gym, taking in the scents of dust and sweaty boys. It took only a minute for play to halt because he walked·onto the middle of the court and stood still, solid and immovable.

Justin White recognized him and darted behind a couple of boys. Coward. He wasn't so tough when facing someone his own size.

Salem grasped the sleeve of his jersey to haul him out from behind them.

"Hey!" Justin yelped. "Don't touch me."

"What's going on here?" Edgar Haynes stepped onto the court. Bald, burly Edgar had been a teacher at the school for years and had taken over coaching basketball after Emily's dad had given up the job. The hand he placed on Salem's shoulder held a message. *Calm down.*

They'd been friends for years. Edgar knew Salem through and through.

"Justin and I are going to have a chat," Salem said, his voice shaking with the strain to keep violence leashed. This little shit had hurt his girl.

"Not without me present," Edgar said. "When these boys are here, they're my responsibility."

"Fine. You can listen in."

Edgar stayed close, as if he was ready for anything to happen. "You can talk to him, but let go of him first." When Salem didn't release the boy, Edgar said, "Salem," his voice ripe with warning. The hum of murmurs from the onlookers penetrated the haze clouding rational thought.

Salem let go slowly, reluctant in case the kid made a run for it. "Stay away from my daughter." The pit bull of Salem's anger strained against the leash, begging for release.

"Don't touch Aiyana. Don't talk to her," Salem ordered. "Don't write lies and crap about her on the internet. Is that clear?"

Justin nodded and backed away.

"You touch her again, you try to *force* her again—" Justin opened his mouth to object, but Salem spoke over him "—and I'll find you and rip your guts up through your throat."

Justin's eyes widened and he croaked, "Coach, you heard this guy threaten me. Call the cops."

"I've known Salem all my life," Edgar said. "He's a reasonable man, which leads me to believe that you hurt his daughter. What did you do to make him lose his temper like this?"

Justin held out his hands, palms up, but his eyes shifted to the side. "I don't know what the guy's talking about."

"Yeah?" Salem leaned forward. "If I go down to the ravine, I won't find a tent you lured my daughter to where you tried to get her drunk? Tried to get her to have sex with you?"

"She's a liar," Justin shouted.

Salem lunged for him, but both Edgar and a kid intercepted him and held him back. "Salem, you need to leave." Salem recognized Cody's voice. Emily's brother. He was strong. Salem couldn't break free of his grasp, not when combined with Edgar's. "Go home, Salem. Coach can handle this."

"Go," Edgar commanded, used to bringing teenagers under control. "I'll talk to Justin."

Salem shoved his finger dangerously close to the boy's face. "You remember what I told you. You stay away from Aiyana, keep your hands off her and take that filth off the internet."

He stormed out, vibrating with rage, as though an alien being maneuvered his body, controlled his normally rational mind.

In the car, he gripped the steering wheel and breathed hard, aware that coming here might not have been the smartest decision, but nothing could have kept him away. What father wouldn't defend his daughter?

Salem didn't drive home. Having his say hadn't calmed him enough. He knew of one place that would help. He pulled the car around behind the Accord Golf and Cross-Country Ski Resort and parked in the farthest corner of the parking lot, a short walk through the woods to the Cathedral. But when he got out of the car, he didn't head that way.

He took a well-trod path to the lake.

Voices down by the water—guests from the main house, no doubt—filtered from the main beach, but that wasn't his destination. He continued on until he reached a rarely used path that led around to the far side, to a tiny enclave he frequented. He needed time to bury the beast.

Craziness still churned inside him, turning him into a person he abhorred, a man who couldn't restrain his emotions.

He'd wanted to kill the kid. Anger swirled in him like clouds of toxic vapor. That boy had hurt his sweet Aiyana.

Once he reached the small beach he called his own, he picked up a handful of stones and tossed them into the lake as far and as hard as he could, one after the other after the other, until his arm ached. He needed the physical release of violence, but couldn't hurt another person. Not even that kid.

When he felt he might be human again, he stopped and shot a heavy breath out of his lungs, hoping to expel the last remnants of anger.

It left him exhausted, spent like the last dollar in a lean wallet.

On the edge of the small rocky beach stood a huge Douglas fir. He rested his hand on the rough bark.

A tree hugger all his life, Salem's only regret was that trees couldn't hug back. Sometimes he felt intensely alone, and had for years, even with Annie, especially toward the end when her mind had been taken over by drugs.

He drew on the sharp scent of pine, on the stillness and peace of the water, on the heat and dappled sunlight against his closed lids.

When the beast skulked away, he sat on the huge

rock at the back of the beach to gather himself. He hated, *hated,* when he lost control like that. It brought back too many memories of his past, of his mom, and the influence she'd had on his life until her death when he was twelve.

His larger-than-life mother could sing like an angel and dance around the house to old rock and roll music all day, but couldn't manage to put dinner on the table every night, or put in a load of laundry so her kid could wear clean clothes to school. She had been passionate, but illogical in her life views. His mother, unwittingly, was the motivator behind his love of rational thought, sound reasoning and quiet living.

He'd spent his adult years crafting a life of peace. Given his explosion this morning, his lack of control over his emotions, he wasn't there yet.

Only when he felt truly like himself again did he head home.

The first thing he did when he got there was to go upstairs and knock on Aiyana's door.

"Come in." She didn't sound happy, but she also wasn't as overtly upset as this morning.

She sat on her bed reading a book, but closed it when he entered. He perched beside her and waggled his fingers toward the book she'd hidden.

"What are you reading? Let me see."

She retrieved the book from her far side and handed it to him.

"Tolkien? Hey, I loved this when I was your age."

"Really? The teachers at school think I should be reading something older."

"Why?"

"Because I'm smart." She wasn't bragging. It was a statement of fact. "Sometimes, I just want to relax and enjoy a book, not always have to work. You know?"

"Yeah. I know. It used to be like that for me with basketball. Sometimes I wanted to forget the drills and just shoot hoops for fun."

He didn't know where to start about last night's incident, so figured he'd just be direct. "I had a talk with Justin."

"You did?"

"I told him to stay away from you. He's not a great guy, Aiyana. You can do better."

A soft flush filled her cheeks. "I know that now, Dad. I can't believe I ever thought he was cute."

Salem couldn't contain his surprise. His daughter had just agreed with him about something. That didn't happen every day. Not these days at any rate. "You're smart and attractive and kind. Don't undervalue your-self with creeps like Justin, got it?"

"Yeah. Got it."

"Okay." Salem stood up. Now for the hard part. "You know I have to punish you for going out last night without permission. You're grounded for the coming week. No TV. No going out after school."

Her mouth dropped open as she scowled, and just like that he'd shattered their fragile harmony.

As he walked downstairs, he felt lower than low. But wasn't it his job as a parent to be tough, even when he didn't want to be?

ON THE DRIVE HOME, Pearl cast sidelong glances at Emily, but showed remarkable restraint in not asking when Emily had left the Jordan home last night and why she had slept at Salem's. Once home, Emily went to her room because she craved time alone to process all that had happened last night and this morning. Salem had given her so much. Tranquility. Breathing room. A fleeting, sleepy memory of him holding her. Even though she'd awakened alone this morning, she didn't think she'd been dreaming about his arms around her. He had been there for her.

She hadn't felt as alone as she had in her father's house, chockablock full of people she loved.

This morning, despite his obvious reluctance to let her get close again, he'd entrusted his daughter into her care.

Dogged by fatigue, by the lingering symptoms of malaria, she nonetheless sat at her desk. *Be proactive. Handle this.*

If she could urge a young girl to stand up and face her problems, then Emily could bloody well take steps to handle her own. She wanted to contact Penelope Chadwick about the relic, but wouldn't email her. What if Emily's account was being watched? She couldn't send a direct message to anyone involved in the dig. What if any mail that arrived from her was intercepted and read? What if she mailed the prayer book to Pen and the authorities opened the package because it came from her? Would Pen then be in trouble?

Civil rights were a fluid concept in some countries.

Instead, Emily wrote a letter to Penelope's brother in England. Arthur lived in London with their aging parents.

She had only ever met him three times when he had visited digs. He had been sweet and nerdy, an English professor to the bone. He'd had a crush on her, but since she'd been with Jean-Marc, neither of them had acknowledged it. While he knew how close Emily and Penny were, maybe he wouldn't want to become involved in Emily's problems. It was a lot to ask of someone she didn't really know well.

It took Emily a while to figure out how to word her strange request. The prayer book had to go back to the Sudan.

She asked Arthur Chadwick to write a letter to his sister proclaiming Emily's innocence and stating that she'd been set up, and that she would fix the situation.

She asked whether, if she mailed him a package, he would re-label it from him and send it along to Penny, so the package wouldn't look suspicious, and whether he minded helping with this.

That done, she put the letter beside the front door. Tomorrow, she would call FedEx to have it delivered ASAP. Then she crawled into bed, because the malaria and the high emotions of the day had caught up to her.

She awoke at about five, still tired, but restless. She

brushed her teeth and hair. Downstairs, she found Laura and Pearl in the kitchen preparing dinner.

Laura left what she was doing at the stove to wrap her arms around Emily. Ah. It was so good to be home in the bosom of her family. When Laura pulled back, she looked deeply into Emily's eyes.

"Are you okay?"

"I will be. In time."

Dust motes danced in the late-afternoon sunlight streaming through the kitchen windows, the quiet of the house a marked contrast to last night's party.

"Where is everyone?"

"Your dad's at the resort, but should be home any minute. Cody's in his room."

Pearl held a carrot and peeler, but watched Emily intently. "How are you feeling?"

"Better. Still tired, but the fever broke last night."

"Where?"

Puzzled, Emily said, "It was all over my body."

Laura and Pearl exchanged a glance then laughed.

"Emily," Pearl said slowly, as though talking to a child. "Why did I have to pick you up at Salem's house this morning?"

Oh. Of course they would ask.

"I stayed there. His dad gave me homemade soup."

"You could have had soup here." Laura took a roast out of the oven, basted it and put it back in.

"There were so many people here, and I was sick. I just wanted peace and quiet."

"With Salem," Pearl said, her smile too knowing.

"Nothing happened." Emily sounded defensive until she realized her sister was joking. "I just wanted to see him."

"How did you get there?"

"I walked to the resort and found him at the Cathedral." No sense mentioning about the need to bury a prayer book.

Laura rinsed dishes at the sink. "E-mi-ly," Laura chastised. "I would have driven you."

Emily hugged her stepmother and said, "Lau-ra, I didn't want to break up the party." She stepped away. "How can I help?"

"You can sit and relax."

Her father walked in and wrapped his arms around her from behind. "How's my girl?"

"Good."

Laura sat down. "Tell us everything, Emily. What happened? Why aren't you going back?"

She explained it all, noticing that her dad ground his teeth when she mentioned Jean-Marc's infidelity. "I should go punch that guy out."

Emily smiled at the thought of the two fathers, Salem and her own dad, protecting their daughters. She was a grown woman, independent, but her father's concern felt good.

When she finished the rest of her explanation, Pearl said, "Good for you. I never liked the sound of that guy. Now you're home."

"Where you belong," her dad added.

"I haven't heard you play in a whole year." Pearl

stood up to finish peeling carrots. "How about if you get your violin and give us a private concert while we work?"

She retrieved her instrument from her room, and when she came back down, Cody was there grabbing carrots while Pearl swatted his hands.

"Don't you ever stop eating?" little Pearl asked her very big brother.

"Nah. When's dinner?"

"As soon as these are cooked, if you've left any for the rest of us," Pearl grumbled.

Emily had lived her first twelve years without siblings, so this whole business of sibling rivalry entertained her. She loved watching their byplay.

"Hey, sis," Cody said. "What was up with Salem this morning?"

"Salem?" What had he done? "Where did you see him?"

"He came to the school during basketball practice and reamed out Justin White. Sounded like it had something to do with his daughter, Aiyana." Cody related everything he'd heard. So, Salem had been mad, but he hadn't gone overboard. Good.

She explained what had happened to Aiyana in broad strokes, keeping the more private stuff…private.

"Aiyana's smart and cute," Cody said. "She can do better than Justin."

Emily tuned her violin. "I gather he isn't the greatest guy."

"He's a jerk, but the girls are on him like flies on shit."

"Cody!" Laura admonished.

"Sorry, Mom," Cody said, but his grin contradicted the apology.

"I can't think about this anymore." Emily had reached her emotional limit for the day.

She played a couple of her favorite classical pieces. The peace of the music washed over her and around her, baptizing her with a familiar sense of renewal. Why had she let herself drift so far away from her music?

It had been her lifesaver during high school. Now here it was, easing her pain, soothing her tumultuous emotions. Saving her again.

But that night, she dreamed about things she hadn't thought of in years. Girls yelling nasty things. Isolation in school corridors. Whispers and pointing fingers.

The question that had plagued her years ago went unanswered in the night. *Why did I deserve to be bullied?*

Home.

Both the word and the place felt good. Right.

On Monday morning, Emily lay in her old bedroom, wondering when the fatigue and the lingering effects of her illness and the pure sweet ache of coming home for good would settle down.

Coming back to Accord to live was big. Huge. She'd walked away from her career. Time stretched before her in all its wondrous glory and terrifying emptiness.

She'd known there would be this gratitude and easing into familiar territory, but there was also the other...the old memories she had shut out for years. Recalling her troubling dreams, she scrubbed the sleep from her eyes and stared at the high peak of the ceiling. In her childish enthusiasm, she'd painted it sky blue and had sponged on white clouds.

Oh, the arrogance of youth. She'd been so sure of herself and her future, had thought she'd known so much about where her life was going and how successful she would be. The best-laid plans...

Shaking off her inertia, she got out of bed, showered and readied herself for the day. She—

Her door slammed open at the bottom of the stairs, hitting the wall with a resounding echo, and she jumped.

What? Who?

Heavy feet pounded up the staircase. Had the authorities found her? Were they coming to arrest her for stealing the artifact? She cast about for escape. The tree! She could climb down and run. To where? She didn't *know*.

When Salem strode into her room, she sagged against the door to the balcony. Only Salem. Thank God. "You scared the *daylights* out of me. Don't ever do that again." She huffed out a breath. "Ever hear of knocking?"

"You have to help me," he said without preamble, about as emotional as she'd ever seen him. No sphinx here today. Yesterday, his rage had been almost cold. Today, he looked hot and bothered, wild and shaken up. And maybe that wasn't such a bad thing.

"Come with me. Now." By his expression, this was more than just being rattled. This was pure fear.

"Where?" she asked, her heart still battering against her ribs. "What's wrong?"

"It's Aiyana. I'm worried about her." Worry didn't begin to cover what Emily saw on Salem's face. Besides the fear, there was raging concern, but also anger. "Those stupid kids. I don't know what else they're writing about her, but she's low, Emily. Really, really low. I've never seen her like this. You're the only one she'll talk to...." His words trailed off and he seemed to deflate.

Emily grabbed a sweater from the back of a chair, threw her purse over her shoulder and said, "Let's go."

Laura was waiting at the bottom of the stairs. "I thought I heard someone come in and then I noticed your car outside, Salem. How about a cup of cof—"

When she saw his face, her welcoming smile faded. "Aiyana?"

He nodded.

"Go." She touched his shoulder. "Call us if you need anything."

Lost but determined, once in the car, Emily buckled herself in. "Tell me what's happening."

"She won't go to school. She looks worse than yesterday. She won't eat. Won't shower. Won't brush her teeth. Won't leave her room."

Emily nodded. "What happened between yesterday and this morning? When I left, she promised she would go to school today."

"I don't know." Salem's frustration rattled around the interior of the old Jeep.

What did he think she could do?

"Talk to her. Please?"

What could she say today that she hadn't said yesterday? "Of course. Same as yesterday, though. I don't know how I can help."

"Just—just try." Salem's worry arced between them like a lightning strike. He might have married Annie out of duty, but he loved his daughters.

"Why me? I know you don't really want me around. Even yesterday, I knew you would rather have had someone else there."

"You're right." Salem glanced at her. "I'd rather it was someone else."

That hurt.

Salem continued, "I know how hard it will be for Aiyana when you leave."

"I'm not leaving."

She could read his skepticism like a novel.

He shrugged. "Aiyana asked for you."

Oh. "Hurry," she said. "Drive faster."

Salem punched the accelerator. "Aiyana is sensitive. Has been since her mother died. You have to help her."

Oh, Lord, no pressure. She'd been useless yesterday. What now?

At Salem's house, Emily found herself in front of Aiyana's closed door for the second morning in a row. She took a fortifying breath and knocked.

"Go away." There was no anger in the girl's voice. In fact, there was nothing.

Emily opened the door. "It's me."

Aiyana lay with her back to the door.

Emily approached the bed. "We need to talk." No response. *Think. Think!* What had Emily needed at that time? Tough love?

She'd give it a try. "You're letting them win."

"They *are* winning." Aiyana's voice was so flat, so devoid of emotion, Emily panicked.

She sat beside Aiyana, reaching a hand to her shoulder but not making contact. Would the girl want to be touched? She'd been violated by a boy the other night, in both her trust and her body. Would Emily's touch be an invasion? Or would it be what Aiyana needed? She didn't *know*. She was flying blind here, hoping female intuition would kick in with a brilliant solution. No such luck so far.

"Talk to me," she urged.

Aiyana rolled over. "What is there to talk about? I'm ruined. Everybody hates me."

"What else has been happening since yesterday?"

"More of the same tweets and emails, but now there's a Facebook page, too."

"Show me."

Aiyana crawled out of bed and opened her laptop, pulling up the page on the internet, her hair hanging in limp strands, cheeks puffy, eyes bloodshot. She'd been crying. She obviously hadn't slept.

The second Emily saw the Facebook page, anger

surged through her. Why were people so cruel? And why were teenagers the worst of the worst? A page had been dedicated to calling this sweet girl a slut.

She couldn't believe what she was reading.

This had gotten out of hand already. So quickly. Wow, life in the internet age moved at the speed of light. Obviously, Salem's warning to Justin hadn't worked yesterday. He needed to go to the school and report this kid. Or even better, go to the cops.

In the meantime, Emily had to help Aiyana.

She studied the girl's face. Aiyana had given up. Already. Before the war had even begun.

"You know what you need?" Emily asked, and knew she was about to sound cold and ruthless, but desperate times called for desperate measures. "You need a backbone."

Aiyana's face crumpled. Tears gathered, ready to spill over.

"I'm not trying to crush you," Emily rushed on. "But instead of getting depressed about this, you should be angry. What these people are doing is appalling. These little shits are trying to ruin your life."

She clapped a hand over her mouth. "I'm sorry! I shouldn't swear in front of you. Your dad would be upset with me."

A smile tugged at the corners of Aiyana's mouth. "You should hear what I call them in my mind. It's a lot worse."

"What? What do you call them? Say it all out loud."

Aiyana did. She shouted swearwords and she called

them dirty names, inventive and pleased with herself by the time she finished.

"That's a better attitude than defeat. Did it feel good?"

"Yes!"

"Good. These people are trying to steal your life from you and you have to fight back."

"I don't know how."

"I'll help you. Your dad will help you. Your grand-father will help you. *You aren't alone.* Understand?" *Yes.* She'd hit the nail on the head. That was exactly what Emily had needed when she'd been bullied—to know that she wasn't alone.

Aiyana looked better. She nodded.

"First, you need to get showered and dressed. Wear something really pretty today."

When Aiyana hesitated, Emily ordered, "Go. Get ready for school." She glanced at her watch. "You still have time."

Aiyana gathered clothes and shuffled out of her bed-room, her baggy Snoopy nightshirt hanging down the backs of her thighs.

In the kitchen, Emily barked orders. "Cucumber. I need two slices," she directed Salem. She turned to Mr. Pearce. "Baking soda," she said, like a general rallying her troops.

They handed her the items. Back upstairs she rummaged around in Aiyana's room until she found nail polish in a soft pink.

Emily glanced up to find Salem watching her from the doorway.

"Thank you," he said.

"Don't thank me yet. I'm flying blind."

"You're doing better than me. I mean it, Emily. Thank you."

Something shimmered between them, and it felt like regret. "You're my friend, Salem. This is what friends do." She wanted so badly for it to be true.

She remembered their conversation a year ago and could tell he did, too, calling her on her use of the word *friend* when he had wanted much more.

He didn't want more from her now, she knew. He'd made that perfectly clear this morning in the Jeep. *I'd rather it was someone else.*

Not that she had any business starting a relationship when her life was so up in the air, but she was and always had been his friend, even when she'd been angry and disappointed with him. Even when he was angry and disappointed with her.

"You need to go to the cops."

Salem's eyebrows shot to his hairline. "It's that bad?"

"It's shocking. When it happened to—" She slammed a door on that statement. She had almost said, *to me,* but she had buried her shame deeply long ago, and wouldn't discuss it, even if Aiyana's situation brought up ghosts from her past. "When things like this happened years ago, it went more slowly, but with the internet, it's everywhere immediately. It's ridiculously fast. You need to stop it now."

Salem looked grim. "Going to the cops will be a problem."

"Why? It should be your first action in this situation. Maybe we should have even done it yesterday."

Salem glanced over his shoulder to his father, who stood in the hallway behind him, worry etching the lines of age deeper into his skin. Mr. Pearce shook his head. "Sheriff White is Justin's father."

Oh. Damn. "You don't think he can be objective?"

Mr. Pearce snorted. "Not about his son."

"We need an alternative," Salem said.

"Okay, this is it. You go to the school and talk to the principal then line up an appointment with a school counselor for Aiyana. We need to make the situation known and protect her."

The frown lifted from Salem's forehead. "Of course. I should have thought of that."

He cursed and Emily said, "Cut yourself some slack, Salem. You've never dealt with this situation before."

"I'll drive Aiyana to school."

"Can you take the time off work?"

Salem looked at her oddly. "It's Monday. The Center is always closed on Mondays and Tuesdays. Always has been. You know that."

"I'm still jet-lagged. I've lost track of my days."

Salem and his father went back downstairs. Emily waited and listened to the shower shut off in the bathroom and then the sound of a hair dryer, while butterflies bedeviled her stomach. Would this all be enough to get Aiyana through the coming ordeal? Emily knew exactly how bad it could get.

Aiyana returned from the washroom wearing a floral-patterned dress. She had good taste. The dress was simple, without the flashy chest- or leg-baring so many kids gave in to these days.

"Here," Emily said, handing her the baking soda. "Make a paste with a little bit of water and exfoliate your skin."

As Aiyana returned to the bathroom, Emily called, "Do it gently then use your best moisturizer."

When Aiyana returned, Emily said, "Lie down for a minute and put these on your eyes." She handed her the cucumber slices. "They'll help with the puffiness."

While the cucumbers did their work, Emily applied moisturizer to the girl's hands and polished her nails.

"I was bullied in high school," she said, because she didn't know how else to help.

"You? But you're so pretty. So full of personality."

These days? Not so much, but Aiyana didn't need to know that. And personality might have gotten her through if she'd had the tiniest bit of support from someone else. She'd been in a high school in a town she hadn't grown up in. Cliques had been formed long before she got here. She hadn't stood a chance. "There were a bunch of girls who didn't like me. They didn't use cyberbullying back then, but they didn't need it. They were mean enough at school, and the rumor mill was healthy."

"Was it bad?"

"Awful."

"So how did you get over it?"

"Music helped me a lot. I played violin. Schoolwork helped. I liked math and the sciences. I loved history."

"Me, too, but don't tell Dad that. He nags me too much about how important studying is."

Emily fingered Aiyana's long hair. "You have beautiful hair."

"I wish it was blond."

"You have this raven-black shiny hair that's like satin and you want blond? Why?"

"Some of the most popular girls in school have blond hair."

Oh, boy. "We need to talk."

"About what?"

"About the grass being greener on the other side. Why on *earth* do you want to look like other girls instead of yourself?"

"I'll bet if I was one of the popular girls, one of the blondes like Madison Williams or Brittany Hardy, Justin wouldn't have tried to do what he did the other night. I'll bet he wouldn't be doing *this* to them." She pointed to her computer.

"Wow. We need to straighten out a few misconceptions." Emily took her hand. "What Justin did the other night was wrong. He was greedy and he tried to take advantage of you. He didn't rape you, thank God, but he did try to intimidate you into having sex. When he didn't get it, he had a snit and slandered you all over the internet. He's a big, overgrown two-year-old having a tantrum."

Aiyana lay on her back on the bed with two slices of cucumber on her face and smiled. "I like that image."

"Even though Justin didn't rape you, let's talk about that for a minute. Rape isn't about sex. It's about power. Justin thought you would be an easy target because you're shy and quiet. For him, getting you to have sex with him the other night would have been as much about winning as about sexual release. It would have been a notch on his bedpost. Do you understand?"

Aiyana nodded.

"Okay. As far as girls named Madison or Brittany, or being blond goes, *some* boys and men will take whatever they can from whomever they can. These are sick men. They prey on everyone. Children have been raped. Senior citizens have been raped. Rape isn't racist. It doesn't respect lines and boundaries. Women of every race, color and culture have been raped."

She removed the cucumber slices to make certain she had eye contact. "Justin didn't try to force you because of your background. I'll bet there are a lot of girls at school who've been pressured by boys. Considering the statistics, I would be willing to bet you know at least one girl who has been sexually abused. It's rife."

Thinking of her amazing father and uncles, and of her brother, Cody, she said, "But that's just some men. Others are real gems. Like your father. He just doesn't know how to relate to a teenage girl."

Aiyana shrugged and Emily knew she'd gotten as far as she would on that point.

Ten minutes later, fingers crossed and heart pumping, she watched Aiyana walk out the door with Salem to drive off to school.

SALEM WAITED FOR Aiyana to enter the school before heading inside himself, guessing she wouldn't want to walk in with her dad.

After Salem explained the problem, the principal expressed his concern and assured him he would take care of it.

Salem drove to the Center because he needed to do something active to expend his nervous energy. There was always work to be done even on his off days, sorting artifacts, changing exhibits, restoring old pieces, paperwork.

This had been his life's work for twenty years, but with the Center firmly established, he had already achieved his goals of preserving Native American heritage and making it available to the public. His passion now was architecture. Recently, Salem had completed his major paper in his quest to be an architect. In a few weeks, he would graduate and start a new career, the culmination of years of part-time studies.

He couldn't stand to be indoors today. He needed to be outside, to sweat away his tension so he wouldn't go after that kid again.

Salem worked around the outside of the Cathedral. He cleaned up the grounds, making his way out from the building, trimming bushes that sat flush with the foundation. They'd become too big and unruly over the winter.

With late-May sunlight warming his back and a light breeze cooling his face, he cleared branches that had come down in a windstorm a couple of weeks ago. He loved physical work. Like academics, it carried him outside of himself. Today, it took his mind away from his daughter's troubles and eased his terrible worry for her while she was at school and he could do nothing for her. Physical labor calmed his nerves and brought order to his universe.

Other than that bit of trimming and clearing, he allowed the surroundings to go natural, just the way he liked them.

Cleaning crews worked regularly around the country club and on the land, but Salem preferred to maintain his slice of heaven on his own.

The land might belong to Emily's father, but the pride of ownership Salem felt in the Heritage Center and its immediate surroundings motivated him to keep it looking good.

When he finished in the clearing, he walked the perimeter and spotted something out of place—a trowel hanging against a tree trunk, on the broken stub of a branch.

What was this doing here? Any and all equipment used on the small archeological digs the center conducted was supposed to be stored in the toolshed after use.

Before Emily's father had built the resort, he'd had to bring together Native American scholars and local elders. More than a century ago, this land had been part of migratory routes. When a tribal member had died, he or she had been buried on the trail.

Once it had been determined that the routes had not come through or near this section of the land, both the resort and the Heritage Center had been built.

Nick Jordan had allowed Salem the incomparable honor of giving input to the architect on what Salem wanted the Heritage Center to look like. Then he'd given the Center to Salem to run. Over the years, Salem had worked hard to make sure Nick Jordan's confidence in him as an untried, but determined eighteen-year-old had been justified. Nick had seen something in Salem, and Salem had since lived up to his potential. He would be grateful to Nick for the rest of his life for his faith in him.

One of the concessions Nick had granted to Salem's people was a small cemetery on the land. Every year, digs were held to uncover artifacts for the museum. A female body had been discovered and reinterred in the cemetery with a beautiful service.

One of the boys Salem had grown up with on the reservation had learned through DNA testing that the woman had been his ancestor. That information had filled Salem with satisfaction and peace.

This was why he had devoted his life to this work—to link the youth on the reservation to their heritage and to instill in them a sense of wonder, connection and pride.

So why couldn't he get his own daughters to revel in that connection? The shoemaker's children...

He grasped the trowel. The carelessness of tools being left out to rust angered him. Hell, his budget didn't allow him to replace these things often.

And why was it even here, so far from the dig?

He turned to leave with it, to carry it back to the shed to clean off the rust and dirt and to store it properly, when he was struck by an image. A memory. The night Emily had shown up sick, she'd had dirt and mud on her hands.

He studied the ground beneath where the trowel had hung. Had it been left as a place marking? The earth had been disturbed recently. Maybe his ancestors had been trackers. Maybe it was in his blood or genes, because the configuration of tree branches and leaves on the ground looked false. The ground had been dug up and then covered to hide that fact.

He shoved aside a large rock that had been dragged into place. He kicked at the debris and scuffed it out of the way. Using the trowel, he dug until he hit a small package, something wrapped in plastic.

He wiped away the dirt. If this was Emily's work, at least she'd dug deeply enough that Sunday night's heavy rain hadn't penetrated.

Maybe he should feel guilty about butting into Emily's private business, but she was hiding something. Why? She'd made the mistake of burying her secret on his land. Again, why?

Carefully, he opened the package, unwrapping the layers of protective plastic to reveal a small book. He didn't understand the language, but the text looked Middle Eastern. His instincts kicked in. He'd handled enough artifacts to know this was ancient. And precious. What the hell was Emily doing with it and why had she buried it in Colorado?

Disappointment twisted through him. *Emily?* Smuggling artifacts out of their native countries?

Could she really have changed so much?

The short answer was no.

There had to be a logical explanation for her having this. What he didn't understand was why she had buried it.

He tucked the artifact inside his jacket, because he couldn't bring himself to put it back into the ground. He filled the hole then covered it with the debris he'd brushed away. Last, he pushed the rock back into place.

He put the trowel back where he'd found it, and walked away satisfied that everything looked exactly the same.

Behind the Heritage Center, he tossed the plastic into the recycling bin. Inside, he climbed the stairs to his office and slid the book into his office drawer with all of the reverence it deserved. Then he locked it.

Let Emily stew. Let her panic. Let her freak out. She should have explained the situation to him. He would have helped her, even if he didn't believe she was here to stay.

She should have trusted him to help her.

CHAPTER FIVE

Aiyana couldn't do this.

She stood in front of the doors of the school with her breakfast, four spoonfuls of oatmeal, scooting up into her throat. She swallowed it down and opened the door.

Emily told her she had to be strong and to face down her demons. Why did it have to be so hard? Why did her chest ache as if she was having a heart attack? As though her heart was going to crack right in two?

She was late and walked through empty hallways. Now she would have to walk into the classroom alone.

At least the door was at the back of the room.

She peeked through the door's window. Mrs. Montgomery was writing on the blackboard with her back to the room, so Aiyana opened the door and stepped inside, closing it with the softest click behind her.

She crept to her seat in the last row, sat down and put her books on the desk then looked up…into Justin's eyes, and his smirk that said, *gotcha*.

While he watched her over his shoulder, with his foot, he nudged the girl beside him, Melanie, who whispered something and laughed. Mel passed a note to Grant in front of her, who read it then turned to look at Aiyana. He smiled, but it was mean, as though he believed Justin's lies about her.

She hated him.

Never before in her life had she hated anyone. She was a good person. She liked people. But she hated Grant and Melanie. She hated Justin. She hated everyone in this classroom.

Justin shouldn't even be in her class, she thought, resentment burning a hole in her. He should be finishing high school this year, but he wouldn't work or hand in assignments, and Mrs. Montgomery had failed him for three years, despite the pressure from the principal and Sheriff White. The rumor Aiyana had heard was that Mrs. M. said she wasn't a teacher who rewarded laziness. Good for her, but it meant that Justin had ended up in Aiyana's class, and he took out his unhappiness with the situation on everyone around him.

As the whispering grew into a buzz, Mrs. Montgomery turned around from the blackboard. "What's all the noise about?"

Nobody said anything, but the teacher glimpsed Brittany handing off a note to Russell.

Mrs. Montgomery approached and held out her hand. She opened the note and read it. Her gaze flew to Aiyana in the back row, but she said to Brittany, "I'll see you after class." She sounded super stern.

When Mrs. M. walked back to the front of the room, Brittany sent Aiyana a venomous look behind the teacher's back.

Aiyana squirmed. What did the note *say?* Her face

burned as fiercely as the sun and she wondered if she looked like she was on fire. Her face, neck, chest, everything got hot. She hated feeling like this. She wanted to wake up as the way she was last week, happy. She wished she'd never met Justin.

The phone at the front of the room rang. Mrs. M. answered, listened and then hung up.

"Justin, you are to report to the office immediately."

He left the room with a scowl.

As soon as the bell rang, Aiyana flew out the door into the busy hallway. She wanted to go home and never come back here, but she had a test this afternoon in math. She'd forgotten about it this morning.

In the lunchroom, she sat alone, as though she had the plague. A shadow fell across the table. Grant sat down across from her. "Hey, Aiyana."

She didn't answer him. He'd never given her the time of day before, let alone sat down with her in the caf.

"Cat got your tongue?" he asked, all smoothlike, as if he was some kind of great playboy. Really? Using a lame old line like that?

"Go away," she mumbled.

"What's wrong? I'm just being friendly. You want to go out one night? Friday night? My parents will be away for the weekend. We can have the house all to ourselves."

She glared at him, at his stupid freckles and his weird cowlick and his crooked front tooth. She knew what he thought, and what he wanted from her.

"Go to hell," she said. She'd never before told a person to do that, but it felt good. Great. Awesome.

He frowned. "You go to hell, bitch."

He stomped away and she was alone again. She wished her friend Alyx hadn't gone away with her family last week. Aiyana really needed someone here with her today.

She bombed on the math test, because her mind wouldn't settle, wouldn't let her concentrate, wouldn't let the numbers make sense. Numbers had always made sense, but right now they looked like hieroglyphics jumping around on the page.

When it was over, the teacher sent her to the office.

She found out she had an appointment with the school counselor. By the time she finished talking to her, she felt better. Apparently, when Justin had been called to the office, it had been about the stuff he'd put on the internet. Dad had come into school this morning to report him to Principal Nevins. Aiyana couldn't hold back her relief. She hoped Nevins told Justin to go to hell.

The counselor said they couldn't prove it was Justin without getting into his computer, which they couldn't do without a warrant, but that the principal, in the counselor's words, had "put the fear of God into him."

After school, she walked past a bunch of kids who snickered and hurled insults, and she didn't even care. Justin had gotten into trouble and that was all that mattered.

Aiyana went home feeling better than she had since Saturday night.

ON TUESDAY MORNING, even before Salem entered his daughter's room, he knew something was wrong. The silence was ominous. She should have been getting ready for school. She should have been playing her favorite music.

He slid the door open cautiously, because the last thing he wanted was to invade her privacy, but what if things hadn't gone well at school yesterday?

Last night, she had seemed better. When he asked if she wanted him to stay home for the evening, she had said no, but had thanked him for talking to the principal.

So, he'd driven to Denver and had taken a couple of his favorite profs out to dinner to thank them for their support these past years. Plus, he couldn't get enough of talking about architecture. Excitement about his new career carried away his worries.

When he'd come home, he'd knocked on Aiyana's door to double-check that she was okay. She'd said she was fine, and had sounded fine. He'd believed her, but now this.

Curled into a ball under her blankets, Aiyana didn't 'r when he called her name. Salem walked around the far side of the bed so he could see her face. Her eyes were screwed shut, ignoring him.

"Hey," he said, trying to ease into the conversation casually. "Where's all of your morning music? Usually I can't hear myself think with it blaring." No response.

"Come downstairs for breakfast." Still no response.

"We have blueberries." She should be giving him

a hard time about getting her to eat a piece of fruit to make sure she got her vitamins. He could almost always tempt her with blueberries, but not today.

He sat down on the bed. Bad sign that she didn't move over to accommodate him. Half his butt hung off the edge.

"Talk to me, Aiyana," he begged, keeping his tone soft. "Tell me what's happening."

"Nothing," she mumbled, and the emptiness, the hollow voice, shook him.

Worry coursed raggedly through his body. His girl was hurting.

"Did you talk to the counselor yesterday?"

Despite nodding, she kept her eyes closed.

"Didn't it help? Didn't Principal Nevins talk to Justin?"

Again she nodded.

"You were okay last night. What's happened?"

She mumbled something.

"I can't hear you," he said.

"Can I have Emily?"

Emily. He shouldn't feel slighted, he shouldn't envy Emily—maybe Aiyana just needed a woman to talk to—but he wanted to be the one who rescued his daughter.

He'd done all of the raising. *He'd* been the one to stick around through thick and thin, and had kissed scraped elbows and changed diapers, had brought home the food and had paid the mortgage. He'd never,

ever, taken a single vacation or jaunt to an exotic country. Or anywhere.

Popping in and out twice a year was not parenting. *He* was the one who had done all of the work, but Emily would get all of the glory for handling this problem.

Man, it set his teeth on edge, even though he didn't know what to do for his daughter to help her.

Well, yeah. He did. The only thing he could do was to give her what she asked for.

He rose above his pettiness and said, "I'll go get her. Okay?"

"Thanks, Daddy."

He was Daddy again. That was worth something.

"Can you hurry?" she asked, words thick. She'd been crying. He ran for the door.

EMILY LAY IN BED drifting in that half state between dream and reality. While she was normally an early riser, the malaria had left her drained. Or maybe it was that mummy wrap that still tied her to Jean-Marc. It wouldn't let her relax until she'd dealt with the prayer

he handled that problem, she was a stranger home, drifting in life, unfamiliar with not having a direction or a goal. She needed something to—

Her door slammed open. She startled upright.

Salem stalked into the room.

"While this comes close to one of my favorite fantasies," she joked, smoothing down her T-shirt for mod-esty's sake, "somehow, I don't think you're here for sex."

When she saw his face, she sobered. Something was terribly wrong. "What is it?"

"Get up. Hurry. Please."

"Aiyana?"

"She's even worse this morning."

"Things didn't go well yesterday?"

"They went fine. I talked to the principal, who talked to Justin. She talked to the school counselor and came home feeling better."

"What's happening this morning?"

"I don't know. She's asking for you again."

She climbed out of bed, showered and dressed in record time, then followed him out the door to help his daughter.

In Aiyana's bedroom, she found out the meeting Justin had with the principal hadn't made matters better, but worse. The things being said online were awful. Bastard.

They went through a repeat of yesterday morning's ritual, with Emily getting cuke slices from the kitchen, but with a change. Salem was colder, a̶n̶d̶ ̶s̶e̶e̶k̶ing help for his daughter, but obviously wishing it were *anyone* other than Emily. He didn't bother to hide the fact that he didn't want her here. That was clear. He'd brought her here strictly for Aiyana. What had changed? How had his initial reluctance turned

Emily picked up a pair of dark skinny jeans. "These. You'll wear these."

"Cody likes skinny jeans?"

She didn't have a clue. "Yep," she lied, because the important thing was to give Aiyana motivation. Emily chose a white T-shirt with lace at the scooped neckline, and a long red boyfriend cardigan. In the closet she found black velvet flats.

"Here's today's outfit," she said. "Cody will love it."

Aiyana rushed through her shower then took care with her skin. When she returned to the bedroom, she lay down and covered her eyes with the cucumber.

"I'm glad you're going in today," Emily said. "Your dad is worried about you."

Aiyana shrugged. "He doesn't care like you do."

What? Holy cow, what was wrong between Salem and his daughter?

"If he didn't care, why would he have rushed over to my place two mornings in a row to drag me out of bed—" Aiyana took the slices from her eyes and stared at Emily "—yes, out of *bed*, looking like a wild-eyed the last one this year." She picked at a loose thread on her blanket. "I haven't asked my dad. Every year, he talks about the same things, about our culture. I want something different this year, but I don't have a mom."

"Uh-huh."

"Can you come?"

"Me?" Emily's heart seemed to stutter. Oh, this was sweet. No one had ever asked her to do something like this. "But I'm not your parent."

"That's okay. Sometimes kids bring other people."

"I'd…I'd be honored." Wow.

"Really?"

"Oh, yes."

Aiyana's smile warmed Emily's heart.

She got too emotional, almost weepy, laughed and rubbed her stomach. "Do you have much food in the house? I've missed breakfast for the third morning in a row. I'm starving."

Aiyana laughed and jumped up from the bed. "Grandpa always has lots of food. Come on."

Emily followed her downstairs and into the kitchen.

made so much worse for him because Aiyana had invited *her* instead.

"What are you going to talk about?" he asked. "Archeology?" He sounded bitter.

"Nope," she answered. "I don't want to tell you, though. I want this to be a surprise. Aiyana can share it with you tomorrow night at dinner."

He only nodded, clearly hurt.

"Are you all right with me doing this? I don't want to come between you and your daughter."

"You're only one of a bunch of things coming between me and Aiyana." His tone implied her part was insignificant. "I don't even know what the other things are. I've lost her."

For a moment, his expression was so bleak Emily wanted to hold him, but whatever was going on between father and daughter needed to be worked out by them. Whatever was coming between Salem and Emily could be dealt with now, though.

"What's wrong between you and me?"

He shrugged and said nothing.

"I've done nothing but help you and your daughter, but today, you're treating me like I'm pond scum. Why?"

"You'll figure it out in time."

"What does that mean?"

"Exactly what I said."

"Whatever. I don't have time for this crap."

She stormed out of the building. Jean-Marc had

done this to her, too, had been hot one minute and cold the next. Never again would she take that from a man.

Whatever resentment Salem had going on toward her had to be worked out by *him*. She had limited emotional resources right now, and her priority had to be Aiyana. Salem was a grown-up, but Aiyana was still developing, and dealing with some horrible stuff.

On that thought, Emily left Salem to brood. She'd done what she could by warning him, and a good thing she had. If Aiyana hadn't mentioned it to her father this evening, he would have found out about it after the fact. Emily could only imagine how hurt he would have been by that, although at the moment she couldn't care less about his feelings.

She drove to Denver.

She had a surprise for Aiyana. She wouldn't be talking about archeology. Instead, she planned to play music. She'd shared with Aiyana that when she had been bullied in high school, her saving grace had been her violin. Tomorrow, she would show her what it had done for her.

At school, she'd thrown herself into science, had especially adored biology, where everything had a name and a classification. She'd loved math, where everything made sense, where things were linear and one thing flowed from another with perfect reason, where even leaps of logic made perfect sense.

And then there had been history. Wonderful, immutable history, the interpretation of events and their impact on history open to debate, but not the facts of dates, people and places, especially where it inter-sected with science, with DNA testing and carbon dating. It had taken her away from the present day, from mean girls and shame and the myriad problems of growing up unpopular and feeling alone. If only she'd had someone to talk to, but she hadn't. Within history, there were wonderful stories of *other* people's lives, deaths and drama, where she'd been safe from her own, where she didn't have to deal with her over-whelming problems.

At home, though, had been where she had really shone, where she could really let loose. She'd buried herself in music, spending hour after hour in her attic room listening to everything that caught her fancy, and playing her violin until her fingers developed calluses.

After all of that time alone, no wonder she had been easy pickings for someone as charming and charis-matic as Jean-Marc. No. She wouldn't think of him. Wouldn't ruin the wonder of this lovely day, when a girl as sweet as Aiyana wanted to bring *Emily* to school to represent her. She would bend over back-ward to do her young friend proud.

She drove to a music store to rent an instrument.

"Give me your toughest violin or fiddle. I need a tank."

"O-kay," the young guy said. Usually people asked for the best, not the worst, but Emily had an idea.

"Throw on the heaviest strings you have. The heavier the better."

By the time she left the shop, she was satisfied she could pull off what she had in mind.

AIYANA WALKED INTO the school with Cody Jordan *holding her hand.* She didn't know why he was doing it, but wow.

At her classroom door, he said, "I have a dental appointment so I can't see you at lunch, but come to watch practice today. Okay?"

She nodded, tongue-tied, because Cody was gorgeous and nearly three years older than her. A few of the girls were shooting her envious glances. Good.

As he walked away, he pulled out his phone and made a call. "Soph?" she heard him say. "I need a favor." Then he was gone, swallowed by the swarms of kids in the hallway.

The morning didn't go well. The kids in her class whispered about her, shot her dirty looks and shunned her. One girl, Fiona, gave her a sympathetic look, but shrugged, as if to say, *What can I do for you against all of them?*

Aiyana wished Fiona would try something, but really, would she herself have enough nerve to help out someone else in this situation? Sometimes, she felt so shy she could barely speak. How could she fight these people?

Lunchtime rolled around both too slowly and too quickly, because she knew she would be sitting alone again. She found a table in the corner.

A second later, someone sat down across from her

and Aiyana glanced up, expecting Grant or one of the other boys who'd been giving her strange looks. Instead it was an older girl she'd never spoken to before. Aiyana was startled she had the nerve to support her. Or was she here to give her grief?

"Hi." She had a cap of curly brown hair, eyes as dark and large as a doe's, and a friendly smile. "I'm Sophia Colantonio."

"Hi," Aiyana answered, then remembered Cody's words. *Soph. I need a favor.* She smiled. "Cody asked you to sit with me?"

"Yes, and I'm happy to. Cody was really nice to me when I was going through a tough time. I owe him."

She picked up a sandwich that looked amazing, obviously not from here in the cafeteria. There were layers of meat that smelled spicy, some red strips Aiyana didn't recognize and dark greens on a thick crusty roll. Sophia noticed Aiyana checking it out, borrowed the butter knife from her tray and cut off a hunk of sandwich.

"Here. Try this."

Aiyana took a tentative bite and it burst on her tongue like spicy sunshine. "This is amazing. What's in here?"

"Salami, prosciutto and provolone."

"And this?"

"Cherry pepper slices. They come pickled for flavor."

"And this?"

"Fresh kale sautéed with garlic."

"Oh, my God, I totally want to learn how to make this. Where did you buy all of this stuff? In Denver?"

"From my family's store here in Accord."

Aiyana had to think for a moment. Grandpa did all of their shopping at the grocery store five minutes from home. She snapped her fingers. "Tonio's?" Tonio's was the organic market on Main.

"Dad shortened it from Colantonio so it would be easy to pronounce." Sophia laughed. "And the sign would be shorter, too. Come in sometime and I'll help you get all of the ingredients. I work there on Saturdays."

Aiyana smiled shyly. "Okay. Thanks."

Sophia stayed with her the entire lunch hour and they learned they had all kinds of interests in common, including being addicted to cryptic crossword puzzles, and thinking *To Kill a Mockingbird* was the best book ever written.

"Someday, I want to write something that amazing." Sophia threw her garbage out and left the cafeteria with Aiyana.

After school, Aiyana sat in the stands in the gym, way up high apart from the others, alone in a crowd. Everyone avoided her as though she had cooties. It hurt. It was okay to be alone when it was a choice, but not when it was forced on you. Then Sophia showed up.

"Hi," she said. "May I sit with you?"

Such good grammar. You rarely heard that around town, even here in school.

"You don't need to babysit me." Aiyana softened that with a smile because, honestly, she was glad Sophia was here.

Sophia leaned close and said, quietly, so no one else would hear, "Justin isn't a nice guy. You're lucky to be away from him. I wanted to tell you at lunch, but there were too many people around."

Aiyana's mouth dropped open. "Did he try to hurt you?"

Sophia nodded and pulled a bag of dried fruit out of her bag. "For a long time, I was angry with him for putting pressure on me, but also with myself for giving in. You didn't give in, did you?"

Aiyana shook her head.

"That's why he's being nasty to you. He's a mean-spirited little prick."

Aiyana chuffed out a laugh.

Sophia held out the fruit. "Want some?"

Aiyana nodded. "Thanks."

"I'll tell you one thing for sure. I'll never sell myself so cheaply again."

"Won't those other girls, his friends, give you a hard time about sitting with me?"

"I've got less than a month of school left and then I'm off to college in the fall. What do I care what they think? They aren't true friends, not by any stretch of the imagination."

They sat together snacking on dried figs and apricots while Cody ran circles around Justin, in effect making a fool of him.

After practice, before leaving to shower, Cody gestured to Aiyana to come down to the court. Before saying goodbye to Sophia, she said, "I'm coming to Tonio's on Saturday, okay?"

"Totally. If you don't see me, ask. Sometimes I work in the back or in the office," Sophia said. "You stuck to your guns the other night with Justin. You're a strong person. I'm really proud of you."

Aiyana smiled and waved. Her praise felt so good. Sophia was a really nice person. When she got to Cody, he leaned close. "Meet me outside the boys' locker room in fifteen minutes. Follow my lead no matter what I do. Okay?"

Aiyana nodded and he ran off.

Fifteen minutes later, she waited for him where he'd asked, alone again. A group of girls waiting for their boyfriends made a point of ignoring her.

Justin came out of the room with some of the team members.

He saw Aiyana and grinned. "Waiting for me? 'Bout time you came around."

The jerk thought she'd come for *him?* After what he'd done to her? Was he really that dense?

Cody came out of the locker room just in time to hear Justin's remark. A cheerleader called Cody's name, but he ignored her and walked over to Justin, grabbing him by the back of his jacket and shaking him as though he were nothing more than a puppy. "I heard you've been spreading rumors about my girl."

His *girl?* What a good brother to do this favor for

Emily, and for a girl he only knew because their fathers were friends.

Justin sputtered, but Cody gave him no time to reply.

"How do you get off on telling lies about someone great like Aiyana? I should kick your ass."

Aiyana scrambled forward. "No!" she shouted. "Don't fight. Don't get into trouble because of him." She jutted her chin toward Justin, angry with him, but also at herself for having ever found him attractive.

She held her breath, afraid that Cody might go too far. You could have heard a pin drop in the hallway.

Cody had three inches and twenty pounds of muscle on Justin. No way would Justin come out the winner, but Cody could get in trouble for instigating a fight. Those kinds of things went on a kid's record.

She touched his arm. "He isn't worth it." Justin was nothing but a bullying nobody.

Cody let go of Justin, who stumbled. "Next time, think twice before you spread a bunch of lies."

Cody wrapped his arm around Aiyana as they walked outside. She died and went to heaven on the spot. "Thank you. That was really nice of you," she whispered.

"We're not done yet." He steered her toward his car. "If you were really my girlfriend, we'd go out for something to eat."

He stopped walking abruptly. "Would that be okay with you? I don't want to force you to do something you don't want to do."

Not want to go out somewhere with Cody Jordan, even if it was only pretend? She grinned at him. "Oh, yeah, I want to."

He grinned back and held open the door of his car. Before she got in, they heard, "Hey!" Justin stood on the school steps surrounded by his entourage.

"If she's your girlfriend," Justin called, careful, Aiyana noted, to keep his distance from Cody, "why did she go out with me the other night?"

"We were fighting," Cody lied glibly. "We made up, though, didn't we, sweetheart?" He kissed her on the lips, quick and hard, making a show of possession.

Justin made some kind of derogatory comment Aiyana didn't catch, but judging by his stiffening body language, Cody did.

He stalked away and Aiyana stared after him. Where was he going? He stopped on the sidewalk at the edge of the parking lot, no longer on school property. "Come over here and say that, if you have the nerve."

Cody wouldn't get into trouble with school if they fought there. Smart. He was also calling Justin's bluff.

Justin's bravado evaporated and he went back inside the school, his friends following, but darted dark glances at Aiyana. No doubt, they were all going out the side door to avoid Cody.

Cody returned to the car. "I guess his true colors are showing. Let's go."

They drove to a family restaurant on Main Street, where they ordered burgers and fries.

Cody stretched and scratched his stomach. "Good practice today. I'm starving."

Aiyana tried not to stare at the rippling of his muscles, at the peek she got of a hard stomach when his T-shirt hiked up. Cody was comfortable in his body in a way that Aiyana had never been in hers.

She toyed with the paper cover from her straw, nervous, because Cody was kind and good-looking, and she didn't know what to say to boys. "I can't thank you enough for what you did for me today." Oh, so lame.

Cody waved away her thanks. "You did the hard part. I saw what those creeps were saying about you. I can't believe you had the nerve to come to school today." He gulped back half of a large cola. "That took real guts."

"Your sister helped me a lot."

He nodded. "Emily's smart." He stared at Aiyana for a long time. "How old are you?"

"Fifteen."

His mouth dropped open and he got a little pale. "I kissed you. I shouldn't have done that."

Aiyana giggled. "Don't worry. I'm not going to report you. You were helping me."

Cody's stiff shoulders eased back against the booth. "When do you turn sixteen?"

"On Thursday."

Their meals came and Cody took a huge bite of his hamburger, taking his time chewing and swallowing. "This Thursday? That's not too long to wait."

"It feels like it's taken forever. I'm tired of waiting."

"What are your plans for the summer?"

"Dad usually sends me to the reservation for a month so I can learn about my heritage." She'd been eating her fries, but put down her fork beside her plate. "I don't want to go. I'm trying to get out of it. What about you?"

"My dad's got me working at the resort."

"What will you be doing? Working at the desk or in the office?"

"Landscaping." Cody grimaced. "Can you believe it?"

"But why? Your dad owns the place. He can give you any job he wants. Why would he make you do that?"

"He says to build character. He says I need to get my hands dirty, that I should learn all of the jobs from the bottom up." He'd finished his burger and wiped his lips. Aiyana liked the way they were formed. "He's right. I need to learn everything."

"Are you going to college?"

"Yep. In September. Business."

She nodded because that made perfect sense. Chances were, he would someday take over his father's business.

When he took her out to his car, he held her hand. He insisted on driving her home, even though she walked all over town by herself. Just before she got out, he said, "Aiyana, don't undervalue yourself."

"What do you mean?"

"I mean you're worth more than a dozen Justin

Whites. There are boys who are worthy of you, but he isn't one of them. Okay?"

"Okay. Thanks."

She got out of the car and entered the house, happier than she'd been in ages. Only when she closed the door behind her did he drive away.

CHAPTER SIX

WEDNESDAY MORNING. The time had come for Emily to talk to Aiyana's class.

She stepped into the school and paused inside the front door. Classes had already started and the halls were empty. The eerie silence held too many bad memories.

Ghostly echoes rang in the hollow stillness.

Emily Schmemily. So childish.

Emily Jordan's got a friend in Gordon's. Intimating alcoholism.

Emily puts out. Here's her phone number. Promiscuity. She'd been a virgin until college. They'd called her a slut and a skank.

In hindsight, it was all stupid, but also relentless. Daily. How could a girl maintain her self-esteem against a never-ending barrage of name-calling and negativity? At the time, she'd been devastated, even though somehow she'd managed to hide her hurt feelings from the world, faking bravado. But it *had* hurt. Terribly.

Emily stood outside the classroom door and waited to be called in, pulse racing.

She didn't usually play for strangers. Her music

was an intensely private thing and she kept it close, usually playing only for trusted friends. Today, she would be playing for a bunch of high school students, possibly the toughest crowd on earth. Maybe this had been a bad idea. Maybe she should just ramble on a bit about archeology.

Standing in the hallway of her former school, she struggled to stop the old panic rising in her chest. It wouldn't do to walk into the classroom hyperventilating. She was no longer that unhappy young girl. She no longer had to pretend to be strong. She *was* strong.

She had survived the ringer washer of her relationship with Jean-Marc and had finally found the strength to call it quits. She'd found the strength to break away from a career that hadn't excited her anymore, and that no longer gave her the "juice" she needed in life.

The final step in severing ties with that past, in breaking the mummy wrap that bound her to Jean-Marc and archeology, would come in time. As soon as she heard back from Arthur, she would know what her next step with the prayer book should be.

Surely, she could survive this school and the bad memories.

The door opened and Aiyana peeked into the hallway, her expression both uncertain and hopeful. "Ready?"

"As I'll ever be." Emily forced a game smile. This was all for Aiyana. Being here was tough, performing even harder, but Aiyana needed her.

This morning, there had been nothing new on the internet, all because of Cody's intervention yesterday.

Please, Emily thought, let today finish off the situation altogether.

She entered the classroom and walked to the front, noting some of the kids Aiyana had described for her, the key players in her abuse. Justin sat in the row near the window. In the tilt of his head and the way his body sprawled out of his chair and into the aisle, Emily detected arrogance and a sense of entitlement. She also saw more. When he looked at Aiyana, anger simmered on his face. The guy obviously didn't like to lose.

So. There might still be trouble there. Maybe she should alert Cody, but Aiyana would need to learn to defend herself at some point in her life. Maybe after all of this support, she would have more confidence to do that.

After an introduction to the teacher, Emily took out the two violins, her own and the one she'd rented.

"Hi." A slight tremor in her voice betrayed her nerves. She hoped it wasn't bad enough for everyone to hear. "As you all must know, I'm not Aiyana's parent, but I am a good family friend, and she asked me to talk to you about the work I do."

She laid the rented violin on the teacher's desk.

"I'm an archeologist, but I decided I'd rather talk today about music. My passion is playing the violin."

She held her violin and bow ready to play. "This is an instrument based on a simple premise—pull the bow across the strings to make music. As you can imagine, with beginners that sounds pretty much like cats screeching in a back alley."

Some kids laughed. "Once a musician knows what she's doing, though, she speaks to us from the heart through her instrument. I know few of you listen to classical music, but bear with me while I play one of the most beautiful pieces ever composed for the violin, Bach's Chaconne for solo violin, from Partita number 2 in D minor."

She set bow to instrument and became immersed in Bach's melody. Standing here in front of the class, everything she had suffered at the hands of arrogant boys and mean-spirited girls flooded her, the loneliness, the isolation and her sense of hopelessness.

She didn't want that for Aiyana. Emily played fiercely. As she had done back then, she opened her heart to the healing power of the music, and the ugliness of the past slowly faded until only beauty remained.

When Emily finished and opened her eyes, it took her a moment to come back to reality. When she did, she found that not everyone had been enthralled. The boys who lounged across the back of the room looked bored. Others looked happy.

One girl's expression arrested Emily's glance around the room. Her hands were cupped one inside the other on her desk, the knuckles bone-white. From beneath her closed lids, one tear trickled down her cheek.

Emily's heart broke for her, for whatever she was going through, especially here where a show of weakness could leave a girl vulnerable to attack by her peers.

Emily had to lighten the mood, both so the girl could collect herself and to engage those bored boys.

"I'm going to play you a fiddle classic, because it's showy and gives you an idea of how different an instrument can sound when playing completely different songs." She played a truncated version of the "Orange Blossom Special."

She was working up a sweat. Some of the kids were engaged. Others, still not so much. She had to get through to this crowd.

"I know fiddle music isn't what any of you listen to, but I hope you can see how versatile an instrument can be. It can be classical, or rooted in folk traditions. Then there's fusion. Melding and blending and showcasing different cultures."

She started some fiddle riffs that morphed into a jig that became a run on some current Irish stuff she really liked then became heavily laced with an East Indian beat that then spun to jazz.

"Instruments are yours to make of them what you will. You can play anything on any instrument."

She had most of the class listening, but the diehards, the four boys sitting across the back looking as if they couldn't wait for lunch hour, were hardcore cynics.

"Now, let's try something completely different."

She picked up the rental violin, the workhorse with the heavier strings. "Who here thinks you need an electric guitar to play rock? How many of you have heard of Apocalyptica?"

The four boys in the back sat up straight and exchanged glances.

"For those of you who don't know of them, they started as four classically trained cellists. They play Metallica. Yes, on cellos."

She ran the heavy rental bow across the strings and adjusted the tuning. She would never play Vivaldi on this, but Metallica? Bring it on.

She explained that she'd had heavy strings put on this violin. "If they can do it with cellos, why can't I with a violin? This is their version of 'One.' Okay, here goes. Fingers crossed that the violin survives."

She played "One," starting by plucking the strings in Metallica's signature opening, then switching to the heavy bow she'd rented.

Further into the song, the sound became harder and heavier, and picked up speed.

Strings on her bow snapped, broken strands of horsehide whipping back and forth with her frenzied sawing motions. Still, she played, wringing youthful disillusionment, defiance and triumph from the violin.

Her hair fell in waves around her face. Sweat bloomed on her forehead and cheeks. On and on she played, wresting sound and passion from these bits of wood and string.

She ended abruptly. Done. Spent.

Dear sweet freaking God, she loved making music. *Adored* it.

The silence after her last notes was broken only by her heavy breathing.

More silence and then…resounding applause. Even the bored boys at the back of the room were on their feet, clapping and hooting, while the teacher tried to quiet them down. That wasn't happening.

Emily swiped her forehead with her sleeve and laughed, joy coursing through her. There was no high on earth quite like this.

The only one not clapping was Justin, his face full of a sullen lack of grace. Too bad. His loss.

She glanced at Aiyana, whose face glowed. Emily had definitely made points for Salem's daughter.

She had done more than that, though. She had conquered the demons that had walked these hallways with her for too many years. The past fell from her like sheets of ice from a 'berg.

She was free, bullies and bad memories vanquished, replaced by joy.

A movement just inside the back door caught her eye. Salem. Oh, he shouldn't have come, especially given how hurt he'd been yesterday, but he didn't look hurt now. He looked proud. Of her.

A tiny frown marred his tanned forehead and he watched her as though sorting out a puzzle.

They'd always had a witchy ability to read other. It had become rusty over the years, but she tried anyway.

Read my expression, answer my question—what's wrong between us?

He looked away briefly. He wasn't going to answer.

When he met her gaze again, though, an understanding passed between them. From Salem came, loudly and clearly as though he'd spoken it, a profound *Thank you.* Her response was an animated smile. *My pleasure. My deepest, happiest pleasure.*

The lunch bell rang, but Emily couldn't leave. Too many of the students asked her about music, about whether she gave lessons, about how they could learn to play Metallica, or any heavy metal, themselves. And, hallelujah, the crowd included the four boys from the back of the room. She'd managed to break through their defenses.

She took down email addresses and promised to get back to them. Aiyana waited patiently, smiling.

Last, the girl who'd been so affected by Bach approached, uncomfortable but determined. She raised her pointy chin and asked, "Can you teach me to play? Can you teach me that song? The Bach?"

"Yes," Emily said and meant it. She would spend years, if she had to, teaching this girl anything to help her get past whatever it was that had hurt her so badly.

By the time everyone cleared out and Emily looked toward the door at the back of the room, Salem was gone and she felt the loss like an ache.

At home, she sat in her bedroom and composed a letter to post on her Facebook page, knowing that everyone she had worked with over the years would see it.

She had done good work this morning in getting rid of those old demons, but what about Jean-Marc and his character assassination of her? She couldn't let that continue without fighting back.

She had helped Aiyana, but it was time to take care of herself.

The resolution to the prayer book problem was on hold until she heard from Arthur, but she could respond to Jean-Marc through social media.

No more hiding her head in the sand as she had done in high school; no more dealing with it all alone. She had a hunch, a strong hunch, that once she responded to him, others would support her. She had treated their colleagues well while Jean-Marc had been his arrogant and opinionated self.

When she opened her page, she found that her friends had already been online defending her. It gave her strength. Not all of her colleagues had spoken up, though. Jean-Marc was their boss, after all.

She wrote from the heart, about her integrity, honesty and her moral character, which her colleagues had all witnessed over the years.

"In closing, I would like to thank all of you for your friendship and professional support throughout my career. I am leaving archeology with a heavy heart, but with excitement for the future, and very much looking forward to the new direction my life will take."

And what direction will that be?

I just don't know.

"Emily?" Pearl called up from the bottom of the stairs.

"Yes?"

"I just made a pot of tea and I have chocolate chip cookies coming out of the oven in one minute."

"I'll be right down."

She clicked the mouse to post her entry, sending it out into the world like a bird of peace, hoping to put an end to this whole crazy problem.

Downstairs she sat at the table where her sister had already put out two cups of tea. Pearl placed a plate of cookies onto the table.

"Those smell heavenly."

"How was the event at school this morning?"

Emily had never told Pearl what had happened in high school—she had been only a toddler at the time—but now she shared that feeling of freedom, of having let go of the past, and Pearl smiled. Emily talked about the music and the resounding enthusiasm from the kids, about how many of them asked her to teach them how to play.

"There it is then," Pearl said.

"There what is?"

"What you are meant to do next, of course."

"What?"

Pearl looked at her as though she were dense. "The next stage in your life is to teach music. You certainly studied it enough when you were in high school."

Yes, she had.

Even so, teaching music? She had never considered it, but as she did now, a warm glow filled her from her heart out. Yes. It felt right. More than right. It felt perfect.

She stood and rounded the table to hug her sister. "You're a genius."

"Of course I am."

Emily burst out laughing and couldn't stop.

SALEM SLIPPED HOME briefly to change for his dinner meeting in Denver with his adviser. The man had gone above and beyond at times to make sure Salem excelled.

He donned a fresh dress shirt and his black dress pants.

"Dad?" Aiyana stood in his bedroom doorway. She still glowed from her successful day at school. Emily had done wonders for her. So how was he supposed to reconcile the godsend with the woman who would eventually leave, breaking his daughter's heart?

And yours.

Yeah, and mine.

"I saw you at the back of class today. What did you think of Emily?"

"She was really good." She was amazing, a genius peddling transcendent music beautifully played.

"I thought she was incredible. I want to study a musical instrument."

"You do? Good." He filled his pockets with his

wallet and keys then combed his hair and braided it. "Which one?"

"I'm not sure. Probably violin. I want to talk to Emily before I decide."

"She can advise you, I would imagine."

"So...can I buy something?"

"Why don't you decide what you want to learn, then rent until we know for sure that's what you really want?" She clattered down the stairs behind him. "If it is, then yes, we can buy you a musical instrument."

At the front door, she threw her arms around him then pulled away too soon, but beamed a glorious smile of happiness. Would wonders never cease?

"Dad? There's something else."

"Yes?"

"Can I invite Emily to my birthday party tomorrow night?"

Thinking of how heavily Aiyana was starting to lean on Emily, and how devastated she'd be when that inevitable break finally came, Salem said, "No." Emily could advise Aiyana about musical instruments, but he wouldn't encourage any more interaction between them than that.

Aiyana stared at him with her mouth open. "But she helped me through all of that awfulness with Justin. She was amazing. *You* asked her to help."

The first time, yes.

She was amazing, passionate and inventive, so far into the music today she probably had no idea how much of her soul shone through while she'd played. But he didn't want Aiyana shattered when she left. And Emily would leave. No doubt about it. They'd been through this too many times over the years.

"She got her brother to help me at school, too," Aiyana reminded him.

She helped you with Aiyana, when you were desperate, and now you want to deny Aiyana a deepening friendship with her.

Yeah, she did, but the crisis is past. Aiyana's fine now and Emily can only hurt her.

"So, why can't I have her over?" Aiyana persisted. "I don't have that many friends, Dad."

No, she didn't, but he wished she could have only the best of friends, not someone who wasn't likely to be here tomorrow.

"I know, but I'd rather you hang out with your peers."

"But I'm more comfortable with adults than with kids my age. I always have been."

True. She'd always been remarkably mature, when she wasn't having adolescent mopes, though he was beginning to understand those more now. High school was a tough place. She would probably make the bulk of her friends in college, when others grew up a bit more. "Emily probably wouldn't want to come to a teenager's party," he extemporized.

"How do you know if you don't ask her?"

"I don't want to embarrass her if she doesn't know how to say no."

"She seems like a person who could say what she means."

Yes, she was. Salem caught his dad watching him from the doorway of the kitchen with a steely glint in his eye. Unless Salem missed his guess, he was going to get an earful later. His dad had always liked Emily.

"You're no fun," Aiyana muttered.

"Hey," Salem said. "Don't talk to me like that." In the blink of an eye, he'd gone from her hero to the worst dad on earth.

She stomped up the stairs, every heavy footfall a rebuke.

The second she turned twenty and stopped being a teenager, Salem was going to drop to his knees and thank the Powers That Be. That thought sobered him. She was already growing up too quickly. He didn't want these years flying any faster than they already were.

"That went well," his father, master of understatement, said.

DEAD TIRED BECAUSE his dinner with his adviser had gone late last night, and everything that could go wrong at work today had, Salem came home wanting nothing more than a hot shower, a quiet evening and an early bedtime.

He opened the front door of the house…into a wall

of sound. Music blared from the living room, along with the worst caterwauling he'd ever heard.

God, no. Aiyana and Mika were singing. They were beautiful girls, smart and hardworking, but they couldn't sing worth a damn. Who on earth was encouraging this? Their grandfather? He couldn't stand their voices, either.

Along with the music and singing, laughter emanated from the living room. Then he remembered and his heart sank. In the chaos of the week, he'd lost track of his days. Today was Aiyana's birthday party. It was going to be a long night.

Even so, Aiyana deserved her fun, especially after this tough week.

He forced a smile and entered the room, only to stop dead. At the center of all the havoc stood Emily.

Figures. It had to be Emily. She creates chaos everywhere she goes.

Aiyana stood beside her sister with a microphone in her hand. When she saw him, she faltered in her singing, but, expression defiant, started up again as if to say, *What are you going to do now, Dad? Kick Emily out of the house?*

She knew he wouldn't. Salem was many things, but he wasn't rude.

When the song ended, he managed to keep his cool and kiss Aiyana on the cheek. "Happy birthday, sweetheart."

Despite her defiance, her smile looked hesitant.

He dug deeply for as much goodwill as he could

muster and said, "I didn't know you planned karaoke." He hated the stuff.

"It was Emily's idea. She bought the machine for my birthday present. Isn't it great?" Salem suppressed a groan. The machine was staying?

Aiyana introduced her guests. "You already know Alyx. She just got back from vacation with her parents. I missed her."

Yes, Alyxandra could have helped her at school this week. "Where did you go?" he asked.

"The Grand Canyon. Dad always takes me out of school early for our trips. He hates traveling in the summer heat."

"Say hello to him for me."

Aiyana gestured toward a pretty girl sitting on the couch. "This is Sophia Colantonio. Her family owns Tonio's. She's going to teach me how to make Italian dishes."

The girl stood and shook his hand. Nice manners. He liked Sophia right away. He hoped Aiyana would keep this friendship. Italian food, though?

"She brought homemade lasagna for supper."

Salem murmured politely. What was wrong with the food they always ate? Roast chicken and mashed potatoes. Fried pork chops and green beans. In late summer, early fall, they ate a lot of Three Sisters— squash, corn and beans. His dad was a good cook. Why did they need to change? They'd bought frozen lasagna in the past. It was only okay.

"What song do you want to do next?" Aiyana asked Mika. "Emily, you join in, too, this time."

"Love to." She squeezed in between them. "I brought a '50s and '60s CD. You guys ever hear of the Supremes?"

"I don't know. Put on something."

The second Emily put on "Stop! In the Name of Love," Salem recognized it. It was long, long before his time, and Emily's, too.

"I'll teach you the movements," Emily shouted above the blaring music then sang the opening verse. At least she had a good voice. The second his girls learned the chorus, though, they'd be belting it out. He didn't want to be in the room when that happened.

Salem hunted down his father in the kitchen, a headache pounding at his forehead.

Dad stood at the counter preparing birthday food with big wads of white tissue sticking out of his ears.

"You look like a demented rabbit," Salem said.

"What?"

Salem removed the tissue and tossed it into the garbage. "How's it going, wascally wabbit?" He got a beer out of the fridge. "I can't hear myself think over all of that racket."

His dad grinned. "Nice to hear the music and the girls laughing, eh? Even if their screeching is hard on the ears, the laughter is good."

"Music's too loud, though."

"You're only thirty-seven and already you're an old man!"

Was that true? Just because he liked peace and quiet did that make him boring? Had he become a stick-in-the-mud? Annie used to tell him he was too uptight. That was usually when she was high on whatever drug she could manage to score in Accord. In his disgust at her behavior, he hadn't taken her seriously. Had it been true? Was he too uptight?

A song by Justin Bieber, Mika's current favorite, followed the Supremes. Mika sang it alone. Oh, his aching eardrums.

Dinner turned out to be an adventure. Salem tried the lasagna and loved it. "Sophia, I've had frozen lasagna before—" the look of horror on her face made him laugh "—but this is awesome."

"Never, ever eat frozen again. I'll teach Aiyana how to make it from scratch. It isn't hard, just time-consuming."

Alyx had brought souvlaki made by her dad. "What's in this?" He pointed to the dollop of white cream with green bits in it that he'd put on his plate beside the meat.

"That's called tzatziki."

"Zat what?"

"Tzatziki. It's yogurt, grated cucumber, garlic and mint. Put it on the lamb. It's delicious."

Lamb? He'd never eaten it before in his life. He put a dab on a piece of meat and ate it. "You're right," he conceded. "It is delicious."

Things went well until they started up the music again after dinner and Salem's headache shot into his temples. When he carried dishes to the kitchen, Emily followed. Damn.

He didn't want to see her, didn't want to talk to her, didn't want to have *anything* to do with her. His rational mind couldn't stop the emotional part that thought she was stealing his daughter's affections.

Her elbow brushed his arm as she passed him and he recoiled. His body liked her touch too much. Always had.

She noticed his withdrawal. How could she not? "Are you going to tell me what's wrong?"

"Nothing." He tried to keep his voice neutral, but disapproval bled through.

Emily dropped a bunch of cutlery into the sink where it clattered. She pointed at his face. "Don't do that."

"Do what?"

"Make that face."

He wasn't making a face. "What face?"

"That human sphinx thing you do. It drives me nuts."

"I'm not doing anything."

"Exactly."

"You're not making sense."

"I'm making *perfect* sense. Whenever you have to deal with the slightest emotion, you close up tighter than a clam's ass."

He knew the punch line. *And that's watertight.*

"So what?"

"So, you can't go giving me dirty looks without telling me why."

He hadn't hidden his displeasure very well. "You should know."

"Should know *what?* Am I supposed to be able to read your mind?"

Emily would be gone soon and he would be left to pick up the pieces, but he wouldn't discuss it here. He refused to ruin Aiyana's party.

When would it end? It was already after nine. "Shouldn't the company be going home soon?"

Emily slid him a sidelong look. "Seriously? Even for a weeknight it's still early. Have you turned into a monk, Salem?"

"No," he shot back. "It's just noisy."

"If you won't tell me why you're mad at me, I'm going to go have fun." Over her shoulder, she tossed, "You can go to bed, old man. The youngsters plan to party until dawn."

Another one calling him *old man.* First his father, now Emily. He wasn't a stick-in-the-mud. He *wasn't.*

The party ended by eleven. Blessed peace and quiet.

Salem hugged his daughter. "Happy?"

"I had an amazing party. Emily's so much fun."

He didn't want to talk about Emily. "I can't believe you're sixteen. Seems it was only a year ago you were spitting up milk on my shoulder and filling your diapers with disgusting crap."

"Dad!" Aiyana giggled.

"Come on upstairs and I'll give you your present."

He'd bought her a dress and hoped she liked it. What did he know about clothing for teenagers?

She waited for him in her bedroom, where he placed the box in front of her on the bed.

When she opened it, she exclaimed, "Oh, Dad, I love it."

That one simple sentence warmed him clear through to his heart. "I'm glad." Damned if he didn't feel teary.

He'd kept it simple with black. A sheath, the lady in the shop in Denver had called it. He thought those were things you kept knives in, but apparently they were also a style of dress. He had bought an adult dress for her. After all, she was becoming a woman.

"Can I try it on?"

"Of course. It's yours."

He left the room and sat on his bed in his room. A minute later, she came in wearing the dress with a pair of flat velvet shoes, and his heart expanded. His daughter was a young woman. Cripes, his eyes were misting again.

"I love it," Aiyana said softly. "Thank you for not buying me a children's dress."

He thought of those children's toothbrushes he'd bought far longer than he should have. About time he got something right.

"We're not finished yet." He retrieved a small jewelry box from the drawer of his bedside table, where he'd hidden it. "Put this on."

She opened it and gasped. "Is it real?"

"Yes." He'd bought a necklace with a single diamond in a white gold setting.

"I love it." When she put it on, it fit into the modest V of the dress's neckline perfectly.

"It's probably the smallest diamond on earth," he admitted.

"I don't care. It's mine and I'll love it forever."

She threw her arms around his neck and he held onto his growing-up-too-quickly daughter for dear life. His eyes misted and he closed them so he could cherish this moment, could record it in the recesses of his mind to keep for the rest of his life.

EMILY HEARD BACK from Arthur Chadwick on Friday morning when a FedEx truck drove up with a letter.

The walk up to her room had never felt longer. She sat on the edge of the bed and opened his letter with hands that shook. What if he'd turned down her request for help? Where would that leave her?

Dear Emily,

It's good to hear from you. Penny has been worried enough that she called to ask whether you had written. She had a hunch you might. She instructed me to give you my full cooperation should you need it. Please be assured you can send me anything and I will make certain it will arrive in my sister's hands safely.

You wouldn't consider bringing the item to England personally? It's beautiful here in May.

Kew Gardens is brimming with lilacs and early roses. The scent is quite astounding.

It would be my pleasure to show you the sights. With the deepest affection,
Arthur

A shaky sob escaped Emily. Dear, sweet Arthur. She'd suspected he'd had a bit of a crush on her. Now she knew.

"Thank you," she whispered. "Thank you, Arthur."

Now she could retrieve the prayer book and start it on its journey home, where it belonged. That dusty mummy wrapping connecting her to her old life and Jean-Marc would finally be broken. She would be free to restart her life. Free most especially of all from the craziness that had been her relationship with a destructive, controlling man. She would take back control of her own life.

After Wednesday's stunning revelation with Pearl, that she loved music enough to make it a career, and that there were people who wanted to learn from her, she'd begun to imagine she could earn a living in Accord.

Thinking of the young girl who'd cried while Emily had played Bach, she knew could share the wonderful therapeutic effects of music. She could help people, real live people, rather than being the caretaker of the dead artifacts of ancient civilizations.

History had been good to her, but it was time for Emily Jordan to live in the present.

On the drive to the Cathedral, she hummed. In the forest, she bobbed on her feet. Life was good.

She'd made sure she was nice and early. The Heritage Center wouldn't open for another hour. None of the resort guests would come poking around this side of the Cathedral. It was safe for her to retrieve the prayer book. She found the trowel where she'd left it and started to dig.

Five minutes later, she sat back on her heels, her heart pounding in her chest. This couldn't be happening.

The prayer book wasn't here.

She tossed branches, leaves, soil. She was in the right place. The trowel had still been hanging where she'd left it.

How could the prayer book not be here? She panicked before realizing she might be slightly off in her calculations. It had been dark and rainy. She'd had a fever. She shifted her search a foot away and dug some more, but didn't find it.

She continued all around the spot where she thought the book should have been. Her trowel hit something. Finally! She'd found it. She slowed down, using only the tip of the tool to clear away soil, careful to do no damage.

She didn't find the prayer book, but what she did uncover stunned her. And sent her panic shooting sky high.

FROM HIS OFFICE WINDOW, Salem watched Emily dig up his forest, watched her motions become frantic, and he smiled grimly as she dug another hole, and another. He'd wondered when she would come to retrieve it. He took a malicious satisfaction in her panic. He shouldn't be enjoying this. To do so was petty and small.

He couldn't hold on to his pique for long. She looked too panicked.

He left the building and strode to the woods, where he found Emily sitting back on her heels in the dirt, shoulders slumped, no doubt shocked her precious artifact was gone.

"Looking for something?" he asked.

She turned an ashen face to him, her movements slow. Maybe she was still sick. He studied her and what he saw—shock and panic—surprised him, her response more extreme than the situation warranted.

"What are you doing here, Emily?" Would she tell him the truth about the artifact?

She opened her mouth then closed it, but said nothing. She really did appear to be in shock.

He retrieved the book from his pocket and dangled it in front of her. "Is this what you want?"

"Yes. I mean no. It's—" She barely glanced at the book, which left Salem bemused. From his vantage point on the third floor of the Center, he'd thought her actions frenzied, so why wasn't she relieved to see the book?

"You weren't looking for this?" Something wasn't adding up here.

"No, I—"

"Did you want money? Were you going to sell it?"

"No—"

"Because I know you're not a dishonest person. So why did you take it from its home?"

"Stop!"

Her shout nonplussed him. "How dare you yell at me?"

She stood, actions slow and shaky, and said, "There's a reason for that—" she pointed to the relic in his hand "—but we have a bigger problem."

"What's bigger than displacing someone's heritage?"

"That," she said, pointing to the ground, and he noticed for the first time what had left her looking so pale.

Three skeletal fingers reached out of the earth toward the sky, obscenely white against the rich dark earth of the forest.

CHAPTER SEVEN

SALEM BLINKED, BECAUSE this had to be a hallucination, or a trick of the sun. "What is that?" he asked, a thrum of excitement warming his blood. Was this one of his ancestors? "Am I seeing what I think I'm seeing?"

Emily nodded.

Salem crouched on his haunches beside her. "Could this be a Ute grave site? But this is way off our calculations of the nomadic routes."

Emily shook her head. "No, Salem. This body isn't ancient. This is new."

"What do you mean *new?* There's no flesh on those bones."

"I mean this isn't an ancient burial. This is recent. Only a few years old."

"Recent?" Could she possibly mean... "As in—"

"People who die of natural causes don't usually bury themselves in the woods. It looks like...murder."

This was so far outside of his experience he didn't know how to react. Maybe Emily was wrong.

"How do you know it's recent?"

She gave him a look that asked, seriously?

Dumb question. She was an archeologist. She would know whether this body was new or ancient.

"For starters, the burial is too shallow."

The implications set in and Salem started to shake. Someone had buried a body on this land in the not-too-distant past. Dread snaked through him and settled in his belly like a lump of mud. This was a hell of a lot uglier than uncovering the wonders of history and heritage, than finding the clues to an ancient way of life—arrowheads, old cooking tools and the like.

Emily patted her pockets. "We need to call the police. I don't have my phone."

Salem nodded and pulled out his cell.

WITHIN HALF AN HOUR, the sum total of Accord's police force, the sheriff and all three deputies, stood around the bones protruding from the hole Emily had dug.

"How did you come to find the body?" Sheriff White, an older, harder-edged version of his son, Justin, held a notebook and the stub of a pencil in his hand.

"I was looking for something else." Emily noticed the sheriff hadn't take down a single of her responses to the questions he'd asked so far.

"Why were you digging here?"

"I was looking for something I'd buried earlier." Emily prayed he wouldn't ask what.

"Mind sharing what that was?" Of course he asked.

"Yes." It was none of his business.

"Uh-huh." Sheriff White glanced at Salem and then back to Emily. "You had no idea this was here?"

"No." Emily squeezed her hands together. "It's freaking me out."

"Freaking you out?" He said it with implied quotation marks. "Aren't you the archeologist? The one who digs up dead bodies all the time?"

Emily barely knew this man, but didn't like him. His arrogant attitude rubbed her the wrong way. Broad-shouldered and tall, with thick hair and a thicker mustache, he might have been handsome if not for the too-forceful jut of his jaw.

"No, I don't dig up dead bodies. Mostly, I uncover ancient artifacts."

"Uh-huh." How did he manage to make two syllables sound so distrustful? And why did he keep narrowing his eyes at Salem and hovering over him? At six feet, Salem was tall, but this guy had a couple of inches on him.

Sheriff White called in help from Denver, and kept Emily and Salem close while waiting for the arrival of the Denver Police Department. He asked the same questions again.

Why was this feeling more and more sinister? They'd found a body and they'd called the cops. They were the good guys, not a pair of criminals.

It grated on Emily's nerves. "I was digging for something. I found the body. Salem called the police. That's the whole story."

She pointed to the body that had been cordoned off with tape. "You think if I had anything to do with putting that there, I would turn around and dig it back up and call the cops?"

Sheriff White tried to stare her down. Good luck

with that, she thought. In her work in the Middle East, she'd run into too many corrupt cops, army patrols who answered only to themselves, and lawless bands to be intimidated by this guy. In the unrest and unstable atmosphere of the Middle East, she'd found herself in danger many times, from coups to revolts to demonstrations.

At least in her home country, there were procedures law enforcement officials had to follow, and a court system that wasn't as corrupt as the ones in some of the places she'd visited.

With all of that, and remembering her terror when she'd nearly been caught at the airport with a relic in her bag, she could handle this guy's suspicions.

When White looked away first, Emily felt a small satisfaction.

DPD arrived with a coroner who suited up to do whatever coroners do before digging up a body. Emily had been away too many years and had watched no television. She'd never seen *CSI,* or *Criminal Minds,* or cop shows, though she'd heard people talk about them on her visits home. Phrases such as *petechial hemorrhaging, lividity* and *exsanguination,* terms that had become a part of the average citizen's lexicon, to judge by some conversations she'd had, meant nothing to her.

The phrases had been tossed around so casually and yet there was nothing casual about the breadth and depth of knowledge required to do this job. Emily's hat went off to the technicians and detectives who could solve these crimes, but she had no desire to learn how they did their work, or to watch them do it. She just wanted to get away.

White finally released Emily and Salem. Inside the Cathedral, in Salem's office, Emily paced. She'd been upset to find the body, but the sheriff's attitude had agitated her beyond belief. "What the *hell* was that about? Did he think *we'd* put the body there?"

Salem took two bottles of apple juice out of the bar fridge in the corner and tossed her one. She drank half of it in one go. They'd been standing in the sun for three hours.

Salem stared out the window to the scene below. "Some would say he was just doing his job."

"It was more than that, Salem."

"Yeah, it was," he conceded. "Since he's Justin's father, I assume he's mad at me for yelling at his kid."

WHILE HE GAVE EMILY a moment to digest that information, Salem watched the army of law enforcement personnel tramp over his land, roping off a broad area with that obscene yellow crime scene tape.

That this should be happening in this peaceful spot, scarring the beauty of his woods, was pure sacrilege.

Evil had invaded Salem's paradise.

They'd found a dead body, mere yards from the Cathedral.

Who was it?

Who had done this?

The sun still shone, the world still turned, and life went on, but someone had been murdered on this land.

Salem crammed his hands into his pockets to still their shaking.

Men and women suited up in protective white garb, armed with booties, latex gloves and the tools of their trade, bent over the exposed bone fingers they all assumed were still attached to a body below the surface.

Once Emily had uncovered them, she'd gone no farther.

"Your dad said the sheriff's crazy about his boy." Emily slumped onto the sofa. "Judging by his behavior, we can assume he knows about you storming into the school on Sunday and giving his son hell."

"Yep. Safe bet."

"He can bluster all he wants. It won't do you any harm."

Salem didn't respond. Life wasn't always fair and weird things happened to people all the time.

"We know where Justin learned to be a bully," Emily stated. "He comes by it naturally."

"The sheriff can be a reasonable man. We'll see what comes of this."

There was a brief silence, which Emily finally broke. "How did you find the prayer book, Salem?"

He'd been wondering when she would ask.

"You had dirt under your nails. Mud on your hands." He crossed his arms, putting a barrier between them. "I found the trowel and saw that the earth had been disturbed. I dug it up."

"You didn't think to ask me about it?"

"Your behavior was strange and so was the fact that you hid it here. It made you look guilty. It still does."

"I'm not."

He didn't know what to believe.

"Why did you bury it here?" He turned back to the window and those disturbing images below, because he couldn't look at Emily. His feelings pinged around like arcade balls. He was aware of her one minute, angry with her the next, then disappointed that his daughter chose her over him, and yet also grateful for what she had done for Aiyana.

But why had she used his land as a burial ground for a smuggled artifact?

"I can see you thinking too hard and I know it's all the wrong things." Emily had approached, her heat close behind him. Too close.

"How can you know that?"

"Because I know you. I know how you honor integrity and honesty. You need to hear my side of this story."

"Go ahead. Tell me."

"Not while your back is to me. I need you to see my face, to know I'm telling the truth."

He moved to sit behind his desk.

"No, I won't be scolded as though I'm a bad employee, either. Let's sit over here, as equals." She strode to the sofa.

He sat in the armchair. "I'm listening," he said, but she would have to come up with a hell of a story to make him understand why she'd taken an artifact away from its homeland.

"I'm holding you to that. You need to suspend judgment and really listen, because I did nothing wrong."

He wanted to believe, because for the life of him he couldn't see Emily as a smuggler or a thief.

"It was Jean-Marc."

That idiot! "He stole it and you're covering for the bastard?"

"No!" He'd angered her. "Just listen. No comments until I finish."

The story she told was fantastic enough to make him skeptical and yet, he did know Emily. He watched her face while she spoke and could see that it was the truth. He could see her being backed into a corner, to either have to take the relic out of the country with her or be arrested. The thought of her in a foreign jail…

"That's the truth, Salem." He could read it on her face. She'd been smart to make him watch her.

A tension that had been sitting on his shoulders like a heavy cloak fell away. "I believe you."

She let her breath out in a whoosh. "Thank you."

At least her story had distracted him from the cops and the grisly discovery below.

"What happens now?" he asked. "You can't keep it."

"I have a friend who also works with Jean-Marc. Penelope Chadwick. I wrote to her brother in England and he's allowing me to mail the relic to him. He'll put a new label on it with his return address and send it along to Penny."

"Cloak and dagger."

"May I have the book?"

He retrieved it from his pocket and handed it to her.

When she took it, she handled it with the reverence it deserved. He might not have been happy that her work had taken her so far away so often, but he didn't doubt her love of it.

"Tell me about it."

She talked about her last dig where they uncovered the book. She spoke about the history of the land and the people who had called it home for centuries.

"This little book would have been treasured by the owners. It's well preserved." Emily turned it over in her hands, touching it as if it was a rare gem. From the first moment they'd met, she and Salem had shared a respect for the past.

"It belongs in a museum, or at the very least, in climate-controlled storage so it won't deteriorate." She tucked it into her purse. "Do you have a small box I could use to mail it?"

"Come with me. I get items mailed to me often since the Museum displays artifacts from all over the Western states." He led her to the storage room, where they found a small, sturdy carton.

"I'll make certain I pack it well for Arthur."

She said his name sweetly, with affection. Salem didn't like to hear another man's name on Emily's lips, and for an intensely civilized man, his jealousy made him feel strangely primal.

WHEN SHE GOT HOME, she checked the internet and found, not surprisingly, that Jean-Marc was fighting back with more innuendo and nasty remarks about their history together.

At least this time, her friends were more vocal in their support of her, despite having to be careful that their boss didn't turn on them, too.

At some point, she was going to have to figure out a more permanent solution. At the moment, all she could think to do was to start the prayer book on its journey home.

Emily called FedEx about picking up a package. She packed the prayer book, almost obsessive in how well she padded it in the carton Salem had given her. She would never forgive herself if it were damaged.

As it was, she'd done such a good job the delivery people could play football with the package and the relic would survive.

Penelope was going to curse her from here to the pyramids when she had to cut through all of the shipping tape with which Emily had coated the box.

The door at the bottom of her stairs opened.

"Emily-y-y-y-y, I have fresh cinnamon buns."

Emily smiled. "Cinnamon buns? Say no more. I'll be right there."

Once Emily had made her peace with her father's remarriage twenty years ago, Laura had always called up to Emily in the same way, drawing out her name to make her smile.

Dear Laura. It was good to be back. If Emily could make a go of teaching music in Accord, she could once again call the town home. After her harrowing escape from the guards at the airport, and feeling so lost after breaking ties with Jean-Marc and archeology, it felt good to have a positive outlook. Her future didn't look as dim as when she'd first arrived.

Package in hand, Emily answered the door and gave the well-wrapped prayer book to the driver. It was on its way. With a little luck, it would arrive in one piece.

Emily had tea and cinnamon buns with Laura and her dad, and explained what she and Salem had found on Turner land.

Their faces reflected the shock she still felt.

Laura reached for her hand. "Are you okay?"

"I'm still processing. It's surreal. I mean, it isn't like finding an ancient burial, you know? It's much more disturbing."

"Speaking of ancient burials…" Her dad sighed. "Please tell me you meant what you said about staying home for good."

Did no one trust her word?

"Yes, Dad, I really have given up on archeology, and yes, I really am going to stay here to live. *Really.*"

He put down his cinnamon roll, wiped his fingers and then stood, pulling her out of her chair with a hand around her wrist.

"What—"

The next thing she knew she was wrapped in a bear hug with the breath being squeezed out of her lungs.

"I've been so worried about you." Her father set her down and gripped her upper arms. "Every time you went to some of those countries, I feared a war would break out, or terrorists would attack. I thought I would lose you."

She'd had no idea he worried so much.

"Welcome home, sweetheart." His voice sounded watery.

He enveloped her in another hug and Laura joined them at Emily's back, wrapping her arms as far around them as she could. Emily's heart did a long, graceful swan dive into a sea of happiness.

ON SUNDAY AFTERNOON, Emily planned to visit her former music teacher, but life threw a spanner into the works.

Still tired after her bout with malaria, she slept in until ten, unheard of in her previous life. When she went downstairs, there was only silence. The house and the garage stood empty. She didn't know where everyone was, but she did know she needed a car to visit Mrs. Gendron, who had retired to a small house in the country on the far side of town.

So much for visiting her today.

Emily could at least walk into town to pick up some items from the pharmacy. After a quick breakfast, she set out.

The trek refreshed her. The balmy May breeze helped to chase the image of the ghostly specters of those skeletal fingers from her mind. Funny that she'd

never minded looking at mummies in museums, but
those bodies had been recovered from burial sites,
buried where they were supposed to have been, not
in the forest floor.

She forced herself to stop thinking about it, but
when she ran into Salem on Main Street in front of
the pharmacy, it all came back.

"Hey," he said, his response subdued and his expression somber.

"Are you thinking about what I'm thinking about?"
Sunshine warmed her shoulders, but ice chilled her
core.

"The body?"

"Yes."

"Can't help but." He held the door of the shop open.
"You going in here, too?"

She nodded and stepped in ahead of him. "Brr. It's
cold."

"Ingram pretty well turns on the air the second he
turns off the furnace for the winter."

Emily laughed. "I think—" A voice interrupted
what she'd been about to say about Mrs. Ingram, the
pharmacist, being menopausal. There couldn't be any
other reason for a man to keep the place as cold as a
refrigerator.

"Hi, Salem. Hello, Emily. Are you here on one of
your fly-by-night visits?"

Victoria Pound approached out of one of the aisles,
the last person Emily wanted to see. Tori had been one
of the mean girls in school.

Throughout the years, Emily had managed to be polite whenever she saw Tori, but there had never been any pleasure in seeing her.

"Hi." Emily couldn't for the life of her manage to sound friendly.

"I'm surprised you ever come back here," Tori said. "What with our town being so small and all. Hardly seems worthwhile for a famous archeologist." Emphasis on the famous.

Emily wasn't famous. Jean-Marc, with his sound bites, charm and good looks, was, and so Emily had sometimes been caught with him in photos taken at parties and fund-raisers that had later appeared in magazines. But *she* wasn't famous, and never would have been known at all without Jean-Marc. Not that obscurity would have bothered her. The media, the parties and contact with celebrities had been seductive, but Emily's career had never been about that. She just loved history, plain and simple.

Tori didn't look well. In fact, she looked tired. Her hair hung in brown strands, not the glossy, pampered blond it had been in high school. She held a baby in her arms. Two children ran from the aisle and handed her a box of tampons.

"Found them, Mom," one of the kids shouted.

Tori's embarrassed glance slid away from Salem. He studied a box of liver pills on a shelf.

"What brings you back to town?" She sounded glum.

"I'm home for good. I've given up archeology."

Tori's eyes widened comically. "Are you crazy?"

Emily's spine stiffened. "Not last time I checked."

"You have this great job, going to all kinds of exotic places and you're giving it up to come back *here*?" Tori obviously had serious issues with *here*. "Do you know how jealous I was when you left this Podunk town and got your amazing career?"

Tori *envied* her? It explained so much—the dirty looks, the unfriendly manner.

"The career ran its course," Emily tried to explain. "It no longer holds my interest."

Tori had no idea how much of Emily's job had been tedious, moving earth by the teaspoonful, finding objects once every few months. It took patience and perseverance, and a certain type of committed personality. Glamour had nothing to do with it, and no country could stay exotic forever.

"You're looking good," Tori said. Despite the earlier sarcasm, she sounded sincere. The baby squirmed in Tori's arms.

"She's adorable." Emily loved children. "May I hold her?"

Tori handed her over and within minutes the baby was laughing. "What's her name?"

Tori paid Mr. Ingram for her tampons. "Charlotte." Mr. Ingram wore a heavy fall cardigan. Yep, the missus was menopausal.

"Oh, what a lovely name. Funny how Charles is such a sober name, but Charlotte so pretty. I hope no one calls her Charlie. That would be sacrilege when she has such a beautiful name." She did this too often. Talked about odd things no one else cared about. "Sorry. I get carried away on weird subjects."

"That's okay." With Emily's interest in her daughter, Tori warmed. "Would you… Do you want to go out for coffee sometime? I'd love to hear about your travels."

It seemed Tori had decided on the spot to handle her envy a whole lot better, even extending an olive branch.

Emily jostled Charlotte and she giggled. "I'd like that."

Tori made a rueful face. "I would have to bring the children."

"Great. I love kids." She had a sudden thought. "If you know of anyone who needs music lessons for their children, let me know. I'm going to teach music here in Accord."

"Music lessons? I might take you up on that for the oldest one here, Mikey."

Tori smiled before leaving the store. It seemed genuine.

"You're staying to teach music? For how long?"

"I said it before and I'll say it again, Salem—I'm home for good."

He kept his skepticism to himself. Good. She didn't feel like arguing today. "What are you here for?"

"Toothbrushes for my girls. I noticed they need new ones."

"Where on earth did you dig up that tiny child's brush I used the other day?"

Under his gorgeous honey skin, his high flat cheek-bones burnished red. "I, um, I've been buying them for Aiyana and Mika. I haven't really kept up with the changes they've gone through lately."

"Boy, I'll say."

"What are you up to today?"

"Remember Mrs. Gendron? She taught me music all through high school. I want to visit her, but all of the family's cars are gone. Everyone's out and about today and I don't know where they've gotten to."

"I can drive you out and back."

"You don't mind?"

"Nope. Give me a minute to pick up the stuff I need."

"Me, too. I'll meet you out front in ten minutes."

Along with shampoo and conditioner, Emily found a postcard of Colorado with a bear in the photo. Maria would love it.

Before driving out, they stopped at Tonio's and picked up a half dozen cannoli for Mrs. Gendron then got back into the Jeep.

Although it looked roomy, the Jeep Wrangler Rubicon, Emily learned, was not a big vehicle. She'd been too sick on her first night back in Accord to notice how close the driver and passenger seats were.

When Salem changed gears, his solid arm brushed hers. The sun shining through the windshield warmed everything, even him, and his soap scent filled the close interior.

She became hyperaware of every breath he took, of

the way he drove with confidence, but not arrogance. That was Salem in a nutshell. A *Bertholletia excela.* A Brazil nut shell with his light nut-toned skin she knew would darken over the summer.

"Can I ask you a question, Emily?"

"Sure."

"What was that tension back there between you and Tori?"

Oh, boy. Other than Aiyana and Pearl recently, she'd never shared those dark secrets with anyone. "When we were in high school, she and three other girls were the definition of mean girls. Once boys started to sniff around me, I guess they got jealous and turned their venom on me. They were ruthless."

She felt his startled glance on her skin like a touch. "Was it bad? Like with Aiyana?"

"Better and worse." She kept her focus on the road ahead, because she didn't want to see pity on Salem's face. "Better in that it was more contained since we didn't have Facebook or Twitter, but worse because there was no one to rescue me. I didn't have an older brother or friends who could pretend I was one of the cool kids, or who had influence and could persuade them to back off."

"Like Cody did for Aiyana."

"Like Cody." She slid off her shoes and rested her feet against the glove compartment, curling her fingers around her knees. "So the abuse went on for a long time. It felt like forever. I was miserable."

"I had no idea."

"How could you have? You'd already finished high school a few years before and were involved with Annie. You didn't really notice me anymore. I wasn't on your radar back then."

They'd arrived at Mrs. Gendron's tiny cottage with the red VW Beetle tucked under a carport on the side of the house. Emily smiled. How like Mrs. Gendron. She'd always been a bit of a free spirit.

Emily slipped her shoes back on. "Besides, when you live with shame, you learn how to cover it really well. I became a master at pretending everything was fine. I don't think even my family knew there was a problem. Dad always said I had spunk, so I used it ruthlessly to fool people into thinking I was okay. I didn't have enough resources to fight everyone at school, but I made them believe I didn't care." Then she'd used the same techniques over the years to hide her troubles with Jean-Marc. "I did care, though. What those girls did really hurt me." As did everything Jean-Marc had done.

"I'm tired of being a victim. It won't happen ever again."

Just as Emily moved to leave the Jeep, Salem touched her arm. "You were never off my radar, Emily, but I made a commitment to Annie. I married her, so I put my energy into making my marriage work. I had to set aside my feelings for you. They surfaced again when you came home last year. Nothing I could do about it."

The look he gave her before he climbed out of the vehicle smoldered.

Saintly jumping...*relics*. What was the man trying to do to her? Was he deliberately confusing her, playing with her emotions? Or was he as confused as she was?

She scrambled out of the passenger seat and followed him as he approached the house, because it seemed safer to ignore the issue and get on with her mission. Salem Pearce could go make some other girl hot and bothered. First he wanted her and then he didn't and then he did. She didn't have a clue what to do about Salem.

When Emily rapped on the frame of the screen door, three yapping Pekinese came running down the tiny hallway. Mrs. Gendron opened the door and the dogs bounded out onto the minuscule veranda. Salem crouched and gave them attention.

Everything about the place, and the woman, was tiny. Barely five feet tall, Mrs. Gendron smiled at Emily from a face with a network of lines crashing into each other when she smiled, like a train wreck of wrinkles.

"Emily, my favorite student. How delightful. Come in. Hello, Salem."

"Hi, Mrs. Gendron."

"Call me Violet, both of you. You're adults now. What brings you here?"

"I want to start teaching music in Accord." Emily

sat in the armchair Violet indicated. "I'd like to pick your brains about it."

Violet's face lit up as though someone had flicked on a light switch. "I'm so glad."

They talked music and teaching for an hour and a half while they drank tea and ate cannoli. No one had taken Violet's place when she'd retired five years ago, leaving the field wide open for Emily.

Emily's thoughts tumbled over each other. "I'll need a place of my own. I can't possibly put the family through listening to new students learning the violin. Or worse, something like the saxophone."

"You played alto sax so well in band. Remember? You had an aptitude for so many instruments. You were my best student ever."

Emily blushed. She knew half a dozen instruments well enough to teach, including piano, but her passion was violin.

Salem carried their dirty dishes to the kitchen and washed them in the sink. "There's an apartment available on Main Street, above The Last Dance."

"The floral shop?"

Salem nodded. "The owner, Audrey, is a super woman. She'd make a great landlady."

"That would be good for living in, but not for teaching music. I would disturb her and her customers downstairs during business hours, and the tenants in neighboring units during the evening."

"True," Violet said. "You'll find yourself teaching

at all kinds of odd hours to accommodate work and school schedules."

Her expression turned thoughtful. "Come." With her thin arms, she hoisted herself out of a cozy chintz armchair and stepped out the back door. Emmy followed with Salem bringing up the rear.

"Look." Violet pointed to a small, detached garage behind the house. "I never use it. It's full of old junk I don't want anymore, but I just don't have the energy to start cleaning it out. It needs a coat of paint on the exterior and a lot of work inside to make it habitable. If you're willing to do the work, you can use it to teach."

"You would let me rent this from you?"

"Rent? No. Use? Yes." She shone her bright, clear-eyed gaze on Emily. Laughter lurked in its depths. "On one condition."

"What's that?"

"Let me sit in on the lessons occasionally. I'm bored. I hate TV and I get tired of my crossword puzzles." Emily had heard that her husband had died about ten years ago.

"You can sit in on every lesson. I would appreciate your support and guidance." Emily held out her hand. "Deal?"

"Deal." They shook on it.

"I'll go to the hardware store tomorrow and pick up supplies." Floating on a cloud of ecstasy, she asked, "Can I see the inside?" Things were coming together quickly.

"This will work for the summer," Violet said.

"If I get enough clients to earn a living, would you mind if I winterize in the fall?"

"You can do whatever you need to do, my dear. I'll love having you around."

Ten minutes later, Emily weighed the amount of work needed. The place would have to be fumigated and cleared out and scoured and painted and, and, and…

She would need help. "Do you think Mika and Aiyana would want to make a little money helping me to fix up the garage?" she asked Salem on the drive back to town.

"Get rid of the pests first and clean, then they can come."

Emily smiled the rest of the way home. She retrieved her shampoo and conditioner from the backseat, shouted her thanks behind her and ran into the house fired up by her new project.

The family sat around the dining room table. "I wondered whether you'd make it home in time for dinner." Laura went to the kitchen and filled a plate for Emily. "Sit."

Throughout the meal, Emily told everyone her plans, how they were firm now that she had a place to teach.

"You'll need a car eventually, but we can juggle until we find something for you." Her dad helped himself to a piece of the rhubarb pie Laura had passed around. His tummy was getting a bit pudgy. How could it not with Laura cooking for him? "You'll continue to live upstairs."

"Just until I'm sure I can make a living doing this, then I'll get an apartment in town."

Laura dropped the spoon she'd been using to stir her coffee. "An apartment in town when you have a perfectly good one upstairs?"

"I'm thirty-one years old. I shouldn't be sponging off my dad."

"You aren't sponging," he said. "You're *living* with your family."

"But what about Pearl? Isn't it time she got to use the attic?"

"I like it up there, Emily, but I like even more that you're here." Pearl wiped a smudge of vanilla ice cream from her upper lip. "Stay. Please. I like having you here with us."

So. It was settled. She would still live here with her family while she taught music in Violet's garage.

She'd spent too many years shunting from pillar to post, from one dangerous spot to another, and always with an unsympathetic man with whom she was never in sync. If she were the crying type, the unconditional support of her family would bring her to tears. What she did instead was smile, a shit-eating grin echoed by everyone else at the table.

Healing, thy name is family.

On Monday, Emily shopped at the hardware store for environmentally friendly cleaning products and tools for fixing up Violet's garage.

She booked an appointment with a pest control

company in Denver to come out that afternoon. Emily wasn't sure, but she thought she might have seen a bat hanging from the eaves. Bats might help organic farming by eating harmful insects that cause agricultural damage, not to mention pesky mosquitos, but Emily preferred her *Vespertilionidae* to live outside, not in. But she did love them. Maybe he would hang around outside.

She drove her supplies to Violet's homestead and found the woman waiting on the veranda.

"I thought you might show up this morning. You were excited yesterday." She and her three dogs approached the car, with the dogs jumping joyfully around Emily when she got out. "What can I carry for you?"

Emily handed her a bag of cleaning supplies and carried the tools around the back of the house to the garage. It looked even more forlorn today with dark clouds hovering on the horizon.

Rusty from disuse, the door creaked when she opened it. She made a note to pick up oil for the hinges.

A faint scurrying heralded their arrival. Emily studied the brown lump she'd spotted in the rafters. Yep, a bat. She loved bats, flat-out adored them, and used to get her dad to take her around the state to study them when she was young.

"Oh," she said, stepping directly beneath it. "If I'm not mistaken, that's a cave myotis. What's he doing this far north? By himself?"

"What do you mean?" Violet had joined her to stare up at the lone bat.

"They're usually found in Colorado only on the Mesa de Maya." She couldn't put him out when he had found a home here.

The interior dimness was emphasized by the approaching storm clouds.

"These windows need to be scrubbed if you want to see what you're doing in here." Violet rummaged in the bags. "You didn't buy window cleaner?"

"I'm using good old-fashioned vinegar. I did, however, get these super-duper, microfiber, glass-cleaning cloths for cars. I figure if they're good enough for autos, they'll work on these windows."

"I remember my mother used to use newspaper."

"Do you want to clean the inside while I do the exterior?"

"Yep. You go on and get out there before the rain starts."

Emily had just finished the last window when a huge drop of rain fell on her head. Violet came outside. "Let's go into the house for lunch. This rain isn't supposed to last all day."

They had lunch, finishing just in time for pest control.

"Can you get rid of the mice by trapping them?" Emily led the exterminator to the garage. "I know I sound a bit loony, but I don't want them killed. I just want them out of the garage."

That way, there would be no unhealthy toxic residue left in the building once she started teaching, and her *myotis velifer* wouldn't die. Surely her students and one bat could coexist. She would be religious in cleaning guano every single day. She could keep the space healthy, no problem.

The owner of the company checked out every nook and cranny. "You've got signs of a healthy mouse population. Give me this afternoon to set a bunch of traps. Tomorrow afternoon, I'll collect them and release the mice elsewhere."

He stood with his hands on his hips. "I don't see signs of insect infestation."

Emily pointed above their heads. "Thank my little buddy."

"He's not that little. What's he doing this far north?"

Emily shot him a surprised look.

He grinned. "I know my pests."

"You sure do. I want to keep that pest, okay?"

"You got it."

Two days later, she and Pearl scrubbed the inside of the garage until their fingers pruned.

On Tuesday afternoon, the pest control guy had carried out dozens of traps filled with mice and had left Emily literature on how to clean up after them, and on how to prevent new critters from moving in.

She'd hunted in every corner of the large room and in every piece of furniture. She didn't know what the guy had used for bait, but it had been effective. Not a single *genus Mus* remained in the garage.

Today, they'd gone through four pairs of heavy-duty

PVC-coated gloves just cleaning out mice poop. After that, they'd scrubbed the walls and the floor and had worn holes in the remaining two pairs of latex gloves, so her hands were wet anyway.

When they'd finished, they stripped off the old clothes they'd worn and bundled them into a garbage bag to throw out. She drove home to have a shower and change into more old clothes. Pearl was meeting friends so Emily picked up more supplies, including another half dozen pairs of gloves.

She returned to the garage for more cleaning.

Then she called in reinforcements.

SALEM DIDN'T BELIEVE for a minute Emily would last in the music-teaching business. Even with her passion for the music, how could she? She'd visited exotic lands, had partied with celebrities and had sampled the best of many cultures. In a few months, Accord would bore her and off she would go again.

Yet despite his lack of faith, here he was driving Aiyana and Mika out to Violet's house. Apparently, Emily had called them after school to ask for their help.

Finding that dead body with her had shaken Salem's ordered world, had given him a different perspective. His life went on in the same way and yet, he lay awake at night with the memory of those pale skeletal fingers reaching toward the sky as though grasping for another chance at life. With that desperate imagery haunting him, he felt changed, moved by this sudden strange development to look at things in a new way. Some poor schmuck had been murdered, his life snuffed out, while all Salem did was worry about the future, about what might happen someday, when the smart thing to do was to live in the here and now. Maybe that dead body was a wake-up call urging him to appreciate every moment for the gift it was. Perhaps the wisest way to live was to experience the moment and deal with consequences later.

He saw clearly now that the relationship between Emily and Aiyana had a life of its own that he couldn't control. He was smart enough to realize that trying to break it up would cause more damage than Emily's inevitable departure. Aiyana would be okay because she would still have *him*. He would never leave.

So, with a feeling of giving in to the inevitable, he drove his girls out to help Emily.

"I'm so happy Emily's doing this, Dad." Aiyana brushed her dark hair then returned her brush to her purse. "I really want to learn a musical instrument. Remember you promised I could?"

"Sure, Aiyana."

"Me, too," Mika piped up from the backseat.

"What instruments are you interested in?"

Mika shrugged, but Aiyana already knew her own mind. "Violin. I loved how Emily played hers."

"How can I know what I want if I don't try a whole bunch of different instruments first?" Mika met Salem's eyes in the rearview mirror. "How can I do that, Dad?"

"I can take you into Denver and we can check out the rental instruments. Okay?"

The corners of Mika's dark brown eyes crinkled when she smiled. "Yeah, I want to do that."

Emily waited for them on the veranda, her hair a wild halo around her.

"You look like you've been pulled through a bush backward." Salem thought she looked cute as hell.

"I've been working." Her overalls were ancient. One knee poked out through a large hole. The T-shirt underneath was miles too big for her. She must have raided Cody's closet. The sleeves, which should have been short, hung down nearly to midforearm.

A smudge of dirt on her nose obscured the few freckles Salem had always wanted to lick.

Hey, none of that. No X-rated thoughts about this heartbreaker, got it?

Yeah, I got it.

Sometimes, though, as had happened the other day when they'd driven out here to talk to Violet, the truth of his feelings burst out of him, like steam exploding from a pressure cooker. Then he had to be careful to not do anything rash.

Even so, he wiped the dust from her nose, just to touch her, even that briefly.

"Come see how much work I've done."

They followed her around back. "There's still a lot to do," she warned, "but you can see the potential now."

They stepped inside and Salem's first thought was,

what potential? But that was Emily. Always the op-
timist. He, on the other hand, was cautious. It saved
a person from a world of heartache down the road.

"The place needs work, Emily."

"Don't rain on my parade, Salem. I have a vision."

"What do you need from us today?" *Us.* He'd only
planned to drop off the girls. So why was he staying?
Because of Emily's infectious excitement. Because the
girls had picked up on it and were exclaiming over the
bat Emily had pointed out to them.

"You're going to leave it there?" He couldn't believe she would do that. "I thought you were going to
teach children."

"Yes, and if they ask questions about the bat, I'll answer them. Not only will they learn music, but they'll
also get a science lesson."

Salem didn't care about science lessons as much as
keeping his daughters safe. "He won't hurt anyone?"

"Bats are the gentlest creatures. They don't attack
people. They don't come down to sit in your hair. They
don't bite. It's only old myths and nonsense about vam-
pires that have scared people for so many centuries."

She brushed a few strands of hair from her face,
adding another smudge of dirt to her forehead. "Otis
won't hurt a soul, and he'll keep the building free of
insects. Considering Violet lives on the edge of these
grain fields, that's a good thing."

"Otis?" Mika asked.

"*Myotis velifer.* His scientific name."

"Otis." Mika laughed. Salem tapped her on the

shoulder. "If you see any raccoons out here, no feeding them, you hear?"

His Intelligent Raccoon scowled. "But, Dad—"

She fed raccoons regularly, leaving Salem to become more and more creative to keep the critters out of his garbage cans. They thought of his house and property as theirs. Damn pests.

Mika had managed to shoot a lot of cell phone videos of raccoons rolling his big plastic bins all over the driveway, trying to get them open. She thought it was hilarious. Salem? Not so much.

"No *buts*," he said. "It's okay for me to handle them at home, but we don't want to leave Violet having to deal with them here." He softened his voice. "It would be hard for her. Okay?"

Mika eased her defiant stance. "I understand."

Not for the first time, Salem marveled at how reasonable his daughters could be when he just explained things to them.

"What should we do?" Salem took the pair of cleaning gloves Emily handed to him. She also gave gloves to Aiyana and Mika.

"We need to get these old pieces of furniture out of here so I can paint." To the girls, she said, "After school tomorrow, do you want to help me look at paint chips for the walls?"

"Yes," they chorused.

"If it's all right with your dad, I'll pick you up after school and we'll head over to Turner Lumber. Okay?"

"What are you going to do with the floor?" Salem

asked. "This cement is only going to keep kicking up dust unless you finish it somehow."

"Like how?"

"How about staining it? Acid cement stains will make it look like stone." He crouched down. The floor was level. "It will look really good. What color do you want it?"

"How about something dark, like a chocolate brown? Do they have dark colors?"

"You can stain it whatever color you want. I can do it for you."

Emily's eyes widened. "You would do that?"

"Yes." He would do just about anything for Emily—anything but have a relationship with her.

"Okay. Thank you."

"I'll pick up the stain on my way to work tomorrow and then leave work a bit early later to come here."

"You left early today, too. Isn't that a problem for you?"

"Since the body was discovered, no one is coming into the Heritage Center." It pained him to talk about it. "They all drive over to look at the hole in the ground. The case has attracted rubberneckers from all over the state."

Emily frowned. "I'm sorry, Salem."

"It is what it is." He'd long since learned to tamp down his feelings when he couldn't control the world around him.

"Any word from the police on who it was?"

"No. DNA testing will take a while."

"Okay, if you would stain the floor tomorrow, I would really appreciate it." She clapped her hands once. "Let's get to work."

They carried furniture out into the sunlight. "Most of this will go to the dump. Violet's already given me permission. But look at this piece." They had just carried out an old desk. "It's solid wood. I'm going to strip, refinish it and use it. What do you think?"

Salem liked that she asked his daughters for their opinions—first, that she cared enough to ask and second, that she listened.

They cleared everything out of the building so they could sweep and then vacuum the floor. By the time they left, the concrete was ready for Salem to stain.

The next day, he found himself in the garage doing just that. He'd picked up a chocolate stain, as Emily had requested.

It looked good. He backed himself out of the building through the side door just as he heard a car drive up. A minute later, the girls and Emily came around the house carrying gallons of paint, brushes and trays.

"We're going to paint tomorrow after school, Dad." Mika set her load down in the too-tall grass surrounding the garage.

"I can drive you over. Does Violet own a lawn mower?"

"She must." Emily rubbed her hands where the paint can handles had dug into her palms. "Her lawn out front was mowed sometime recently, but it's getting a bit ragged. The backyard is decidedly rough, though."

"When I drop the girls off to paint after school, I'll cut everything."

Emily pulled open the large doors. "Let's make sure Otis isn't exposed to too many chemicals. Ooh, look at that beautiful color. Salem, it's gorgeous."

As if Mika had conjured a raccoon from midair, one sauntered around the corner, not the least bit intimidated by them all milling about.

"Eek!" Emily squealed. "Don't let him walk on Salem's freshly stained floor."

They chased the raccoon away, shooing him farther and farther into the field, laughing like a bunch of children.

Aiyana and Mika laughed easily with Emily, more than they had with their own mother. Who could blame them? Annie had had a heart of gold, but what good was it when she was stoned, her addictions more powerful than her love for her family?

Emily brought out the best in his children. It warmed his heart, and he resisted that warmth because he didn't want his daughters depending on her, not after what their mother had put them through, and what Emily would certainly put them through when she left.

He'd made his decision, though, to allow this relationship to grow, and swallowed his sadness. *Let them live for this moment.*

FRANTIC KNOCKING ON the front door that evening had Salem rushing to open it. Who on earth would that be at nine-thirty at night? Emily stood under the porch light, gripping a couple of cheap aluminum and nylon-webbing lawn chairs.

"Emily, what's going on? I thought there was something wrong."

"There will be if we miss the meteor shower that's forecast for tonight. I heard about it an hour ago." She thrust the chairs at him. "Take these to the backyard. I'll get the rest."

The girls had joined Salem. Aiyana slipped into a pair of shoes. "I'll help."

They retrieved more chairs from Nick Jordan's SUV then trooped through the house to the backyard to set them up.

"Salem, I picked up snacks. They're in bags on the backseat of the car. Would you get them, please?"

He did, then found everyone in the kitchen. Emily filled big bowls his dad had taken out of cupboards, with popcorn and chips. She handed around juice boxes.

"Let's go," she said. "Do you own a plastic table we can use outside?"

"I have folding dinner trays." His father pulled them out of the laundry room at the back of the house.

Salem stopped Emily just before she stepped outside. "Why aren't you watching this with your own family instead of coming over here?"

"They left for a party in Denver two hours ago. I was really pooped from working on the garage and didn't feel like going. I'd rather watch shooting stars anyway."

Disappointment slid through him, bitter like a dose of cod liver oil. Why had he hoped for a different answer? For something like, *I wanted to be with you.*

You're hopeless, buddy, resisting her because of guaranteed future heartbreak, but wanting her to desire you just the same.

Out in the backyard, his dad opened the trays in the middle of the circle of chairs and Emily put the food down. Aiyana and Mika had carried out the drinks. They chose their seats.

"You want to tell us what this is about?" Salem reached for a handful of chips.

"The earth is passing through debris from a comet's orbit tonight. It should look like a rainfall of shooting stars."

In the faint light shining through the back windows of the house, Emily's face glowed. He'd forgotten how much she used to love this stuff, how much of a nerd she'd been as an adolescent, despite not looking the least bit like one.

"Can we turn off the indoor lights?"

"I'll do it." Salem turned them off then returned through the darkness to take his seat again. An owl hooted in the distance. Even back here, he heard those crickets that had taken up residence under the front porch.

Down the street, someone was just closing up his grill for the night. Overhead, stars sparkled.

"How does a meteor shower happen? What causes the debris?" Salem's own teenaged nerd, Aiyana, burned with the same level of curiosity as Emily had at that age. He crossed his fingers. If only high school didn't burn it out of her.

He listened with half an ear while Emily explained. This came close to his idea of heaven, sharing a piece of nature with people he loved.

"Look!" Mika cried.

Once the shower started it didn't let up until they were hoarse and their throats spent after too many oohs and aahs. Nature's fireworks, brought to them because Emily had been vigilant, and had thought to include his family in the event.

"That was amazing." Aiyana sounded breathy and happy.

"Yeah. Thanks, Emily." Mika's juice box straw made rude noises when she sucked the remnants out of the bottom.

Everyone laughed.

"We are happy, eh?" Salem's dad gathered the empty bowls and carried them to the back door. "Thank you, Emily, for going to this trouble."

It was a dig at him, Salem knew. It was his father's way of saying, *Look, here she is again bringing* fun *trouble into this house.*

Salem had scooted down in his chair earlier so he could rest his neck on the back to watch the show. He rolled his head to admire Emily in the chair beside him. She had scrunched down in her chair, too.

She must have felt him studying her. She rolled her head to meet his gaze, hard to see in the spare ambient light. Yet he knew an understanding passed between them, of a love of nature, and a love of friends. Their awareness of each other became pronounced, palpable.

Her hand rested on the arm of her chair and he set his on top of it. She turned her palm up, and it was natural to thread his fingers with hers.

He smiled, floating in a serenity that blocked out any problems the future might bring. This woman gave his children so much.

Thank you, with all of my heart.

She returned his smile.

You're welcome, from my heart to yours.

CHAPTER EIGHT

SALEM DROVE THE GIRLS into Denver on Thursday evening after work. They found the music rental shop without a problem and spent a couple of hours trying out instruments.

In the end, Aiyana stuck with her original plan. No surprise there. She had a habit of knowing her own mind.

Mika chose the clarinet. Fine by Salem. He loved New Orleans jazz and envisioned his daughter belting out some lively stuff one of these days.

They left the store with their rented instruments. If the girls liked the music enough, and stuck with it, he would buy them their own.

Aiyana said, "I want to buy Emily and Cody gifts to thank them for helping me with the bullying, but I don't know what to get."

"I can help you. Let's do it now."

Aiyana's lovely smile warmed his soul. "Thanks, Dad. I don't have much money. Do you think they'd be okay with something small?"

"Yes. They'll be touched by the sentiment—the cost doesn't matter."

"Okay," Aiyana said. "I want to get something for you, too."

"Me? What did I do? I was totally useless."

"You got me the right help."

He didn't want to tell her how little he'd wanted to ask Emily because, in the end, his daughter's needs had been more important than his own discomfort.

"One of my teachers once said that having a lot of knowledge is great," Aiyana said, "but even more important is knowing where to look when you don't have the answers. You knew where to look. Emily was perfect."

If only Emily really were perfect. Sometimes, though, only Emily came close enough to that ideal to tempt him. If only she would stay put.

They found a gift shop where Aiyana bought her dad a journal. She chose a bright scarf for Emily and a black leather wristband for Cody. The band had a pair of silver hands that clasped together to keep it closed.

"This is so cool, Dad. It's like jewelry, but it's still really masculine. I'm not sure, though. Is it appropriate to give something like this to a guy I'm not dating?"

"Good question, Aiyana. On the one hand, it's a nice thought and a generous way to thank him. On the other hand—"

Mika grabbed it from her sister. "Honestly, you guys think too much." She plonked it on the counter beside the cash register. "You're buying it, Aiyana. It's perfect."

Salem took his daughters out for dinner as a kind

of celebration. Occasionally, he treated the family to dinner in Accord, but between working and studying so much and paying tuition for years, it hadn't been a regular thing.

He couldn't remember the last time he'd taken them out in Denver, even though it was only a little over an hour up the road from their hometown.

Over fish and chips, coleslaw and milk shakes, Salem broached the subject that had been troubling him. How was Aiyana doing now? As a parent he should know, but he'd never been one to open a can of worms if he didn't have to, especially since he wasn't sure how he would help her if she was still struggling.

He jumped in before he lost his nerve.

"Aiyana." He must have sounded serious because both girls stopped chewing, the easiness of the meal gone in a moment.

"What, Dad?"

"Are you okay?"

"Okay?" A puzzled frown formed between her brows. "What do you mean?"

"I mean, you know…with the whole Justin thing."

"Oh, Dad, that's so over. Thanks to Emily and Cody, it became a nonissue fast. Everything's back to normal at school."

She cut up her battered fillet and scooped out the fish to eat first, saving her favorite part, the batter, for last. Salem hid a bittersweet smile behind his hand, happy to see that his growing-up-too-fast teenager still had some of her childish habits. She'd had this one for years and he'd always found it endearing. How much longer would this tiny piece of her childhood last?

Another thought had been troubling Salem since the Justin debacle, when Aiyana hadn't had a mother to turn to for help. Had his girls recovered from their mother's death? Salem had been clumsy in his attempts to console them at the time while also trying to protect them from the harsher reality of what had happened. Mothers weren't supposed to die from drug overdoses. It might somehow have been more acceptable if it had been a prescription drug, but that crazy Caleb Brown had sold her some kind of dirty meth. The fact that the cops hadn't followed up and charged Caleb still burned Salem to this day. Then the coward had skipped town.

Annie might not have been a pillar of society, might not have held a significant position in town, and might not have had influence, but she had been important to her children.

"Girls?" Again they stopped eating and stared at him.

"Do you ever miss your mother?"

Mika stared down at her plate. "I feel really bad, Dad. Some days, I can't see her face anymore. I have to look at her picture to remember her."

"That's normal and you have nothing to feel guilty about. I think it's the mind's way of dealing with grief, of making it easier to accept loss." That was advice Salem felt comfortable giving because he'd lived with that guilt himself before he realized it was a waste of energy. "How about you, Aiyana?"

"I felt guilty for a long time after she died because I was so mad at Mom for doing drugs. I know she was a good person, but I *hated* when she was using. Why did she do it, Dad?"

How could he tell them the truth without hurting their feelings?

"Just tell us, Dad. We can handle it."

Man, these women who knew him so well could run circles around him. First Emily, and now Aiyana.

"Whatever it is," she continued, "you need to be honest with us. We're growing up. We're not little kids anymore."

The waitress came, cleared their plates and took orders for dessert. While Salem doctored a coffee, he decided his daughters deserved the truth.

"Your mom had kids too young." He rushed to reassure them. "Don't get me wrong. She really loved you two. Ever notice all the photos of you as babies and toddlers around the house? She loved making photo albums of those pictures. That was her favorite hobby."

"So, what does that have to do with her taking drugs?" That was Mika, ready to face reality.

"She wasn't yet thirty and you girls were growing up, and she realized she'd become a wife and a mother before she'd had much of a chance to find out who she was, or to have fun. She went straight from working in that upholstery factory as a teenager to marriage.

I guess she saw me as a way out, but in time came to see it as a different kind of…bondage, I guess?"

"Oh." Aiyana's voice sounded small. Salem took her hand then also held Mika's.

"That's why I told you how much she loved you first. Her problem wasn't with *you,* but with something inside her. She left school and started working at sixteen, came straight into marriage and motherhood at barely nineteen and missed her adolescence after the fact."

"I guess she started work early because she needed the money?"

"Yes, Aiyana. That's why I'm always stressing how important education is. I want you to have choices. Annie felt trapped."

"I get it, Dad. By the way, I really like school. I just wanted to go out with Justin because I wanted some fun, too. But don't worry—I'm more like you than Mom."

Salem smiled. "Yeah, you are. Mika, you have your mom's free spirit. But because your upbringing has been stable, you are, too. You like your fun, but you're smart about it."

"That's because of what I saw in Mom."

"Good."

"I've been thinking about if Mom had still been alive—" Aiyana cut into the lemon meringue pie she'd ordered "—she might not have been able to handle the trouble I had with Justin as well as Emily did."

"That's possible, Aiyana. Can you tell me what makes you think that?"

"Mom might have been stoned, anyway, but even worse, she didn't have Emily's experience to understand what I was going through. She would've thought they were just teasing or that they didn't really mean to hurt me. Mom was really generous, but she didn't always have a lot of common sense."

Ain't that the truth, Salem thought. He had slammed up against that so many times during their marriage. If he hadn't had his own mother's faulty example, he might not have found it so hard, but all Annie did was bring back bad memories for him.

After they finished dessert and paid the bill, they left the restaurant together. "So, we're good?"

Mika threw her arms around him and hugged hard. "Yeah, Dad, everything's great. Can't wait to start playing the clarinet."

Aiyana wrapped her arm across his back and rested her head on his shoulder. "Thanks for tonight, Dad. I really enjoyed spending time with you."

Like an awkward three-headed beast, they walked to the Jeep giggling.

At home, Salem thanked his lucky stars that Emily had unwittingly brought him and his girls together this evening.

His emotional high lasted until both Aiyana and Mika went to their room and started wailing on their new instruments, every note discordant and harsh. Amid the screeching cacophony, he entered the kitchen.

His dad had stuffed his ears with tissues again. Salem reached for the tissue box and did the same, muttering, "Heaven help us."

SALEM DROVE TO Violet's garage on Friday evening after work with the warm June breeze slipping through the open windows and resting gentle hands on his shoulders like an old friend, heralding his favorite time of year. Days were growing longer and warmer, but weren't yet humid.

He drew a deep comforting breath. The scent of fresh earth and burgeoning corn in the fields outside Accord mingled with the aroma of green peppers and pepperoni inside the Jeep. Two large pizzas sat on the passenger seat beside him.

Tonight, they were celebrating. Emily's garage was renovated and ready for her first clients. Nothing like pizza and soft drinks to commemorate a job well done.

Emily, Violet, Aiyana and Mika sat on lawn chairs in the backyard beside the garage when he arrived. The dogs yipped and jumped around him, trying to reach the pizza boxes. Emily had scraped the outside of the garage and had painted it white with periwinkle trim. Salem thought it just looked blue, but Mika had set him straight. "*Periwinkle* blue, Dad."

He put the food and drinks on a plastic table. "Place looks really good. Love the flowers."

"Violet bought the window boxes and planted them." Emily pulled a lawn chair close for him.

A riot of purple and yellow pansies, with hot-pink geraniums, filled the *periwinkle* blue wooden planters.

Violet handed around cups of ginger ale.

"You do fast work, Emily." Salem handed her a couple of slices of pizza on a paper plate. He couldn't believe she could get so much done in a little less than two weeks. "You should be a contractor. I didn't think you'd pull the place together this quickly."

"I'm dying to start teaching." Emily took the food. "My first students are booked for tomorrow."

Her eyes shone. She sparkled with energy.

"Tomorrow? That's soon." Pride swelled in him in her accomplishment. "How does the inside look?"

She put down her pizza. "Come have a peek."

He hadn't seen it since he'd put up molding around the windows and doors.

She and his girls had painted the walls a subdued gray with a hint of lavender and the moldings a glossy white.

"Aiyana did a great job on the moldings. Both girls were amazing, Salem. I couldn't have done it without them."

Again that sense of pride blazed through him, this time for his daughters.

"This gray is a good color. Makes the room feel calm."

"I agree," Violet said. "It's a beautiful backdrop for music."

"That's what I think, too." Emily ran her hand across one wall. "All of the color will come from the music and the kids. I thought it would be a good idea to have a calm atmosphere."

Her attitude surprised Salem. He'd thought someone with her strong personality would choose bold colors. She didn't seem to be the impulsive woman he'd thought she was. Or maybe she had matured, as she kept trying to tell him. Actions spoke louder than words, though, and while painting a room a soft gray seemed like a great idea, it wasn't enough to convince him.

He hadn't been able to help last Saturday or Sunday. They were his busiest days at the Center. Recently, he'd been training a young band member, Raymond Harris, to take over. Ray had a passion for the Heritage Center and had worked there for years. It was time for Salem to pass the responsibility on to him. Ray had gone away last weekend, though, so Salem couldn't help here. Aiyana and Mika had been here and all over the project, telling him about it in the evenings. He had turned a corner with his daughters at the dinner last week. Aiyana was opening up to him, and blossoming now that Justin had stopped slandering her online, and she'd made a new friend in Sophia. It seemed that Salem could stop worrying and just enjoy Aiyana's company.

Throughout this week, Salem had managed to help a bit after work, hauling trash to the dump and stripping the old desk Emily had wanted to keep. It looked like a million bucks with fresh stain and varnish.

They stepped back outside to continue with their

dinner. "How's Otis been? Not too disturbed by the changes?"

"I made sure all of the windows were wide open while we painted, and kept the big doors open, too. I bought low VOC paint, so I don't think he was exposed to too many toxins."

"Little guy seems happy enough." He caught Mika's eye. His animal-loving daughter grinned. "Don't even think about trying to catch a bat to bring home."

At her mock scowl, everyone laughed.

A second later, he watched her surreptitiously sneak bits of pizza crust to the three dogs. At times like this, Salem's heart expanded as though all of the goodness in the universe had been captured in that tiny, defiant, generous gesture.

They had just finished the pizza when they heard cars pull up out front.

"You expecting company?" Salem asked Violet. She shook her head and put the barking dogs inside the house. Everyone trooped toward the front of the house.

Two sheriff's department vehicles sat in the driveway, with Sheriff White and a couple of his deputies stepping out of them. Salem raised his eyebrows in question to Violet. She shrugged. Obviously, she had no idea why they would be here. What was up?

Violet stepped forward. "What's going on?"

"We've been looking for Salem," White answered. "Don't give us any trouble. Come along peacefully."

Come along? What did he mean? "Where to? Why?"

"We're arresting you for the murder of Caleb Brown."

"*Arresting* me? What are you talking about? Murder? *Caleb?* He hasn't been around Accord for four years."

"That's right. He's been buried on your land."

Salem choked. A chill ran through him. He hadn't thought about the man since Annie's death, but had remembered him recently when he talked to his girls about their mother. Now all of a sudden Salem was being arrested for the man's murder. Caleb had been only yards away from the Cathedral all of that time. "That was Caleb? He didn't run off somewhere?"

"You should know," White said. "You put him there."

"Sheriff," Deputy Matt Breslin admonished. "He's only under arrest. A court of law will decide whether he's guilty."

White stepped around behind Salem's back and cuffed him.

"Hey!" Mika yelled.

"You can't be serious." That was Emily.

"Really, Sheriff." Violet.

Salem forced himself to stay calm because White seemed to have a beef against him, and Salem knew exactly what that beef was, but he wasn't going down without questions. "What are you doing?"

"Like I said, I'm arresting you. You have the right to remain silent…"

Salem didn't hear the rest, detached himself from what was happening because never, in his wildest dreams, could this scenario have occurred to him.

"This can't be happening. You've got to be kidding. Matt, you can't believe this is true." He'd gone to school with Matt. They'd played basketball together.

"He's Deputy Breslin to you." Sheriff White tugged Salem's arms up behind his back and pain shot through his shoulders.

"Mmmph."

Mika squealed. "Stop hurting my Dad!"

Aiyana folded in on herself like a wounded animal.

"Do you have to do this in front of his daughters?" God bless Emily and her natural defiance. Felt good to have her turn it on for him.

"Just following the letter of the law, ma'am."

"Sheriff," Deputy Breslin started, but White quelled him with a silencing glare.

"I didn't do anything," Salem protested. "What evidence can you possibly have?"

"We found him on your land."

Emily stepped beside Salem and the warmth from her body reassured him. Surely between the two of them they could set the world to rights again. "*You* didn't find the body. *I* did." Emily sounded calm, but Salem sensed the banked fight in her. "And the land isn't his. It's my dad's. Are you going to arrest him, too?"

"Nope. Only Salem."

"Why are you arresting him? Why aren't you just taking him in for questioning?"

"Because we have it on good authority Salem had an argument with the deceased."

"What argument?" Salem struggled with panic. White led him to the car, hiking his arms high again. "Hey, that hurts. What the hell are you doing?"

"You going to resist arrest, Pearce?"

White wanted him to do exactly that so he could get in a few good hits. Animosity rolled from him like mist from the ocean, chilling Salem.

"No." Salem kept a reasonable tone, unwilling to be provoked by the sheriff. "What argument are you talking about?"

"You were seen quarreling with Caleb before he died."

"A month before he left town. So what? He was giving my wife drugs. I was understandably angry."

"Yeah, and a week later, your wife died of an overdose."

Jesus. It sounded bad.

Emily got into White's face. "You arrest people on so little? Since when? Again, why aren't you just questioning him? Why are you charging him? You sure you're doing your job properly, Sheriff?"

"Emily, cool it," Salem warned. He loved that she was on his side, but he didn't need the situation to escalate, especially not in front of his girls.

"I'm calling my dad's lawyer, Salem. I'll get this straightened out."

That kind of help he appreciated.

White shoved him into the back of the cruiser. "Breslin, you go on ahead. We'll see you at the station."

"But, Sheriff—"

"I said you go on ahead." White's face might as well have been carved out of granite. Breslin drove off with a spray of gravel.

Deputy Hammond rode shotgun in the sheriff's cruiser as White pulled out of the driveway and drove toward town. Salem wished Breslin hadn't left. He didn't trust White. He didn't know Hammond well enough to know whether he'd stop the sheriff from doing anything illegal or if he would cover for him. Hammond had been a few years behind Salem in school, more in Emily's circle than his.

When White pulled off the highway onto a dirt side road instead of driving straight into town, Salem's heart dropped. *Here it comes,* he thought. *Trouble.*

White screeched to a halt, rounded the car and hauled Salem out of the backseat. The first punch opened the skin on Salem's left cheek. The second punch knocked him to his knees.

White's black boots came into view. "That's for my boy."

"VIOLET, CAN YOU KEEP the girls with you while I drive to town to figure out how to fix this?"

"I'm coming, too." Aiyana, who'd seemed tiny and frail, came to life. "He's got my dad. I need to be there."

"You do understand Sheriff White is Justin's father?"

"Yeah. I know. I don't trust him. That's why I have to be there. I'll sleep in jail with Dad to keep him safe."

"Okay. Come with me." Emily opened her car door.

"I'm coming, too. I don't understand what's happening."

"Mika, it would be best for you to stay with Violet."

"No."

What could Emily do? She had no authority over Mika. The girl had just seen her father arrested.

"Wait for me to get my sweater." Violet headed toward the house. "I'm coming, too."

The second Violet returned, Emily pulled out of the driveway and drove hell-bent for leather into town.

Partway there, Aiyana shouted, "Stop!"

Emily slammed on the brakes so hard the car fishtailed.

"What?"

"Back there. Down that road. I saw the sheriff's car."

Emily's fear shot through the roof. Oh, dear God. Was Sheriff White taking revenge on Salem for yelling at his kid?

She pulled a U-turn and shot back down the two-lane highway, turning onto the road Aiyana indicated.

The scene she pulled up behind turned her stomach. Salem was on the ground with White and Deputy Hammond standing over him. The sheriff was pulling back his foot to kick Salem in the ribs.

Emily laid her hand on the horn and didn't let up until White glared at her, but at least that heavy boot hadn't made contact.

"Bastard," she yelled, running from the car to confront White.

The deputy held her back with a fist around her arm. "Ma'am, get back in your car."

"Not a chance. Put Salem into the cruiser and take him to a hospital."

White stepped in front of her, hiding Salem from her view. "The prisoner was resisting arrest."

"Sitting alone in the backseat behind a screen with his hands cuffed?"

"Yes, ma'am." White's expression gave nothing away.

"Liar. I'm going to have you charged."

Mika and Aiyana had gotten out of the car and hovered over their father. Aiyana bent down to check on him and then flew at the sheriff, claws bared.

She got a good scratch to his face before the deputy pulled her away.

"You want me to arrest you, too, little girl?"

"Don't you touch her," Emily said, her tone sharp enough to draw blood. "You are in a whole shitload of trouble. Unless you want to make it worse, put Salem back into your cruiser now, gently, and we'll drive into town behind you."

"I can arrest you, as well, for obstruction."

"And me, too?" Violet had gotten out of the car. Emily was glad she'd allowed the older woman to come.

Violet, with her air of dignity, said, "Shame on you, Brent Hammond, for allowing this disgusting, *illegal* behavior. You're the *law*. You're not supposed to be above it. When I taught you in school, I instilled integrity and ethics. Where are they now?"

Rage boiled underneath Violet's dignified façade.

The deputy turned bright red and helped Salem to his feet.

Oh, his face. Salem's poor face. Blood trickled from a cut on his right cheekbone and his eye was swelled shut.

"Aiyana?" Emily barely held herself back from going after White.

"Yes?" Aiyana's voice shook.

"Do you have your cell phone with you?"

"In the car."

White tried to hustle Salem into the cruiser before Aiyana could retrieve it, but Mika was right there whipping her own phone out of her pocket and shooting pictures of her dad's face.

"Get a long shot," Emily said. "We need the world to see where this happened."

Mika pulled back and took another shot.

"Give me that phone." White advanced on Mika.

"Get into the car," Emily ordered, stepping between White and the girl. "You could erase those photos, but what are you going to do? Erase our memories, too? We're four credible witnesses."

Just before she followed the girls and Violet into her car, she said, "Take Salem to the station and we'll follow behind you. And, Sheriff? Say your prayers. You're as guilty as sin, just like your son."

Emily slammed her car door and backed out of the road onto the highway. She waited on the far shoulder until Sheriff White pulled out then followed him into town.

Down the street from the sheriff's office—and his jail cells—was her dad's lawyer's office. Her father had once said that John Spade was the most cutthroat lawyer he'd ever known—and he'd dealt with plenty of lawyers over the years.

Emily decided to make it her first stop. That the office was locked for the weekend wasn't surprising, but the note on the door was. Spade would be away for the following week on holidays.

"What do we do now?" Emily whispered.

Aiyana's and Mika's fear shimmered from them like heat from asphalt.

"Let's go." She took them to the sheriff's office.

Emily opened the door, but White was there, blocking the way and keeping them outside on the sidewalk.

"Thought you'd come around to cause trouble."

"We're not causing trouble, Sheriff. We're here to make sure Salem is being handled properly. That this arrest is being handled according to the letter of the law." Emily used his own words against him.

"I'm handling this just fine. No one gets in to see him."

"He's my dad," Mika shouted. "You can't keep me from him."

"I sure enough can, little girl. Unless you want a

charge of obstructing justice, or causing a disturbance, I'm advising you to leave. All of you go home."

"Not until I see my dad." Aiyana's hatred of the sheriff blazed.

"We don't need a bunch of rubberneckers here."

"Rubberneckers?" Emily's rage hit the roof.

Violet touched Emily's arm to hold her back. "Dear, it's time to regroup. We'll be back, Sheriff."

"Wait. Doesn't he get a phone call to a lawyer?"

"Emily, come." Violet had a strong grip for an aging woman. She urged Emily and the girls toward the car.

They left and the sheriff went back inside the office, but not until they were all seated inside the car.

"What was that about?" Emily started the engine and drove away slowly, gazing at the closed door of the attorney's office as she passed. Salem was in jail and there wasn't a damn thing she could do about it.

She pounded the steering wheel.

"The sheriff isn't going to be reasonable at the moment." Violet sat beside Emily in the passenger seat. "We need to be smart so he won't have a thing to complain about, or use against us, later."

"Good thinking." Emily accelerated. "Let's go talk to my dad. He'll know what to do." They drove to the Jordan house.

Emily's dad had taken to spending a lot of time in the garage building a canoe. The man he used to be when he first came to Accord twenty years ago would have said that sort of pastime was a waste of time. Thank goodness Laura had been able to tame the workaholic in him, or he might be dead of a heart attack by now.

When they drove up the driveway, he stepped outside. His smile of greeting dropped the second he saw their faces.

"What's happening?" he asked even before Emily was fully out of the car.

"Salem's been arrested."

"Salem? What on earth for?"

"For murder," Mika blurted, and the usually confident girl sounded scared. Her voice wobbled. No wonder after what she'd just seen.

Emily's dad stopped wiping his hands on the rag he held. "*Murder?* Is this a joke?"

"I wasn't here at the time," Emily said, "but do you remember a man named Caleb Brown?"

"Sure. Local gossip was that he'd run out of town ahead of some drug dealers who'd come from Denver looking for him."

"Remember Salem and I found a body behind the Cathedral?"

Her dad understood. "Caleb."

"You guessed it."

"Fine, but why arrest Salem?"

The girls crowded close to Emily while Violet hovered off to the side. "Because he had an argument with Caleb before the man disappeared."

"That's it? That's all the evidence they have?"

They followed him into the house. "Violet, I haven't seen you in town in a while. How are you?"

"I've been better, Nick. I'm in shock."

"No wonder. Laura," he called.

Laura popped into the hallway from the living room, her welcoming smile dropping as quickly as her husband's had.

"Can you make us a pot of tea? I'll fill you in on what's happening." Emily's dad followed her down the hallway to the kitchen, where they all sat around the table.

Just as Emily was about to start, Cody came downstairs and joined them. "What's up?"

Emily repeated the news.

"Salem? Murder?" Cody leaned against the counter and crossed his arms, his big, solid presence reassuring. At the moment, Emily needed every assurance that the world hadn't gone completely insane.

"Is White for real?" Cody asked.

"It gets worse." When Emily made sure she had everyone's attention, she told them about catching Sheriff White assaulting Salem while Deputy Hammond watched. Cody straightened away from the counter and her father shot up so quickly his chair fell over.

"Mika got pictures." At Emily's urging, she took out her phone and showed them around. Silent tears coursed her cheeks.

"These are excellent, Mika. We can nail the sheriff with them." *Thanks, Dad,* Emily thought.

Aiyana nudged Emily's knee with her own. "Tell them about Justin."

"They already know."

"I was in the gym that day," Cody told Aiyana. "Your dad was really angry, but he didn't put his hands on Justin. He wasn't going to beat him, but he did want the kid to know he was serious about staying away from you."

"I don't know what Salem argued with Caleb about, but he wouldn't have become physical then, either." Emily scooted her chair over to make room for Laura. "It isn't in his nature."

Laura put mugs and a teapot on the table.

"I know what it was about." Everyone turned toward Aiyana and the quiet words that had landed like a bomb. "It was about my mom." Aiyana fiddled with the hem of her T-shirt. "Caleb used to sell her drugs. My dad was trying to get Mom to stop taking them, but Caleb kept getting her to use more."

"Oh, Aiyana. How did you know? You were so young."

"I was already twelve when she overdosed. Parents think kids don't know what's going on, but we know a lot."

Emily pressed a mug of hot tea with sugar into her hands. "Do you know whether your dad threatened him?"

"The big fight was after Mom died and Caleb came to the burial." Aiyana trembled and she wrapped her fingers around the warm mug. "Dad was so mad. Mom wasn't perfect, but she loved us, you know? Dad was angry that we didn't have a mother anymore and he blamed Caleb. He always wanted the cops to arrest Caleb, but they never did."

Mika stared down at her lap, still with those tears falling silently. Violet took her hand and wiped her cheeks with a tissue from her purse.

"A verbal altercation shouldn't be enough grounds for an arrest." Emily's dad scrubbed his hands through his hair. For the first time, Emily noticed it wasn't as thick as it used to be.

"There was more."

Emily turned her attention back to Aiyana. "It was more than a verbal argument?"

"No, I mean, there was more between my mom and Caleb." She twirled her hand in a funny little circle. "I mean, they were, you know…" Her voice trailed off, and the room became uncomfortably quiet.

"Oh, boy," Emily's dad said. "If Sheriff White finds out, then he could claim that Salem killed Caleb out of jealousy."

"Dad wouldn't do that," Mika cried. "My dad doesn't kill people."

"No, he doesn't." Emily's dad's authoritative voice had a soothing effect on the girl. "It's just what the sheriff might think."

"You know, Dad," Emily said, "I think with White it comes back to Justin. I think he's angry that Salem humiliated his son in public and is taking it out on him now, arresting him on flimsy evidence. I'm sure that's why he beat him."

"We'll get John Spade on it."

"John's on holiday for a week. There's a sign on his door."

Her father swore and then apologized to the girls for doing so, even though what he'd said was tame compared to what they probably heard at school, and on the radio. Most rap lyrics were more graphic that what he'd said.

"Should we contact the state police about charging White, Dad? He can't be allowed to get away with what he did."

"He won't, but let's leave that for John to take care of when he gets back. Investigating cops is tricky. John will know the best people to contact. He'll make sure everything gets done."

"But he's out of town. What do we do in the meantime?"

"I'll call around to the lawyers in neighboring towns to see who's available."

"Can you do that tomorrow?"

"Yes. Also, the sheriff might not be motivated to investigate as well as he should. Remember that fraud case I had a couple of years ago when that couple tried to sue the resort for nonexistent negligence?"

Emily nodded.

"I hired a great private investigator from Denver. I'll get him on this to see what he can learn. Maybe with a little competition, White will be more dili-gent."

Her father left for his study. Emily stood. "Come on, girls, Violet. I'll take you home."

Cody stood, too. "You look tired, sis. I was just heading out. I can drive them."

"Thanks, Cody." Emily snuck a peek at the tiny smile on Aiyana's face. Any distraction was a good thing.

As the four walked toward the front door, Emily heard Cody ask, "Did Justin stop bothering you?"

Laura and Emily leaned against the kitchen door-way for a better chance to catch what they were saying.

"Yes, thanks to you," Aiyana answered.

"That's good," Cody said. The rest was lost as Cody closed the front door behind them.

Laura smiled at Emily. "Oh, my. He likes her. I can tell."

"How would you feel if Cody dated Aiyana?"

"Happy. She's a lovely girl."

"It would do her some good, too. She needs a sym-pathetic shoulder right now."

Emily shivered. She could use one of those, too. She had to get Salem out of that jail cell. "I'll be back soon."

"Where are you going?"

"To the sheriff's office. I want to make sure Salem's okay."

"Need company?" Good old Laura. So dependable.

Emily hugged her and held on hard. "I love you, but I can do this alone."

Parking was at a premium on Main Street. It was Friday night and a lot of people would be dining out at the inn, or at the diner, or the family restaurant. Emily parked way down the block from the sheriff's office.

Good. The walk will give you a chance to get your emotions under control.

She entered the courthouse and saw Sheriff White huddled with Deputy Hammond.

"You say one word to anyone about what happened and I'll—" White cut off what he was saying when Brent jutted his chin toward Emily in the open doorway. They were planning their cover-up of Salem's beating.

Emily lost her control.

"You're going down, White."

"That's *Sheriff* White to you, girl."

Girl? That didn't bode well for the evening. She was thirty-one years old. Bully.

"Where's Salem? I want to see him."

Deputy Breslin came out of the back corridor from around a corner where Emily assumed the jail cells were. He was frowning, but smiled when he saw her. "Hey, Emily. Remember me? Matt Breslin. I was a couple of years ahead of you in school. Salem's back here. I'll show you." He gestured for her to join him.

White put one arm out in front of her like a bar blocking a car from exiting a parking lot.

"Are you his lawyer?"

"Of course not."

"Then you can't see him."

"Sheriff…"

"Shut up, Breslin. Salem's a prisoner. He gets one phone call and he already used it to call someone about work."

Oh, Salem. Do you have to be so super responsible? You need to worry about yourself right now. Not work or anything else. Just you.

Breslin swore under his breath. Perhaps his thoughts were running along the same lines as hers.

"We have photos of what you did to Salem," Emily said. "I know what he looked like when you brought him in. We're pressing charges. My dad will make sure of it. If I see one more bruise, one single more cut on him, it will only get worse for you."

White sneered. Wow, people really did that? She thought that happened only in bad novels. "You rich kids think you're special and look down on the rest of us working-class slobs."

"Seriously? Knock the damn chip off your shoulder. My dad's done a lot for this town. The employment rate skyrocketed when he opened the resort. Those employees pay the taxes that allow you to hire deputies. They pay your salary."

She reined herself in and continued in a calmer voice. "Besides, Salem isn't rich. He's working class. Like you. Like your deputies."

White's impassive expression said it all—he wasn't

going to let her in tonight. She opened the door to leave.

"I'm warning you. Don't touch him. Keep your hands off him, or so help me God, I will slay you in the courts."

CHAPTER NINE

AIYANA SAT IN the passenger seat of Cody's car while Mika huddled in the back after they'd taken Violet home. Her little sister was taking it hard. Mika would turn fourteen in a few weeks, but at the moment, she felt very young to Aiyana. And Aiyana felt very old.

Cody's presence in the car beside her steadied her nerves.

He used some kind of soap that smelled really good, that seemed to have worked its way into the fabric of the seats. She expected most teenaged boys to smell a little sweaty and maybe greasy from eating too much fried food, but Cody smelled clean.

Dad was in jail accused of murder. Too strange. Too crazy weird. She couldn't take it in. She needed to talk to Grandpa.

"You okay?" Cody asked. He might be only eighteen, but he had a man's voice, deep and reassuring.

"No. I feel helpless. I don't know what to do."

"One thing you need to do for tonight, both of you—" he raised his voice to make sure Mika heard him "—is to try to have faith in my family. Neither Dad nor Emily will let this thing rest until it's taken care of. Okay?"

Aiyana nodded and heard Mika say, "'Kay."

"You need to sleep tonight." She felt Cody take his eyes off the road for a moment to glance at her.

"That's not going to happen." Aiyana could already map out the sleepless hours ahead of her. "My dad wouldn't hurt a soul."

"I know. What about that day in the gym, though? He didn't hit Justin, but man, he was mad. A good prosecutor will use that against him."

"He was defending me. The thing about Dad is that he bottles up a lot of stuff. He doesn't think letting emotion out is the right way to deal with things, so he holds it all in. When it comes out, it *really* comes out."

"But he doesn't *kill* people," Mika wailed.

"No, he doesn't." Cody sounded so confident, Mika's sobs subsided. "Dad will hire the best lawyer."

"I don't know how we'll pay him back." Aiyana thought of all of that tuition Dad had been paying over the years as well as carrying a mortgage and taking care of his family. Until now, she'd never thought about his responsibilities, his burdens.

"He's the best dad," she whispered, but even Mika caught it in the backseat.

"The *best,*" she said vehemently.

Mika had always been happy and carefree. Had she just lost her innocence? Aiyana recognized the signs. Justin had done it to her, and now his father had done it to Mika.

None of this "done it to" business. Stop being a victim.

"This sucks. This totally sucks."

"You keep that anger simmering, Aiyana." Cody pulled into their driveway. "It's better than feeling helpless or sorry for yourself."

There were things she needed to say to Cody, in private.

"Mika, can you go tell Grandpa what happened? He needs to know."

After her sister left the car, Aiyana turned to Cody. "Cody, I really appreciate what your family is doing," she said. "I also want to thank you for helping me with Justin. I don't think he would have stopped without your confronting him."

Boy, oh, boy, she couldn't seem to talk to him without sounding like a forty-year-old. But what else could she do? Throw her arms around him as if he was a rock star? That's what he was to her.

He didn't respond, but got out of the car and walked around to her side, while she wondered what he was doing. He opened her door and held out his hand, palm up. Oh, wow. Like a prince in a movie.

She took it and he helped her out of the car. Not that she needed it, but the action was so polite, so caring, she reveled in it. They walked to the porch, with his big palm curled around hers like a warm baseball glove.

Grandpa hadn't turned on the porch light, thank goodness, so Cody wouldn't see how red her face was. This hand-holding with boys was still so new.

"Aiyana, I don't want you to take this the wrong way, but I'm going to hold you for a minute 'cause I think you need it. I'm not taking advantage of you like Justin tried to do. Okay?"

"As if I would ever thi—"

She lost her train of thought, because Cody's chest was big and hard, and his arms across the back of her waist were exactly what she needed right now. Boys were supposed to be clueless. Someday she was going to have to tell Mr. and Mrs. Jordan what an amazing job they had done raising Cody.

Then, even that thought flew from her mind. True to his word, Cody didn't make a move on her. He just held her, and it was the most beautiful thing she'd ever felt.

The crickets under the floorboards sang a melody. The night pulsed around them in cadence with Cody's strong, solid heartbeat. She didn't cry, but it was a near thing. Instead, she let his comfort in, let it wash over her like a hot shower, easing the tension and shock out of her body.

The porch light flared on and they jumped apart.

Grandpa stepped outside. "Who is this with you, Aiyana?"

Cody, not the least bit rattled, put forward his hand. "It's Cody Jordan, Mr. Pearce."

Grandpa shook his hand. "Can't believe how you've grown. Terrible thing about Salem, eh?"

"Yes, sir. My family will help. Call if you need anything."

"I thank you. Thank your father for me. He's a good man. Aiyana, don't stay out too long."

He went back inside and closed the front door. A second later, the porch light went out.

For a moment neither of them said anything. "Does that mean I have his approval?" Cody ventured.

Aiyana giggled. "Yeah. I think so."

"Good." Cody leaned forward and kissed her, softly and sweetly. "You need anything from me, even just to talk, you call."

With that he was gone and Aiyana was left in the darkness with only the crickets for company while she played her fingers across her lips.

SALEM LAY IN THE DARKNESS of the jail cell and stared at the ceiling. A single desk lamp in the main room cast only a dim light this far back in the building.

Deputy Breslin, so new that he worked the night shift every night, had left to do his rounds an hour ago. The silence should have been a comfort. Instead, it stifled. *Well, this is what you've always wanted. You asked for this. Peace and quiet.*

He laughed bitterly, the sound piercing the stillness of the lonely night. He hadn't meant incarceration. All those years when Salem had fought for peace, order and solitude, he'd thought it would bring him joy. This terrible silence brought him nothing but isolation. A terrifying aloneness. The sure knowledge that, in the end, everyone was alone in this vast, dark emptiness.

That realization should be coming with old age, with accepting the end of a long life, not in the prime of life.

He was only thirty-seven. It was too soon to have to confront that truth. He should be home with his family. He should be learning to trust a woman like Emily and loving her.

He missed his girls, his dad and Emily. He missed their laughter and vibrancy. They had offered him treasure, but he had resisted it at every turn.

Earlier this evening, he'd heard Emily come to the office. He'd heard every blessed word she'd said, fighting for him like an Amazon, but never going too far. A man needed a woman like her in his corner. He wished he could have seen her. In her fury and her tawny-haired, odd-eyed beauty, she would have been magnificent.

His father had been right when he'd said that Emily was nothing like Salem's mother or Annie. Emily wasn't *trouble* trouble. She was fun trouble, but also so much more. She was loyal, honorable, hardworking and generous. Salem could lie here listing adjectives for hours. Or he could imagine her sunny smile, her thick hair entwined through his fingers, or those beautiful, unusual blue-hazel eyes laughing at him. But to do that would make him even more miserable, and he had a whole night to get through in the darkness.

There was no window in his cell, only flat gray walls. He'd gone from the glass wonder of the Cathedral to this. How?

The front door opened. He heard Breslin moving about in the outer office, pouring himself a coffee. He sat up. "You have enough of that to spare a cup for me?" He wasn't sleeping anyway. Caffeine wasn't going to hurt him at this point.

Breslin came to the back. "You having trouble sleeping?"

"Yeah."

"Guilty conscience?"

From White, it would have sounded like an accusation. From Deputy Breslin, it was a joke. Matt Breslin was a good guy with a sense of humor.

"Nah," Salem said. "I've done nothing wrong."

"I'm not supposed to say stuff like this, but I believe you, Salem. You're no murderer. White's got it in for you 'cause of his kid. You'll get off."

Matt wandered back to the front. "What do you take in your coffee?"

"One sugar and cream."

"Don't have cream. White won't keep it in the office 'cause his wife has him on a diet. Homo milk is all I got."

"Double up on the milk then."

A minute later, Breslin returned with two cups of coffee. He handed one to Salem through the bars then sat on the cot in the cell across the hall and sipped his coffee.

"Where'd you go when you finished high school?" God, the coffee was awful. Salem set it aside to cool. "Why did you become a deputy so late?"

"I went to New York to become a stockbroker. Wanted to make big money. What a joke. I made money, but couldn't stand the rat race. What about you? You like working at the Heritage Center?"

"It's a great job, but I want more. I loved designing it, so I've been taking college courses at night. As of this month, I'm officially an architect."

"Hey, congratulations, man." Matt stood and they clinked cups through the bars. "You going to stop working at the Heritage Center?"

"Not yet. Not until I get work as an architect. With luck, I'll get something in Denver and commute or work from home on the computer." Salem took a gulp of his coffee. "Didn't they teach you how to make a decent cup of coffee in the city?"

"Yeah, but White will only buy the cheap stuff."

They didn't say much more, but it helped to have another human being nearby. Even just hearing Matt's steady breathing eased the darkness inside Salem, which was a good thing because as much as he knew he was innocent, Salem also knew that people had been convicted on less than they had on him, especially with someone like Sheriff White out to get him.

The worst part was that Salem could never tell the truth, that he suspected he knew exactly who had killed Caleb. Never in a million years would he turn that man in.

EXCITED ABOUT HER new business venture, Emily had booked lessons through the whole weekend. As soon as the townspeople had heard she was teaching music, they'd started booking appointments for their kids.

This morning, all she wanted to do was to see Salem at the sheriff's office, to give him hope, to reassure him that she wouldn't let this rest until she'd set him free. But she had to honor her commitments here first.

Tori dropped Mikey off on Saturday morning. He brought a rented tenor sax with him, from which he managed to wrench some truly god-awful squawks. Emily shared a rueful grin with Violet, who sat in the corner listening.

She learned how hard it was to teach *embouchure* to a ten-year-old boy who couldn't care less what he was supposed to do with his lips. He just wanted to make noise.

She got out her iPod and put it into the small stereo system she'd bought.

"Okay, listen, Mike. Playing saxophone isn't a free-for-all. *This* is what you get if you learn how to play properly."

She selected the song she'd been looking for and soon Bruce Springsteen's "Born to Run" was blaring from the speakers. Emily fast-forwarded to Clarence Clemons's sax solo in the break.

Mikey's eyes lit up and he blew into the sax in his hands, turning Clarence's sublime notes into duck calls.

Emily bent over laughing until tears streamed down her cheeks, and wasn't that great. After last night's tension, she needed this.

One way or the other, she was getting Salem out

of that jail cell. In the meantime, she'd enjoy children trying to massacre classic songs with too much enthusiasm.

Mikey bounced on the balls of his feet. "I want to hear more."

Emily played the sax solo at the end of "Thunder Road."

"So, do you want to learn to play like that?"

Mikey nodded so hard, his hair curtained his forehead.

He put the sax to his lips and another duck call rang through the tiny building. Otis flew to the farthest corner.

"What's that?"

"That's a bat. His name is Otis." Emily launched into a short lecture about bats.

Mikey nodded and smiled. "Cool." When his mom picked him up an hour later, he said, "Bye, Emily and Mrs. Gendron, thanks. Bye, Otis."

There was a lot to be said for enthusiasm.

SOMEONE NAMED IRIS had booked a violin lesson in the afternoon. She had registered by phone, so Emily was surprised when Iris turned out to be the girl from Aiyana's class who'd cried while listening to Emily play. If she learned to play with that same depth of emotion, she would be a force to be reckoned with.

The violin Iris pulled out of a brand-new case was also new. Iris obviously thought she was committing to the long haul.

She noticed Emily's look. "I fell in love with the violin the day you played it. I won't quit until I can play that well. You'll see."

By the grit in her tone, and the determination in her expression, Emily believed her.

"Besides, my dad was so happy I showed interest in something for the first time in two years, he would have bought me a piano if I'd asked for it."

Wow, didn't that say a lot about Iris's state of mind, and of how much her father loved her.

The first thing Emily noticed was that Iris didn't like to be touched. In fact, she flinched when Emily came too close in an attempt to show her how to hold the instrument properly. Emily handled her gingerly.

The second thing she noted was a pair of hands that looked like war zones, ragged fingernails chewed to the quick, and hangnails picked until bloody.

Emily remembered how Iris had clenched those hands so tightly her knuckles had turned white, the color of the bones apparent through her thin skin.

Everything about her brittle, Iris lacked an average girl's fluidity and playfulness. Along with passion, a lot of music was about just having fun. Emily doubted Iris was ever going to just have fun. The music, for Iris, was about healing.

Emily was no psychiatrist, but part of her lessons with Iris was going to have to involve gleaning clues about what happened to her.

Emily skirted that issue for now. It wasn't her place

to pry. The music would do the healing, not any words of wisdom Emily might impart.

She managed to convey to Violet with one glance that she shouldn't sit in on this lesson. Violet stood. "I'm going to put on a pot of tea, Emily. Join me when you finish this lesson."

After she left, Emily warned Iris how long a process it was to learn how to tease beauty out of a stringed instrument. "You won't hear anything pleasant for a while, but we'll start today, and that's all that matters. What I need from you is a commitment to practice at home."

"I can do that. I spend a lot of time in my room."

Wasn't that sad? Oh, but so familiar to Emily. Been there. Done that. *Concentrate on the positive, Emily.* "Let's get started."

As she'd feared, Iris left frustrated. "The violin isn't easy, Iris, but it is worth the effort."

"I could tell by the way you played it. I'll practice. I promise."

EMILY DIDN'T MAKE IT to the sheriff's office until after five that evening. Because it was Saturday, she was hoping to catch one of the deputies in the office without the sheriff.

Matt Breslin had seemed sympathetic, and willing to let her see Salem. Unfortunately, when she arrived, the deputy on duty was Brent Hammond. She turned herself inside out pleading with him to let her see Salem. No go.

Ten minutes later, the sheriff walked in. How on earth he knew she was here flummoxed her. Hammond hadn't called him, but he'd let White know somehow. Did they have an emergency button under the desk, like in banks in case of robbery?

"I told you he wasn't allowed visitors." White moved to stand between her and the hallway with his arms crossed over his chest.

Emily challenged him. "This is only meant to be a holding cell. Why didn't you transfer him to the county jail where he would have a larger cell and a shower?"

"County jail's full," White intoned.

Emily didn't believe it for a minute. "This whole procedure is ludicrous."

The sheriff wanted to keep Salem close, under his control, as a way to intimidate him and to show who was boss. Maybe, too, White wanted to keep the evidence of his own bad behavior under wraps. The fewer people who saw Salem for the next week until his bruises healed, the better for White.

"There are laws in this country that even law enforcement officials have to follow." Emily pointed at White. "Even you." She nodded at Hammond. "And you. There are consequences for breaking the law." She went through the sequence again. "Even for you. And you."

"Salem tripped when he got out of the squad car. That's how he hurt his face."

"And us? The witnesses?"

"All you saw was a man on the ground. You never saw me hit him."

"Four of us saw you with your foot hauled back ready to give him a kick in the ribs."

"But you didn't see me kick him."

"Why were you parked down the side road to begin with? There was no reason to stop. You were supposed to be going to town."

"Your boy needed to take a whizz."

"That couldn't wait until you got here?"

"Said he had to go bad."

"You're full of crap."

White hovered close. "You watch your step. You can be thrown into jail just as easily as Salem was."

"Are you threatening me?"

"Did you hear a threat, Deputy Hammond?"

"No, boss."

Emily lifted her cell phone to her ear. She'd had it in her hand and turned on the whole time. "Did you hear all of that, Dad?" When White realized he'd been overheard, his face contorted. Good. Let him fill with the same rage she'd carried since he had arrested Salem last night.

"Every word," her father said from the other end of the line. "Now get the hell out of there and let the lawyers handle it. I haven't yet found one who isn't booked solid for the week, but White won't know that. I'll keep looking."

"I should be home in about ten minutes. If I'm not, come to the sheriff's office to make sure I'm okay."

Disappointed that they still didn't have a lawyer, she pasted on a poker face, turned off her phone and left without a backward glance, not giving a flipping fig what the sheriff thought of her tricks.

Just after eleven that night, Emily sat in Laura's car on Main Street across from the sheriff's office. The night had turned chilly and she shrugged into a sweater she'd brought with her. She had come back to watch the schedule the deputies kept and was over-the-moon happy that Hammond had gone home when Deputy Breslin's shift started for the night a half hour ago.

An hour later, when the front door of the office opened, Emily hunkered down in her seat so Matt wouldn't see her. He left on foot, walking his beat. Once he was far enough down Main that he wouldn't notice her, Emily scooted across the street and tested the door. Unlocked.

Emily slipped inside and closed the door behind her without making a sound. A small desk lamp cast a lonely glow around a tiny portion of the office. The rest of the place was as dark as a cave.

She approached the turn in the hallway from which Matt had emerged earlier when Emily had been questioning the sheriff.

"Salem?" she whispered.

She heard rustling from farther down the hall. "Emily?"

"Yes." She found her way carefully toward the voice.

"What are you doing here? Did Matt let you in?"

She found her way by following the sound of his voice. "No, I waited until he left to do his rounds. The man is too trusting. He left the front door unlocked."

"This is a small town, Emily. We trust each other here. Or used to."

"Man, it's dark."

"White doesn't allow lights back here after ten, and there are no windows."

"The man's a sadist. How are you holding up?"

For a long, long time, he said nothing.

"Salem?"

"I'm doing fine, Emily."

He wasn't. She could hear it in his voice. This was a man who loved the outdoors, who revered nature. It had to hurt like hell to be stuck in this small space where the air was stale and darkness complete. She gripped the bars of his cell.

"I'm going to get you out of here, Salem."

He didn't respond.

"I mean it. I'm getting you out of here and I'm going to keep you with me forever. No more of our wimpy fooling around. You and I belong together. We're going to get together and stay together."

Still no response.

"Salem, come here. I want to touch you. To hold your hand."

"No, Emily. Get out of here."

"Why?"

"I don't want you to see me like this, caged like an animal. Stay away."

"I can't. I need to know you're okay."

"Fine. I'm okay."

He'd tried to make himself sound stronger. It hadn't worked. Emily could still hear the despair below the fake confidence.

"Salem. Please. Come here."

He stood and made his way to the bars. Gripping them, he shook the door but groaned when it refused to yield. "This is killing me, Emily."

Fumbling, she found his cheek. She wished she could see him clearly, as more than just this shape in the darkness. He exhaled roughly and took her hand in his, hurting her fingers with his hard grip. When he whispered her name, it sounded like both an imprecation and a plea.

He touched her face through the bars and leaned forward. Somehow, they managed to find each other's mouths, a simple chaste meeting of their lips because the space between the bars was too narrow for the blending and delving and oblivion they really craved. It would have to do. Salem rested his mouth on hers for long silent moments of pure bliss.

In this desperate situation, Emily couldn't deny what she felt for Salem. She would do anything to get him out of here, but for now she would savor his touch in this wasteland.

She'd craved his kiss for years, but had never imagined their first one would be like this. It wasn't enough, but she would take it.

He drew away slowly. "I needed to touch you, but

I need you to stay away, too. Don't come see me in the daylight. Please. I don't want you to see me, here, like this. It's…"

"Undignified."

"Yes."

"That's White's point."

"Salem?" Damn. Deputy Breslin had returned. "Are you talking to yourself back there?"

"No, Matt, it's me." Emily figured she might as well be open. Was she going to crouch back here like a criminal waiting until the next time he went on rounds so she could leave?

"Emily?" Matt rounded the corner and turned on the lights. Emily blinked. Thankfully, Salem had let go of her and sat on the cot on the far side of the cell. Smart man.

"Sorry, Matt. Sheriff White wouldn't let me in to see Salem earlier. I wanted to talk to him, to tell him what we've been doing to get him out of here. It isn't right that White hasn't let anyone visit, not even his children."

"You shouldn't have done this, Emily. I guess there's a reason why the sheriff didn't let anyone, especially his daughters, come." He nodded his head toward Salem.

When Emily saw Salem's face, she gasped. His injuries looked so much worse than the glimpses she'd caught of them on the side road, his face swelling and turning color. His beautiful high cheekbones were black and blue. The gorgeous lips she'd just been kissing were split. One eye was swollen shut. He looked like he'd gone a few rounds in a boxing ring. White had obviously got in more than one punch before they'd arrived to stop him. It must have hurt to have her touch him, but Salem hadn't said a word, had behaved as though it was wonderful.

"Can you see anything out of your left eye, Salem?"

Angrily, he said to Matt, "Get her out of here. I didn't want her to see me like this."

Rage boiled through her. "I'm glad I did. It fires me up even more to get you out of here."

She turned on the deputy. "Surely you don't think what Sheriff White did was right? Beating up on a prisoner?"

"No, I don't. I would have stopped him if I'd been there."

"Which is exactly why White sent you on ahead and kept Hammond with him."

"Yeah. Brent's father is a friend of White's. They get along well. Brent wouldn't do anything to damage that friendship."

"I meant what I said. I'm going to sue White for this. Have criminal charges brought against him."

"You do what you have to do, Emily. White's not a completely bad guy, but he's got his blind spots. His son is one of them. I heard what Salem did, calling the kid out in front of his basketball buddies. White didn't like that at all."

"No, I guess not, but it had to be done. I have a feeling that boy's gotten away with murder in this town."

Emily flinched when she unwittingly used that phrase in front of Salem.

He didn't seem to notice, seemed to have pulled back inside himself once Matt turned on the lights and Emily got a look at his face.

"I'll head home now, Salem. Matt, I would appreciate it if you wouldn't mention this visit to the sheriff."

"Of course not, Emily, but don't do it again. It puts me in a really rough spot."

"I can see that. Sorry." She turned to say goodnight to Salem, but he'd lain down with his back to them, and Emily left quietly. She really had no words of wisdom for him, and any she tried to offer would probably be rebuffed.

ON SUNDAY EVENING after the joy of another day of teaching music, commingled with her terrible worry about Salem, Emily entered his house with her arms full of groceries.

Aiyana had called to ask her to stay here a few days. Her grandfather had gone to the reservation to consult with the elders about Salem's predicament, and to pray.

Aiyana sat in the living room with Alyx and Sophia.

"Hi," Emily said, happy to see that Aiyana had friends over. "Where's Mika?"

"She has a sleepover at her friend's down the street. It will be good for her. A distraction. I think that's why the parents invited her."

"Makes sense. Very kind of them. Are you girls hungry? I picked up nacho fixings."

Sophia perked up. "I've never had nachos."

Emily, Alyx and Aiyana stared at her. "Girl," Emily said, "you are in for a treat. I'll go throw some together."

"Can I watch?" Sophia asked.

Emily shot her a puzzled smile and said, "Sure."

"Sophia likes to cook," Aiyana explained.

Emily put Aiyana to work putting away groceries while she grated a hunk of Monterey Jack.

"Sophia's family owns Tonio's."

Sophia picked up the bag of tortilla chips. "Can I help?"

"This is dead simple. Three ingredients. Chips, salsa and cheese." Emily told Sophia to sit at the table. "I love your family's store. So, do you get to use whatever ingredients you want? Can you just go pick up a chunk of aged parmigiana reggiano whenever you want to?"

Sophia laughed. "Yes."

"You're so lucky."

"My dad doesn't let us take the really expensive stuff, though."

"What's more expensive than imported Parmesan?"

"Caviar."

"Ah. You have a point."

Ten minutes later, when Sophia tried the nachos, she closed her eyes while she chewed. "Oh, wow, that is soooo good."

Emily, Alyx and Aiyana laughed. Aiyana sobered

quickly. "Sophia and Alyx came over because I was feeling bad about Dad."

"No wonder." Emily wiped her fingers on her napkin, appetite gone. "I wish there was more we could do. Sheriff White is going after your dad just because of the way he confronted Justin. He's being a real jerk."

"I feel funny sitting here eating with my friends while my dad sits in that jail cell." Aiyana wiped her eyes on her sleeve.

Emily got a tissue for her from a box on the counter. "I'm sorry, sweetheart. I'm very angry, too." That put it mildly. "We need to do something, convince the sheriff your dad had every right to be mad at his son."

Aiyana snuck a glance at Sophia and said, "Can I share your experience with her?"

Sophia nodded.

"Justin gave Sophia trouble, too."

"He put a lot of pressure on me to have sex with him," Sophia said, "telling me he loved me, that I was special and if I really loved him back, I'd show him how much."

She put the nacho chip she was nibbling back onto her plate. "I wasn't as smart as Aiyana. I thought he really cared about me and I gave in. The second I did, he lost interest and moved on to another girl."

Aiyana picked up the tale. "It really devastated her. Cody helped her through it."

"Yeah? I'm beginning to think my brother's a saint."

Sophia giggled. "No. Trust me, he's a teenage boy.

He thinks it's hilarious to burp the alphabet. He's nicer than most boys, though. And smart. He's a good guy."

A seed of an idea began to form. "Sophia, do you mind if I ask how long ago your relationship with Justin was?"

"Two years ago. I was fifteen."

"Same age as Aiyana was. He likes them young."

"He wasn't yet sixteen at the time, so I guess it was reasonable that he was dating me. The problem is, he's still dating girls that age even though he's older now. Mainly, though, he's really good at ferreting out a girl's vulnerabilities. He looks for weakness."

She put another nacho onto her plate. "If he'd had sex with Aiyana, would that have been statutory rape? He's nearly eighteen now."

"I think so. I'm not sure," Emily mused, still thinking hard. She turned to Alyx.

"Did he ever come on to you?"

"Nope. I'm not pretty enough."

Aiyana swatted her arm. "You are too pretty."

"Thanks, Aiyana, but Justin wants real eye candy on his arm."

"Okay, listen," Emily said. "Here's what I'm hearing about this guy. He's got an ego. He likes girls young. He doesn't like to take no for an answer. He jumps from girl to girl. Am I right so far?"

"Yes."

"That sounds like Justin exactly."

"So, if he jumps from girl to girl so easily, and he pressures them, is it possible he's gone too far and has maybe, if not forced some, at least pressed too hard? How many girls do you think this guy has hurt?"

Sophia nodded. "I see where you're going with this. The problem with Sheriff White is that he thinks the sun rises and sets on Justin. Maybe he needs a reality check."

"Exactly. What if the sheriff found out what kind of bully his son is and how many girls he's hurt, and how close the kid comes to breaking the law? Maybe if he realizes that Salem had a right to defend his daughter, White will back off on his persecuting him."

"I totally get it." Aiyana refilled their glasses of ginger ale. "I'm in. I'll talk to girls at school to find out if he did this to anyone else."

"I can guarantee you there's no *if* about it, but *how many*."

"We need a plan," Sophia said. "Aiyana, you talk to some of the younger kids at school and I'll talk to the older girls. I can almost guess some of the names now."

"He shouldn't have been allowed to get away with it for so long. How did he?" Aiyana asked.

"Shame." Sophia and Emily said it at the same time.

"Girls feel ashamed that they let him use them," Emily said gently.

Aiyana nodded. "And they feel ashamed when he verbally beats up on them if they don't."

"This guy's gotta be stopped." She raised her ginger ale. "Ladies, let's bring this boy *down*."

They clinked glasses, then dug into the nachos

again. Now that they had a clear plan, hope swelled and a solution seemed possible.

Emily had an idea she knew where to find one of Justin's victims. Following a hunch, she got Iris's phone number through directory assistance. "Iris? This is Emily Jordan. I'm over at Aiyana Pearce's house with Alyx and Sophia Colantonio. Do you know Sophia?"

"I've never spoken to her, but I've seen her around school. What is this call about, Emily?"

How in character that Iris would come straight to the point.

"We need to talk to you. Would it be possible for you to come here and join us? I can pick you up."

Iris was quiet for so long, Emily was sure her answer would be no. "Yes, I'll come over. Dad says I spend too much time alone."

"Give me your address."

"No. My dad likes to drive me everywhere. Tell me Aiyana's address and I'll be there in twenty minutes."

Twenty minutes later on the dot, Iris arrived.

Emily liked Iris. She was prickly and hurting, but underneath the cactus exterior was a lively mind.

Iris nodded to Aiyana, Alyx and Sophia when she entered the living room. Warily, she sat across from Emily on a love seat.

"Iris, I know you're using the music as therapy, and that's great. I have many times, too." She chose her words carefully, scared to death of spooking the girl and sending her running off. "I know something happened to you."

Iris stood, knocking against the coffee table in her haste. "Why are you saying that?"

"I don't want details." She kept her tone soothing. "I just need to know whether it had anything to do with Justin White."

Iris bolted. *Bingo.* Emily chased her to the front door.

From behind her, Aiyana said, "We need to get that dirtbag Justin put out of commission so he can't keep hurting girls."

"Hear us out, please, Iris. There's a reason we're asking."

Iris faced the door, back rigid.

Aiyana said, "You're not alone."

Iris turned. Her eyes blazed. Her cheeks burned. "What do you mean?"

"He's hurt other girls, too."

"Who?"

"Come back and sit down," Emily said. "We'll explain."

Once they were seated again, Emily asked, "You know that Salem Pearce, Aiyana's dad, has been arrested for the murder of Caleb Brown? Did you hear that Salem went to the school and confronted Justin about trying to force his daughter to have sex with him?"

Iris's eyes widened. "Aiyana?"

"Yes." Aiyana answered before Emily could. "You didn't hear about it?"

"Nobody at school talks to me. I'm not exactly popular."

"Because I wouldn't give in, Justin put ugly messages about me all over Facebook and Twitter saying that I had gone all the way with him and with other boys, too, and that I was a slut."

Iris's lips turned white. "That sounds like Justin."

Emily took over. "The upshot of Salem giving Justin a piece of his mind is that Justin's dad, the sheriff, is pursuing Salem as a suspect aggressively and refuses to look elsewhere."

She outlined the plan that she, Aiyana and Sophia had come up with—to pull together as many of the girls as possible who Justin had hurt, and confront Sheriff White with the truth about his son.

"He hurt you, too?" Iris asked Sophia.

"Yes. He talked me into having sex with him by telling me he loved me and then dropped me like a hot potato the next day."

"And you?" Iris asked Alyx.

She shook her head.

"Of course not," Iris said. "You're too strong. It would be hard for Justin to find your vulnerabilities."

She looked at all of them.

"Aiyana's right." Iris worried the sleeves of her shirt with restless fingers. "Justin is a dirtbag, and he thinks he can get away with it because his father is sheriff."

"That's right," Emily said. "I don't know how it

will change things, but Sheriff White needs to know what his son is really like. At the very least, maybe it will keep Justin from taking advantage of other girls."

She leaned forward and covered Iris's hand with her own. "Did Justin hurt you?"

The tears that welled in Iris's eyes turned them into huge gray prisms in her petite face. She nodded.

"Can you share your story with us, or would you rather not?"

"I've never told anyone, not even my mom. My dad knows something happened. That's why he drives me everywhere. He doesn't want anything else to happen. I can tell he's angry. He wants to know who hurt me."

"What happened?"

"Justin—" She stared down at her hands, where she'd cupped one inside the other, the knuckles white as though the skin had disappeared, and Emily saw through to the bone, as she had the first time Emily had seen her in the classroom. "He raped me."

Emily went cold.

CHAPTER TEN

RAPE. NOT *HE SEDUCED ME,* or *he tried to have sex with me,* or *he persuaded me.* But rape.

"He actually forced himself on you?"

She closed her eyes and nodded while tears leaked down her cheeks. Aiyana moved from the sofa to sit beside her on the love seat.

"Yes. I said no, but he wouldn't listen. Then he put his hand over my mouth so I wouldn't scream."

"How old are you?"

"I just turned sixteen. This was two years ago, though."

"You were only fourteen and he forced you?"

"Yes."

Emily covered her mouth because she felt a little sick. Mika was just shy of fourteen, barely more than a child. She imagined a boy like Justin forcing himself onto a girl that young. It would ruin her.

Poor Iris. No surprise that she needed music for healing. Fourteen was far, far too young to be forced to grow up in that way, to face some of the cruelty of humanity. The wonder was that she hadn't hurt herself, and that she'd recognized what she needed, music, and had started to take steps in her own healing.

A huge rage cleaved Emily with the force of an ax. "This boy is dangerous. He won't get better, only worse. We need to get him off the streets. Do you want to bring Justin to justice? To make him pay for his crime?"

"How?" Iris asked. "His dad's the sheriff. My dad is one of the sheriff's friends."

Oh, so tricky.

"If you told your parents about this, what do you think they would say?"

"Dad might hurt Justin, even though he and the sheriff are friends. Dad would get into trouble and I don't want that."

Emily couldn't help but compare his response with Salem's. Yes, these men loved their daughters.

"What would your mother say?"

"She would comfort me."

"For what it's worth, here's my opinion. You've been through a terrible, harrowing experience, and you have a right to your feelings."

Iris's mouth got tight. "Even anger?"

"*Especially* anger."

She smiled grimly. "Good, because I'm so mad I could scream. I want to murder Justin, but first I want him to suffer like I did. Like I do every single day."

And with no one to turn to, where would these feelings go? She was carrying too heavy a burden for someone so young.

"Iris, you have a right to everything you feel. You also have the right to deal with this in your own way. If you want to help us, good. If you can't, I understand." She snagged a handful of tissues from a box on the coffee table and handed them to Iris. "You need to take care of yourself. Be kind. Be forgiving of yourself. *You* did nothing wrong. It was all Justin. First and foremost at this time, think about yourself and what you need. Okay?"

Iris thought about it. Emily could almost see the wheels turning beneath her alabaster brow.

"Okay, I'll help. What do I have to do?"

"We're going to confront Sheriff White, the sooner the better, but we need to be strong. Strength in numbers. We're going to try to find as many girls as possible who Justin might have hurt."

"Start by asking Madison Williams."

"Madison?" Aiyana sounded shocked.

Emily remembered their discussion about how the blonde Madisons of the world didn't get hurt by boys. She raised her eyebrow as if to say, *See, I told you so.*

Aiyana got the message, but frowned. "She's one of Justin's friends. She helped to spread the rumors about me."

"Because she has a terrible crush on him. She still wants him for her boyfriend."

Emily's heart sank. "She might not speak against him."

"Madison might be dumb in love at the moment, but she's not completely stupid." Iris seemed to have gained strength since her arrival. Maybe she didn't feel so alone anymore. "Once she hears about our experiences with Justin and that we're telling the truth, she'll see it's time to cut the ties."

Emily's hope for Salem grew. This just might work.

That night, she slept in Salem's bed. Funny how she had spent so much time abroad, traveling all over the world, and yet she missed Salem more here when he was only a few blocks away. She wanted him out of jail so badly. She wanted him in her arms. In this bed. She wasn't letting *anything* separate them ever again.

Aiyana had got her fresh sheets from the linen cupboard, but Emily didn't use them. She needed to feel close to Salem, and the sheets on the bed held his scent of soap and the forest. She imagined herself surrounded by his arms and his love.

On Monday morning, Emily managed to catch five minutes in the sheriff's office alone with Salem. This morning, Brent Hammond seemed to be more sympathetic.

"Hurry," he said. "I can give you five minutes, and then I have to call Roger to warn him you're here. If anyone saw you come in, he'd find out at some point. I'm supposed to let him know if anyone visits. I need this job."

Emily raced to the back and ran through the details of their plan with Salem. "That's good, Emily." He sounded low, almost as though he didn't care.

But she did. "Don't give up on me, Salem," she ordered. "You're innocent. We're going to win this. All they have is circumstantial evidence."

"Emily, that kind of thing can stick in court."

"Dad's hired you a private investigator."

"Why?"

"To do the job White's supposed to be doing. To find out who really killed Caleb."

Salem finally showed signs of life. "No, Emily. Don't. Cancel the investigator."

"Are you crazy? Of course we won't cancel. We're getting to the bottom of this."

Salem paced the length of the cell, all twelve feet and back, then approached and grasped her wrist through the bars. "Stop him. Please, Emily," he begged. "Do this for me."

His desperation worried her. She didn't have a clue what was going on, and why Salem wouldn't take all the help he could get. "Don't you care that you could spend the rest of your life in jail?"

Salem returned to the cot and slumped onto it. He buried his fingers in his hair. Greasy, it hung to his shoulders instead of in the tight braid he usually wore.

"Don't even think about falling apart on me, Salem. I'm getting you out of here."

"Okay," he mumbled, "but tread carefully."

She had no idea what he meant by that. "Aiyana, Sophia and I are mounting a campaign to get the sheriff to see who his son really is. We're going to beat this."

Salem didn't respond, and she felt the frustration that had been building since he'd been unceremoniously tossed into jail. Why wasn't he fighting back? Why wasn't he as spitting mad as she was?

She opened her mouth to ask, but Sheriff White walked in. "What are you doing here?"

"What do you think? I'm planning a jailbreak." The man brought out the worst in her.

With White's big body blocking the hallway into the office, she couldn't breathe. How could Salem stand the stale air back here?

Both a ceiling and a floor fan hummed in the office, but back here where the cells were the air hung like a wet blanket.

"Give him a fan," she ordered.

"This ain't the Holiday Inn. We don't do our prisoners favors."

"You know what? You're a mean son of a bitch."

"Emily, don't," Salem admonished.

The light that shone in the sheriff's eyes was dirty and cruel, proving Emily's point.

"Careful, lady, or you'll be spending time in the cell across from your boyfriend."

He made *boyfriend* sound like a dirty word. His son was out forcing young girls to have sex, and he stood here looking at her as though she were trash.

"I've done nothing wrong and you know it. You throw me into that cell—" she nodded across the hallway "—and I'll have lawyers breathing down your neck so fast you won't know what hit you. Then I'll sue the shirt off your back."

Sheriff White clenched his jaw. "Don't threaten me."

"Let's keep the facts straight. *You* threatened *me*."

There was no point in staying here any longer. She wouldn't get another private minute with Salem.

Salem approached the bars. "Don't give up on me." He kept his voice low, perhaps hoping White wouldn't hear.

"Never," Emily whispered, the fierceness of the word echoing what was in her heart. "I'm never leaving you again. How's that for a commitment?"

When she tried to pass Sheriff White, he didn't budge.

"Please step aside so I can leave."

"You've got a smart mouth on you. One of these days, it's going to get you into trouble."

Sheriff White had come to town a little bit before Emily and her father and had married Sylvie Therrien. Emily remembered the woman who'd been a cashier at the grocery store. Her memories were fond. Sylvie had been kind and friendly. Never mean. Never in a bad mood.

But she'd married this man. Why? He couldn't possibly be all bad. He had to have some redeeming features. For the life of her, Emily couldn't see them.

"How's Sylvie?" she asked.

His expression flattened. "Leave my wife out of this."

"Just wondering whether you bully her as much as you do other people."

"I love my wife. I take care of her." He stepped close and she whipped her cell phone out of her purse.

"Who're you going to call?" he asked with a mocking grin. "The cops?"

"Step aside or I'll call my dad's lawyer. He's only two doors down and can be here in five minutes."

"John Spade's on holiday."

He knew! Damn. That was why he'd been in no hurry to move on dealing with Salem, and why he thought it was safe to leave him in that cell without fear of retribution.

Sheriff White did step aside, but he took his time doing it, making the point that she didn't intimidate him one bit. Maybe not, but her dad's lawyer would when he eventually returned to town.

Just before leaving, she said, "If I see one more bruise on Salem, I'm calling in the State police. Got it?"

She couldn't help herself. She'd antagonized the man again, but she hated to see Salem hurt. And she wanted to see Sheriff White taken down a notch.

EMILY STORMED INTO her dad's office at the Accord Golf and Cross-Country Resort. "I'm so angry I could spit."

Her father put his pen down on the papers he'd been reading. "Hmm. I won't offer you a coffee. Doesn't look like you need the caffeine. What's up?"

"Sheriff White. He's just letting Salem rot in the jail cell. He won't move him to the county jail where he could at least have a shower. Why doesn't he have a bail hearing set? We need to get charges laid against White for assault and battery."

Her dad stood, walked around to the front of his desk and leaned back against it, crossing his legs as though he didn't have a care in the world. "Stop pacing. Sit."

Didn't he get how serious this was? "How can you be so calm? What is this due process everyone always talks about? Shouldn't White be doing something to get Salem into the system? Shouldn't we be getting Salem a lawyer from Denver? And where's that private investigator you said you were going to hire?"

"He's been in town all weekend asking questions. He's been discreet. He hasn't advertised his presence."

That pulled her up short. "Oh. What did he learn?"

"That Caleb had a bad reputation around town. He committed a few petty crimes to support his habit. When he disappeared, everyone thought he'd skipped out on bail after robbing the supermarket or was running from drug dealers There were a lot of rumors floating around. That's why no one looked for him." Her dad took her hands in his, his grip firm. "Doesn't mean the man deserved to be killed, but there isn't a lot of affection for him around here. There won't be too many people up in arms demanding a pound of Salem's flesh."

Slowly, her father's calm manner seeped into Emily. "Good."

"Also, and even better, I got in touch with John Spade and he's agreed to cut his vacation short and come back to help Salem."

Emily's mouth dropped open. "Are you serious?"

"Dead serious. I've given John a lot of business since I moved here to build the resort. Even so, this is going to cost me a bundle."

She threw her arms around her dad and held on tight, a little bit weepy and a whole lot happy. "I love you." Then she pulled back. "Where is John vacationing?"

"Barbados."

"You're bringing him back from *Barbados?* No wonder it's costing you a fortune. Poor guy."

"Want me to cancel his flight home and let him finish out his week?"

"No!"

Her father grinned. "Didn't think so."

"When will he get here?"

"Tomorrow, and he'll start working on the case right away."

"Tomorrow isn't soon enough, but I'll take it." Something had been bothering Emily since talking to Salem this morning. "You know what's weird, Dad?"

"What?"

"When I told Salem you'd hired a P.I. to investigate, he got really upset. He wanted me to ask you to cancel the contract and send the guy home."

Her father reared back as though she'd hit him. "That doesn't sound good. Could mean Salem's hiding something."

"Not murder. Salem didn't kill anyone."

"No. He wouldn't. But it's possible he knows who *did* kill Caleb."

"You mean he could be an accessory? I feel sick."

"Not necessarily. Maybe he has a suspicion and is protecting someone."

"Who would he care that much about that he would protect them with his life?"

"Len Pearce?"

Emily shook her head hard. "No. I can't see Salem's dad doing it. I really can't."

"Me, either, but I'm going to tell the investigator about this and get him to look at anyone Salem might be close to. A friend, maybe? Who are his friends?"

"I don't know, Dad. I've been away too often."

Emily left the club feeling only marginally better than when she'd arrived. The lawyer would be here tomorrow. Excellent. The investigator had been working in Accord all weekend. Also excellent, but what if he found out something that actually implicated Salem instead of clearing him?

What did Salem know that he wasn't sharing with her?

BETWEEN THEM, EMILY and the girls found ten other girls who agreed to help with the case against Justin. They had all called in sick this morning. This was so much more important than missing one day of school. Every one of them had a grievance against him, of various strengths. Iris's experience seemed to be the worst.

Maybe Justin had been drawn to her ethereal beauty, whether to own or to dominate. Emily couldn't know for sure. She'd never tried to delve into the mind of a rapist before.

Emily was certain there must be more, but ten was an excellent start. With Aiyana, Sophia and Iris, and Mika to offer support, that made fourteen, plus Emily who marched into Sheriff White's office on Tuesday morning. The sun shone through the window in stripes through horizontal blinds.

Deputy Hammond raised his eyebrows when he saw them crowd his small office. "You can't all be here. You can't visit Salem at the same time."

Emily stepped forward as their spokesperson. "We're here to see Sheriff White."

"He isn't here."

"Call him."

He did right away. He knew something serious was up, not only because this many young girls never walked into the sheriff's office at one time, but also because of how angry they were.

While they waited, Emily, Aiyana and Mika slipped to the back hallway and greeted Salem. He approached the cell door. "I heard a commotion." He wrapped his fingers around the bars and his daughters touched them. Salem might be feeling a bit out of his element with them as teenagers, but he'd done a good job raising them under difficult conditions.

They loved their father. Tears formed in Mika's eyes. "Oh, Daddy, look what they did to your face."

Aiyana's look of militancy, the one she'd worn since

they left the house, gathered all the girls and walked into this office together, softened for her father.

"How are you, Dad? Did you get the cinnamon buns I bought? Laura said she would bring them over herself to make sure the deputy or sheriff didn't eat them instead."

A smile formed on Salem's lips and he linked his fingers with Aiyana's. "Laura sat on the cot in the other cell and watched while I ate. White was furious."

Emily laughed. "That sounds like Laura."

"Yeah. She brought me coffee, too. Hot and fresh. Better than the rotgut stuff they brew here."

"What else can we bring you?" Mika piped up. "Are you cold at night? Do you want my blanket?"

Apparently, Mika owned a fleece blanket with raccoons all over it. She never slept without it. The fact that she would give it up for her dad brought a mistiness to Emily's eyes she had to blink hard to dispel.

"No, honey," Salem responded. "You keep your blanket, but if you go to Tonio's, get me some of their homemade lasagna. Okay?"

"You got it, Dad."

"What the hell's going on here?" Sheriff White's voice boomed in the outer office. "What are y'all doing in my office?"

Emily squeezed Salem's arm then led Aiyana and Mika back out front.

When White spotted her, he frowned. "I should've known you'd have something to do with this. What do you want?"

"We want you to open your mind, to consider other suspects besides Salem. We want you to stop harassing him just because he yelled at your son."

"He *bullied* my son."

"It's about time someone did," Sophia said.

White spun around, in search of the source of the voice. When he spotted Sophia, he said, "You're the kid of that wop who owns that fancy store on Main, aren't you?"

Everyone in the room gasped. Brent Hammond shot his boss a dirty look.

"We don't use racist words like that."

"You should be ashamed of yourself using a racial slur."

"That's a disgusting thing to say. Apologize."

"I was taught by my parents to be better than that."

"What century are you living in?"

The statements came so quickly, one on top of the other, Emily didn't know who was saying what, only that the reaction was blessed, right and universal.

"These girls have better manners than you do," Emily said.

"That's unprofessional behavior, Sheriff." Brett Hammond's voice oozed disgust, even though he was the sheriff's friend.

White looked chastened. "You're right. I apologize. I shouldn't have said that." He turned stern again. "Now tell me what the hell this is about. I'm not letting a murderer out of jail."

"An *alleged* murderer," Aiyana said. "You're per-secuting my dad just because your son is a bast—"

Emily gripped the girl's arm to cut her off. "We're here to tell you exactly who your son is, and why Salem felt he had to defend his daughter. Aiyana, tell him what happened."

The look that Emily sent her said, *Keep it cool.*

"Justin pretended he wanted to be my boyfriend. On our first date, when we were supposed to go for ice cream, he took me down into the ravine and tried to get me drunk. Then he…did stuff that I didn't like. When I told him to stop, he got angry because I wouldn't have sex with him. He ran away and left me alone in the dark."

"So you sent him the wrong signals. Not my son's fault if he misunderstood."

"Tell him how old you were at the time," Emily prodded.

"Fifteen."

"That was two weeks ago," Emily clarified. "How old is Justin?"

White looked a little green. "Eighteen."

"Right." Emily cocked her head to one side. "If he'd gone through with it, even with Aiyana's permis-sion, that would have been statutory rape, wouldn't it?" She'd done some research and discovered that the laws were more complicated than that, but was count-ing on the sheriff not knowing everything about these things. Emily couldn't remember there ever being a rape case in Accord. She just hoped he wouldn't call her bluff. All she needed was for him to be intimidated enough to see reason.

"That's not a legal term."

"Fine," Emily huffed. "Rape of a child. Corruption of a minor. Carnal knowledge of a minor. Sexual assault. I'm not a lawyer. Take your pick of whatever it would be called here in Colorado."

The other girls spoke up, all at once, all with the same complaints, angry and wanting their say. They'd kept their emotions pent up for too long about a kid who didn't deserve the time of day from them let alone sex.

"He had sex with me when I was only fifteen," Sophia admitted, stepping forward to get into the sheriff's space. "He was sixteen. He said he loved me. After that night, I never heard from him again. He saw me at school and laughed at me. Age of consent in Colorado is seventeen."

"Justin's only a year older than you. It'll never stick."

"It doesn't matter whether or not it's legal." Sophia sounded exasperated. "We're talking about a matter of principle. We're trying to get you to see who your son really is. He's a bully."

"He gets mad at the drop of a hat and uses his temper against people." Aiyana moved forward beside Sophia. "The morning after I wouldn't have sex with him, he posted all over Twitter and Facebook that I had, and that he wasn't the first. He called me filthy names. He said I was a slut."

She got into his face. "I've never had sex with anyone!" she shouted. "I've never even been out with a boy. I thought Justin was my first boyfriend, and on our first date, he tried to force me to have sex with him. Your son is a waste of a human body. He stinks."

Sheriff White didn't look so hot, but he still came out swinging. "It's only your word that you're a virgin."

"I'm willing to be examined for the record. That point can be proven."

For an intensely private girl, this stood testament to how much she loved her father.

"I'm a good girl," Aiyana continued. "I get straight As at school. I dress modestly, but even if I didn't, your son wouldn't have the right to try to force me."

"He's done creepy stuff to all of us," one of the other girls said amid a chorus of "yeahs" and "me, toos."

"I still say he could have been misinterpreting signals. My kid's not a rapist."

The only one who hadn't spoken was Iris. She stood across from Emily with her skin pale and her hands curled into fists so tightly they looked painful.

Emily waited. Iris's story was her own. No one could force her to tell it. In this she needed control.

"Yes, he is." Iris spoke so quietly, people almost didn't hear her.

Sheriff White's glare was designed to intimidate. "What did you say?"

She quailed for a moment, but rallied. "I said he is a rapist. He raped me." Her voice rose. "He had sex with me without my permission. He forced me and he hurt me." All of that anger finally had a place to go. Iris finally found her voice. "After I said no, he put his hand over my mouth so I couldn't scream. There were no signals for him to misinterpret. I didn't agree to go out with him. I never wanted to have anything to do with him. He dragged me into an alley and took what he wanted."

"You can't prove it." The sheriff no longer sounded confident.

"I can. I went to the hospital. I had a rape kit done. I was torn. He wasn't gentle. There were people who saw him with me that night after he finished. I can prove it in a court of law."

"If that's all true, why haven't you?"

"Because I didn't want the trial. I didn't want the scrutiny or the ridicule from his stupid friends. I didn't want everyone to know what he'd done to me. I was too ashamed, but you know what?"

White stared at her with a deer-in-the-headlights fascination. He shook his head.

"The shame wasn't mine. It was his. I was only fourteen. Not only did he rape me, I was a *minor*."

Sheriff White's Adam's apple bobbed nervously.

Iris held her arm wide to encompass all of the young women in the room. "Your son hurt a lot of girls. Unless you stop him, he'll hurt more. This is how many we found in *one* day. How many more are there? How can we be sure I'm the only one he *raped*?"

Clearly puzzled, White said, "He's popular. He doesn't need to force girls."

Emily spoke up. "Maybe he likes to. You need to check his computer. Get into his social media accounts. Find out what he's doing online. What kind of websites he visits. There is a dangerous pattern emerging. Your son likes young girls. You should be monitoring him."

"My dad had a right to yell at Justin after what he did to me," Aiyana added. "Personally, I would have been happy if he'd beaten him up, but that would have gotten him into trouble. Just because he told your kid to stay away from me and to stop posting lies about me on the internet, you arrested him for murder on flimsy evidence. You need to look for the real killer and not my dad. Do your job."

The sheriff looked lost. If he hadn't been such a hard-ass every time Emily had dealt with him, she would have felt sorry for him now. But it was good to see him look human, and less cocky.

"I'll talk to my son." He sent Iris a hard glare. "You aren't going to have him charged with rape, are you?"

Whoa. That sounded too much like blackmail, or bribery. *I'll ease up on Salem if you promise not to charge my son.* Emily opened her mouth to warn Iris, but she got there first.

"Your son needs to change. You're an officer of the law. *You* need to monitor him. You need to make sure he doesn't retaliate against any of us. That's your job, not ours."

She turned and left the building, almost as though she couldn't stand to stay in the same room with Justin's father another second. Iris hadn't, Emily noted, made the sheriff any promises.

The girls departed amid grumbling, not everyone convinced anything would change.

"I don't blame them for their skepticism." Emily lingered for a final word with the sheriff. "Your son has been getting away with this crap for a long time. He's probably felt immune from consequences because of your position in town. That has to stop."

The sheriff didn't say anything, just nodded, his jawline hard. Emily wasn't sure who he was most angry with—her, the girls, Salem or his son—but she hoped like crazy it was all against Justin.

She left the office and found everyone waiting for her on Main Street. They looked unsure what to do next. They'd finally had their day in court, so to speak, but needed more. "Let's celebrate," she said. "Let's go to Sweet Temptations for sugar and chocolate. My treat."

The girls laughed and headed to Laura's bakery and café.

Emily stepped inside and was immediately transported back twenty years. The colors of the walls might have changed over the years, but the essence of the decorations, the ambience, was still pure Laura. Big, bold and colorful. Sensual and lively.

A wave of sadness swept over her.

So much time passed. So much water under the bridge. How much had she missed over the years?

And now that Salem was in jail, was it possible she'd waited too long to come home?

After they all had their snacks, they sat around two tables.

Emily bit into her date square. Apparently, Laura had sold out of cinnamon buns early today. A pair of arms wrapped around her from behind and she was washed by patchouli and incense. She smiled. Laura.

Laura pulled away and asked the girls, "How did your meeting with Sheriff White go?"

"We think it went well," Sophia said. "He seemed to at least listen to our stories. It's hard to know what he'll do about it, though."

Aiyana put down her brownie and wiped her fingers on her serviette. "I got the feeling he took us seriously. He looked a lot less like a bad guy by the time we left."

"Yes," Emily said. "More human."

"Not as cocky. I think he'll talk to Justin." Aiyana picked up her hot chocolate and blew on it. "I just hope he doesn't buy any of Justin's lies."

The door opened behind them and an extraordinarily good-looking boy walked in, set apart by olive skin, dark wavy hair and, oh my, the most gorgeous pair of bedroom eyes Emily had seen in a long time.

"Hey, Tony," Sophia called. "Join us."

He dragged a spare chair from a nearby table and straddled it. "Hey, sis."

Sophia introduced her brother to everyone. Aiyana's cheeks, Emily noticed, turned pink. Holy relics, so sweet.

Tony glanced at her sideways and then said hi to everyone else. "What's good today?"

Laura tapped him on the shoulder. "Everything's good here, buster."

Tony laughed, white teeth flashing against tanned Italian skin. Had Hollywood come knocking yet? It was only a matter of time.

"Soph," he said, "can you take my shift on Thursday night?"

"Sure. Hot date?"

"My secret." Tony grinned, stood and ambled to the counter. Two tables full of female eyes tracked his progress. He seemed oblivious, natural in his skin.

In a strange way, he reminded Emily of Salem. He'd always been comfortable in and with his body, too. It was one of the things she'd first fallen for, while watching him play basketball for hours. Later, her dad had taught her how to play, and she'd loved it, but had never become really skilled. Music had been her thing.

Tony left and the room breathed an audible sigh.

"Oh. My. God. Sophia, your brother is so hot." One of the girls, Jane, fanned herself with a napkin. "His eyes are amazing. Sleepy. Dark. So Italian."

"He's my pesky younger brother, Jane. I so *don't* see him as hot."

"How old is he?" Aiyana asked quietly.

"Sixteen."

"He's dating already."

Sophia picked up on the same apprehension in Aiyana's voice that Emily heard. "He is *not* like Justin.

He likes girls and they like him. He knows he's good-looking, but my parents raised him right. He has fun with it, but doesn't let it go to his head."

When Aiyana wasn't looking, Sophia met Emily's gaze with her own and smiled. Emily could tell Sophia was totally going to promote something between Aiyana and Tony.

Maybe that was a good thing. Maybe a date with Tony, and maybe one with Cody. Wouldn't it be sweet for Aiyana to get some experience with boys who were safe, even if it was only one or two good dates, just to restore her faith in the opposite sex?

Emily nodded, letting Sophia know she had her full support. If Sophia could get her brother to ask Aiyana out, it would be the best thing that could happen to her.

SALEM LAY ON THE COT staring at the gray ceiling, stunned by everything he'd just heard.

Aiyana hadn't been the only girl Justin had victimized. And in their way, all of them had just taken themselves out of the *victim* role. By testifying against Justin, even if only in the sheriff's office rather than in a court of law, the girls had turned themselves into *survivors*.

He was proud of Aiyana for fighting back, both for herself and for her father, for displaying spunk and backbone.

The worst, though, was what had happened to the one girl who had said she'd been raped at fourteen. He thought of Mika. It would kill him if it happened to either of his daughters, but so young? That would be even more devastating.

The front door of the office opened and closed. More girls?

Salem heard the sheriff's voice. "What are you doing here? You should be in school." Who was it?

"I heard rumors there were a whole bunch of girls from school here this morning."

Justin was here. Salem stood and crept to the corner of the cell nearest to the office so he could hear.

"Brent," White said, "why don't you go on your rounds?"

"But I only just got back before those girls showed up."

"Go. I need to talk to my son alone."

Salem heard the front door open and close.

"What do you think those girls were doing here, son?"

"I don't know." Justin sounded surly.

"Think about it. Apparently, all of them know you."

"Yeah? So?" Salem imagined the boy's shrug. "We all go to the same school. Of course they know me."

"They all had complaints about you. Serious ones."

"Like what?" Now he sounded worried.

"About you trying to pressure them to have sex with you when they didn't want to."

"That's a lie. I don't have to force girls. They're all over me. Dad, you know that. You've seen them."

"Yeah, but there was more to their allegations."
Sheriff White sounded about as serious as Salem had

ever heard him. He'd taken what the girls had said to heart. "Some of the girls you tried to have sex with were underage."

"So? They wanted it. They went out with me when I asked them on dates."

"You were asking fourteen-year-old girls out when you were sixteen and seventeen? There are plenty of lovely girls out there your own age. Why go after the young ones?"

"So? It's not illegal if they're willing."

It was interesting, Salem was learning, how much could be heard in a voice when you couldn't see a person's face. What he heard now was a careless bravado.

White groaned. "It doesn't matter if they're willing. They're too young for it to be acceptable. And that's another thing. What about when they aren't willing?"

"What do you mean?"

"Have you ever raped a girl?"

"No," he snapped. "Who said I did?"

"Harold's daughter, Iris."

"The pretty one. Man, she looks like she should be in an old-fashioned Italian painting or something." The tone of Justin's voice had taken on a sensual air, had, as one of the girls had stated about him, become creepy.

"Come off it," Sheriff White snapped. "Did you rape her?"

"No. She's lying."

"She didn't say no?"

"Never."

"You didn't drag her into an alley and put your hand over her mouth so she couldn't scream?"

"Nope." The kid was lying. Salem could hear it. He wondered if White could, too.

Standing here in the dimness listening, but not seeing, was like being a lie detector. He could hear so much in a person's voice without the distraction of seeing a face.

"You know something, son? I believed her. She was one of the most convincing victims I've ever seen. That girl hates your guts, and it sounds like she has good reason."

"You're gonna believe a girl over me? What about all the stories you told about when you were young? Sowing your wild oats, you called it."

"I never forced a girl. I never pressured. I never even seduced. And I certainly didn't drop them after one night unless they wanted to be dropped. You've moved into a whole other category altogether, and it's not only disgusting, it's illegal."

Salem actually heard one of them swallow, and he was pretty sure it wasn't the father. "What are you going to do about it?"

Sheriff White sighed. "Legally? I don't know. No one's pressed charges. Yet. Morally? I'm suspending all privileges. No car. No dates. No allowance. No going out nights. They said you use the internet to tell lies about them." Salem heard a drawer slide open. "Goddamn it. Do you see all of this stuff? This is training material they keep sending us, teaching us to recognize cyberbullying. It's a *crime*. Jesus. My own son."

The drawer slammed shut. "No internet. I'm confiscating your computer. School and studies and that's it. You've got another week of classes left. After that, I don't know what we'll do. For now, you stay away from all girls, y'hear?"

"That really sucks. I can't believe you won't support your own son."

"I've supported you for years, even when your grades slipped and the teachers complained that you goofed around too much and slacked off. Even when that old teacher kept holding you back year after year, I argued for you. I thought, so what, the kid's young, but I was wrong. You've been screwing up big-time behind my back. I haven't been strict enough. That changes as of today."

Salem heard the sheriff move and what sounded like a minor scuffle.

"Hey! Let go of me!" There was no missing the shock in Justin's voice.

"Your mother and I indulged you. We were wrong. No more. This summer, you'll go to a counselor, as often and as long as it takes to fix whatever is wrong inside you. A sex counselor, if I can find one. And if I ever hear of you forcing a girl again, I will personally lock you up and throw away the key."

The silence that followed hummed with an electrical charge Salem swore he could feel all the way back here in his cell.

"I hate you." The door slammed, shaking the building.

The office chair squeaked as though White had sat down and either leaned back to stare at the ceiling, or forward to put his head in his hands.

As a parent, Salem commiserated, but he wasn't so dumb that he didn't also feel good about this turn of events. Maybe the sheriff would get off his back. Salem heard a car start and roar off down the street and crossed his fingers the kid didn't kill anyone on his way home.

CHAPTER ELEVEN

EMILY LEFT THE CAFÉ with Aiyana and Mika. Just as she did, farther down the street, John Spade stepped into the sheriff's office.

"I was going to drive you to school for the afternoon," Emily said, "but we need to return to the jail. I want you to see that your dad is being taken care of." She wanted it for their peace of mind.

"What do you mean?" Aiyana asked.

"Did you see that man who just entered the office?" Aiyana nodded.

"He's the cavalry."

"Who?"

"That was John Spade, your father's new lawyer."

"Let's go."

They practically fell over each other to get there first. They stepped into the office just as John Spade handed the sheriff a sheaf of papers.

"I would advise you to let my client out of here right away."

"Um." Sheriff White didn't look very good. "I thought you were gone for a week."

"I was. I came back." John Spade was the epitome of a lawyer who'd made good money, his suit expensive, his white shirt perfectly pressed, his face and body buffed, scrubbed and pampered by the best money could buy. "What's the problem? Let me in to see my client."

White rubbed his hands over his face. His goose was cooked and he knew it. White had banked on the only lawyer in town being away and hoping he could throw Salem in jail and sit on the case from last Friday and for the full week through until next Monday, when John should have returned. By then the bruises would have been gone, and the cuts healed.

Steps heavy, White brought John around back. Emily followed and could feel the girls behind her.

When John Spade saw Salem, he stopped short. "You're in a shitload of trouble, Sheriff."

"He fell—"

John raised a hand to shut him up. "Save it for the courtroom."

Emily wasn't sure she'd ever been in the presence of a more confident man. Jean-Marc had been arrogant, but wasn't that sometimes a function of insecurity? An overcompensation? Hadn't Jean-Marc's excessive need to philander been a means to cover his fear of isolation? He couldn't stand to be alone, ever. Every minute of every day had to be filled. His need for attention had exhausted Emily.

Jean-Marc had never learned the difference between loneliness and solitude. He had never experienced the rejuvenation that moments of solitude could bring.

John Spade, on the other hand, could probably spend

endless days alone happily, and had the cojones to back up Emily's dad's claim that he was the best. So great to have a ruthless man on one's side.

"Open the cell door. I need to meet with my client."

"He's a criminal. A murderer."

John's ice-blue eyes cut through White's B.S. "He's a suspect. Every suspect has the right to legal counsel, and to private meetings with that counsel. If you don't allow that, I'll file a complaint and have you fired. Open the door."

Whoa. The implacability in his voice intimidated even Emily. Sheriff White hadn't managed to intimidate her with his mean spirits no matter how hard he'd tried, but Spade did with his ice. If there was even a trace of warmth behind those eyes, Emily couldn't detect it.

The sheriff unlocked Salem's cell and left them alone, returning to the office around the corner. Before Spade could enter, Aiyana and Mika scooted in ahead of him and threw themselves into his arms.

"Daddy, I missed your hugs."

"I hated not having you home with us. Oh, Dad, your poor face."

"I'm going to kick the sheriff."

"Hush. You'll do no such thing. I won't have you tossed in here with me." Emily thought she detected a damp gleam in his eyes. "I missed you, too." His butter-soft voice sounded hoarse today, whether from emotion or disuse Emily couldn't tell.

"The sheriff wouldn't let us in to see him." While

she told John this, she gripped the bars, holding herself from running in to claim any tiny spot left in that hug for herself, but Salem had his hands full. And rightly so. His daughters mattered to him. "Other than Laura bringing him the buns, he's had no visitors."

Both girls started to talk, speaking over each other, cutting each other off, sharing with their father details of what they'd done that morning.

"I heard you when you came to the office." Salem ran his hand over their smooth raven-dark hair that matched his. "I heard it all. You were brave warriors."

John turned his cool gaze on Emily, but she thought she detected a spark. "I heard he had one other visitor, after midnight on Saturday night." He kept his voice low enough that Sheriff White wouldn't be able to hear him.

"Dad told you about that, huh?"

John nodded.

"I was angry and I wanted to make sure Salem hadn't been mistreated even more than when he was arrested."

"Good. Next time, be more careful. Don't get caught."

"I don't think Deputy Breslin reported me. He's been very sympathetic."

"At this point, the sheriff isn't going to do anything about it even if he does find out. He's in more than enough trouble himself. His energy will be spent figuring out how to save his own hide."

"True. We have incriminating photos."

"So your father said. I need copies."

"I'll get them to you."

"You need to get into that cell for a brief visit before I have to boot you all out." The sparkle in his eyes actually became laughter and a smile. "I know you want to."

Without further encouragement, Emily flew inside and against Salem. He staggered then righted himself. His arms became steel bands across her back, hard and reassuring. "Thank you," he whispered. "You were the fiercest of all."

He pulled back. "When the darkness threatened to eat me alive, I thought of you three fighting for me, and I knew I would get out of here one day."

"Time's up," John said. "I'll get Salem's case into the court system today, but I need to talk to him first. I'm stronger if I have all of the information."

"Come, girls," Emily said. "Mr. Spade is right. He has to get this show on the road. The sooner he does, the sooner your dad can come home."

Salem kissed and held each of his daughters before turning to shake John's hand. "Thank you for coming."

When she left, Emily looked back over her shoulder. Salem watched her go with an expression she thought she understood. He didn't want any of them to leave. He didn't want to be left in that jail cell even one more day. And he wanted Emily to see the depth of his love.

In those dark, deep-set eyes, it smoldered. Again with that gorgeous smoldering.

Oh, saintly relics, did he smolder.

JOHN SPADE WAS able to get Salem into court but not until Thursday morning.

Salem's dad hadn't yet come home from the reservation, so Emily was still staying with Aiyana and Mika.

Emily spent Wednesday in a state of frustration. Late that afternoon, Iris came home from school with Aiyana.

"Iris wants to talk to you, Emily."

"Sure. You girls hungry? Should we go to the kitchen and I'll fix us a snack?"

"No, we need to sit in here." Iris led the way to the living room and sat on the sofa. Aiyana joined her and Emily sat in the armchair opposite.

"What's up?"

Iris had her hands locked in their familiar position, one fist inside the other, but Emily noted that her fingers were more relaxed. It wasn't a death grip. "I've been thinking a lot since we talked to the sheriff yesterday. It wasn't right for me not to report Justin after he raped me. If I had, other girls might not have been hurt since then."

"You had been through a terrible ordeal. You didn't have anyone to talk to. How could you possibly have known what to do?"

"Yes, Iris. I was lucky to have Emily here the morning I woke up and found all of those awful tweets about me. What you lived through was much worse, and you had no one to confide in."

"I wish I'd had someone like Emily."

"Or me. You can call me anytime you need someone to talk to. The lesson I learned from all of this is that you have to reach out. If you need help, ask for it."

Iris's smile lit up her face. "I'll probably have to take advantage of you in the future." She turned her attention to Emily. "I've decided I'm going to press charges against Justin. I want him arrested and taken to court."

Hallelujah! "That's amazing. I'm not surprised, Iris. You're a strong person."

"Most days I don't feel strong."

"Aiyana's right. On the days when you don't, you have to reach out."

"I have a confession to make." Iris started to wring her hands again. "I lied about the rape kit. There wasn't one. I'm usually the most honest person you'll ever meet, but I wanted to shake up the sheriff, to get him to take us more seriously."

"You certainly did that," Emily said dryly. "So you didn't go to the hospital?"

Iris shook her head.

"May I ask why not?"

"I wasn't sure if they'd have to call my parents because I was so young. I didn't know. I love my mom and dad more than anything. All I could think was that I didn't want my dad beating up Justin. Not for Justin, but for my dad. I don't want him in jail. He loves me and he'd be really angry with anyone who hurt me." She looked at Emily with a plea for understanding in her eyes. "I know it sounds stupid now, but I didn't want them hurt by this."

Oh, Iris. I understand. I really do. "They've probably been hurt anyway, though. Haven't they?"

Iris looked down at her white fists. "Yes. I changed a lot after that night. They knew something was wrong. They might even have guessed what kind of thing. That's why my dad drives me everywhere. To protect me."

Glancing at Emily, she asked. "Have I screwed everything up? Do I still have a case without the rape kit?"

"I honestly don't know."

"What does having him charged entail? I mean, I can't go to the sheriff, can I?"

"I haven't got a clue, but John Spade will know. Let's go now. Aiyana, will you come with us?"

The three walked to John's office ten minutes away. His receptionist was still on vacation, so they called out to him when they entered the reception area. He came out of his office.

"Hey, it's the cavalry. I heard what all of you did yesterday before I arrived at the sheriff's office. Salem brought me up to speed."

Emily laughed. "I thought you were the cavalry."

"Nope. You shook up the sheriff. He was already reeling by the time I got there. Did you know his son showed up just after you left?"

"I wish I could have been a fly on the wall at that meeting," Emily said. "Do you think his dad gave him hell?"

"There was a fly on the wall. They didn't bother to keep their voices down. Salem heard everything."

"When he comes home," Emily vowed, "we're getting the complete conversation. I want to know every single word."

"The sheriff was angry with his son. He's grounded from here until eternity. Nothing. No car. No dates. No internet. They're also putting him in counseling."

"Good."

"So, what can I do for you?"

Emily urged Iris forward. "This is Iris Walker. She has something she wants to discuss with you. Are you hiring John, Iris?"

"Yes, but I want Emily and Aiyana to sit in on our conversation. I need them with me."

"This sounds serious. Come into the office, all of you."

John snagged his receptionist's chair and dragged it into the room so they could all sit. "Go ahead."

"I haven't talked about this with many people. This is hard." Her knuckles were white again. Emily took her hands and massaged them, then held one. Aiyana took the other. Iris gave them both a look of gratitude.

"Two years ago, when I was fourteen, Justin White raped me."

John sprang forward, opened a black leather binder and started taking notes. "I understand this will be difficult for you, but I need every detail."

Emily hadn't thought the man would show much

emotion, but when he looked at Iris, his compassion leaked through while the girl told her story.

At the end, Iris said, "I didn't go to the police then. I didn't want it to become public or for my parents to be hurt, but what he did was wrong and now I realize I have to be strong and see him punished, so he'll never do it to anyone else."

"You've changed your mind?" John asked. "You want to have him charged now?"

"Yes, but I can't go to the sheriff. Where can I go?"

"Let me take care of it. I'll get it to the right people."

"So, you'll be my lawyer?"

John smiled with a hard glint in his eye. "I already am."

Emily suspected John was fired up by the challenge, and the probability of putting Justin out of commission.

"I didn't get a rape kit done," Iris said. "Will it matter?"

John leaned back in his chair. "I don't know. It might be hard to win the case without solid proof. It would only be his word against yours. But at the very least, the hassle would make Justin think twice about ever forcing another girl. Plus, the publicity would alert other girls to who he really is, even if he's not convicted. He won't find it easy to fool as many in the future."

That seemed to be good enough for Iris. "That's exactly what I want. To protect other girls."

They left John's office feeling more hopeful than they had when they went in.

Emily took Iris and Aiyana out for dinner. Afterward, she called Mika at her friend's house to see whether she could stay there a little longer while Emily took care of one more thing.

"What do you need to do?" Aiyana asked. They stood on the pavement outside the restaurant.

"We need to go home with Iris. I'm guessing you're going to tell your parents tonight. Correct?"

Iris nodded. "Surprisingly, what happened in the sheriff's office hasn't got back to them yet. People have been discreet, I guess."

"Do you need support?"

"Yes. Please."

They went to Iris's house, where she introduced Emily and Aiyana to her parents. Emily had lived out of town for so long, she didn't know much about them.

Mr. Walker would be considered a handsome man if not for a nonexistent chin. His nervous energy contrasted with his wife's warm welcome. A woman of delicate bones and a fragile air, she smiled, and in that smile, Emily saw her youth.

"I brought Emily and Aiyana here to help me talk to you."

"Talk to us?" Her father frowned. "About what? Why do we need strangers here for you to talk to us?"

"It's about something that happened a couple of years ago. Aiyana is helping me to get through it. The same thing almost happened to her."

Her parents' expressions sharpened. Of course, they'd seen changes in their daughter. They must have known something was terribly wrong and perhaps hidden that from themselves. Now, here it was about to come out, and Mr. Walker looked ready to spit nails, while Mrs. Walker withdrew. Her smile became vacant.

Iris told them about the rape. Mr. Walker covered his face, because he didn't seem to know what else to do. His breathing roared in the quiet room. Then he paced as though being driven by a giant itch he couldn't scratch. When he stopped, he took a pack of cigarettes from his pocket and shook one out. He glanced at the front door and then at Iris, clearly torn between smoking and staying with his daughter.

"Just this once," Mrs. Walker said. "Go ahead. Light up."

He did and the smell filled the room, even though he'd moved away from everyone. "You should have told me. I would have taken the bully down for you. I would have killed him."

His voice resonated with anger, yes, but also with grief.

"That's what I was afraid of, Daddy."

Emily wondered whether Iris realized she'd used the childish term and how young she sounded.

The pain on Mr. Walker's face broke Emily's heart.

Mrs. Walker, who'd started to cry, sat beside her daughter and took her into her arms. She rested her daughter's head on her shoulder and caressed her hair. "I'm so sorry. What can we do for you?"

Overcome by the tension in the room, in her father, Iris withdrew into herself. She looked tense, so Emily and Aiyana told them what had been happening.

"Yes, we heard Salem had been arrested." Mr. Walker pulled himself under control. "I can't believe Roger didn't follow the book. He's usually a stickler for details."

Emily described how Salem had gone to the school to confront Justin after he'd found out about Justin's Facebook and Twitter nastiness, and how that had angered Sheriff White.

"It would," Mr. Walker said bitterly. "He thinks the sun rises and sets on his son."

"Not anymore. It's kind of hard to deny the truth when ten girls are accusing your son of hurting and taking advantage of them. And worse. There would have to be a massive conspiracy for it not to be true."

"I'm pressing charges." Iris pulled out of her mother's embrace. "He needs to pay for what he's done. I don't want this to happen to more girls. This guy isn't going to stop. He's hurt other girls. We don't even know if I'm the only one he's raped."

Mr. Walker flinched. "The whole town will know what happened."

"After yesterday in the sheriff's office, Dad, it's going to get out anyway."

"But—"

"Harold." Mrs. Walker's tone took on a thread of

steel. "Iris has made up her mind. We will support her in this."

Mr. Walker lost his steam. "You're right. Okay. What do you need us to do?"

Iris started to cry. "Help me. Support me. Don't judge."

Emily and Aiyana left Iris with her parents.

Despite how exhausted she was from the intense emotion, Emily was also happy. "How do you feel about all of this, Aiyana?"

"Ecstatic. Justin will finally get what's coming to him. He won't have a chance to hurt anyone else."

Emily whooshed out a relieved breath and started the car. "Yes, and it's all because of you and Sophia and Iris being such strong women."

"Iris is amazing. I hope we can stay friends."

"I think you will. I have to stop off at home for clean clothes and to pick up my mail." Emily drove them both to the Jordan house and Aiyana followed her upstairs.

"Wow, this room is awesome. I love it. I could so live here."

"Isn't it wonderful? It was a great retreat when I was a teenager."

"Is this where you came when the girls at school were bullying you?"

"Yes. I threw myself into schoolwork. Math, science and history. I wanted to excel so I could get into the best college and get a good job and leave this town far behind."

"But you did come back."

"I did." Emily threw clean clothes into an overnight bag.

"Are you glad?"

"Yes. There is a time for everything. I've healed. I have you to thank for that."

"Me? What did I do?"

"I was in a very bad place when I came home. You took me outside of myself. I couldn't retreat inside to lick my wounds. Instead, I was motivated to help you. You forced me to look at everything that had happened to me in high school and to finally put it to rest."

"I thought *you* were helping me."

"I hope I did."

"Oh, you really did. I'll never forget it."

On impulse, Emily hugged Aiyana, the warmth between them real and necessary. She'd thought life had thrown her a few unfair punches, but here in Accord, where she'd least expected it, she'd found affection and support.

Aiyana touched Emily's music stand. "This is where you played your music, too, isn't it?"

"My lifesaver? Yes."

"I'm glad you had something to help you. Now Iris has music, too."

"She has a lot more to overcome than I did."

"Yeah, but she'll have us. Right?"

"Right. We'll stick by her."

"I heard Dad tell Grandpa you won't be staying in town." Aiyana sounded worried. "Is that true?"

"Nope. I'm home to stay. Your dad just hasn't figured that out yet." Emily added fresh underwear to the bag. "He has reason to doubt me. History. But I'm going to do my best to change his mind."

"Good. I want you to stay. I would miss you if you weren't here."

"I would miss you, too. And Mika."

"And Dad?" There was a smile in Aiyana's voice.

"You're too smart, you know that?" They started downstairs. "Yes, I would miss your dad terribly."

At the bottom of the stairs, Laura appeared. "Hi, Aiyana. I brought more cinnamon buns to your dad this morning, and guess what?"

"What?"

"Sheriff White didn't try to stop me. He seemed subdued. Just let me waltz right on to the back without saying a word. Whatever all of you did yesterday was powerful magic."

"We just made him see the truth. Right, Emily?"

"You received a couple of letters while you've been staying at the Pearces', Emily." Laura retrieved them from a small desk in the foyer. "I love the exotic stamps."

Exotic? Penelope, maybe? Please, please, please.

"Yes!" She had two letters, one from Arthur and one from Penny. She opened Arthur's first. He had sent the package to his sister by express delivery.

The second letter was from Penelope, short and to the point.

The eagle has landed. What do I do with it?

Penelope had the prayer book. Thank God. Relief left Emily's knees weak. Good question, though. What now?

She finished reading the note.

Sad news, dear. The young student you found with Jean-Marc discovered him in bed with her roommate. She was distraught. She tried to kill herself. Fortunately, she was found in time and was taken to hospital. Her parents have since taken her home, poor thing. That man needs to be stopped.

Emily reeled. Once she had found out the student had been sleeping with Jean-Marc, she'd been furious. She hadn't wanted to have anything to do with the woman she had privately called everything from a slut to a witch. But a suicide attempt? The poor girl.

There had to have been some imbalance there. Either that or she had truly believed herself in love.

Something had to be done. Jean-Marc couldn't go on hurting women, chewing them up and then discarding them as though they were apple cores.

Something had to be done. Something…

She couldn't leave this alone.

The scene in the sheriff's office the other morning flashed. She thought of all of those young girls fighting back, of the courage they'd shown, especially Iris.

No way was she asking Penny to take care of this.

Emily would take care of it herself, would pay Jean-

Marc back for all of those years he had treated her badly.

She was going to have to go back to the Sudan, to Jean-Marc, the last person on this earth she ever wanted to see again.

"Good news?" Laura asked.

"The best." It really was. *Look at the positive.* She had a chance to right years' worth of wrongs, and stop a man from hurting anyone else—just as they'd done with Justin—and she would take it. But, first, she had to finish rescuing the man she loved.

EARLY THURSDAY MORNING, Emily went to visit Salem. She'd been bothered by something her dad had said. It had eaten away at her, rubbing like a stone in her shoe.

"Emily." Salem stood when he saw her. He was clean, his hair glossy, combed and braided. He wore the fresh clothes Emily had delivered for court, black dress pants and a white dress shirt. She drank in every detail.

"How did you manage to wash your hair in that tiny sink?"

He approached the bars and curled his fingers around hers. "I didn't. John Spade finagled it so Deputy Breslin could take me to the B and B and supervise while I showered."

"Ew. Matt had to watch while you showered?"

"No. John paid for the top-floor suite. Breslin sat in the bedroom while I showered. The window was too small for me to climb through and the ground too far below for me to jump. Not that I would have. And not that Matt thought I would. Sheriff White was just covering his ass."

"We need to talk." Emily lowered her voice. The last thing she wanted was for White to hear this conversation. "What are you hiding? Why didn't you want my dad to hire an investigator?"

Salem swung away, leaning his hands against the cement wall. "We're back to that? For God's sake, Emily, let it go."

"I can't. What do you know?"

"Nothing."

She thought of her dad's suspicion. "Do you know who did it?"

His flinch was so subtle she almost missed it.

"You do know," she hissed. "And you're not telling?"

He came back to her. "I don't *know*. I'm only guessing."

"Is it a likelihood? An educated guess?"

He shrugged.

"Ooh, don't do that. Don't do that sphinx thing again. Not now. If these bars weren't in my way, I'd wring your neck."

"I've told you all I'm going to."

"Then I'll have to find out on my own, and then I'm going to tell the sheriff my suspicions. Do you know why?"

Salem looked as if he'd bitten into something sour. "Why?"

"Because I can't stand to see you in here. Because it's tearing me apart." Her voice had risen and she tempered her tone. "Because it's the right thing to do, just as telling Sheriff White about his son was the right thing for Aiyana to do. She showed real courage, Salem, on your behalf. She deserves to see you set free. I'm going to find out who did this."

"Don't."

She walked away. Outside, she called her dad.

"He knows who did it and won't say." Her voice caught. Damn the man. She loved Salem and she wanted to rescue him, but how could she when the darn man wouldn't allow himself to be rescued? She paced the sidewalk in front of the sheriff's office. "How is the P.I. doing? Any leads?"

"He thinks he has an idea, but won't name names without proof. He's still working on it."

"Okay, thanks, Dad."

She didn't want to lose Salem's respect over this, but it was a chance she would have to take. The true criminal needed to be behind bars instead of the man she loved.

EMILY CHECKED THE driveway again for the fortieth time since Aiyana and Mika had come home from school, hoping that John Spade might drop Salem off. The bail hearing had been today and Emily had still heard nothing. On tenterhooks and afraid to hope, she'd called Spade's cell a dozen times and left messages because the blasted man wasn't picking up.

Why hadn't he called her back? Did that mean they were still in court? What if the judge denied bail? Was Salem back in jail? What if bail was set so high Salem couldn't afford it? Should she call her dad?

"Emily?" Aiyana and Mika sat on the sofa side by side.

"Yes, Aiyana?"

"Can you stop pacing? I'm getting dizzy watching you."

The girls had gone to school, but Aiyana had called Emily between classes to find out if her father was home.

Emily fell into an armchair. "What do you two want for dinner?" She had no desire to cook or to eat, but she had to make an effort for the girls.

They shrugged, looking as anxious as Emily felt. They weren't interested in food, either.

The front door opened. Had Mr. Pearce finally come home from the reservation?

They heard footsteps in the foyer and then Salem stepped into the living room with a mile-wide grin on his face.

"Dad!" Aiyana and Mika screamed and converged on him. They hugged and kissed their dad, and laughed.

"Salem." Now that he was here in all his handsome, quiet glory, Emily's brain flat-out stopped working.

"How did this happen?" Emily absorbed the happiness around her. Salem's face glowed while he held his girls. He closed his eyes and breathed deeply as though inhaling the essence of his family. "Why didn't John call?"

"I asked him not to. I wanted to surprise all of you." When he stared at her over his daughters' heads, there was no sign of the sphinx, only his intense smoldering. It would have to wait for later when they had a private moment, or two, or a million.

"When is the trial set to start?"

"Not until August, so I have time to mount a defense."

"I'm so happy you're here, Dad." Aiyana curled her arms around him. "We'll worry about the future later. Tonight, we need to celebrate your freedom and have fun."

Mika ran to get her camera and Salem held open one arm. Emily stepped into his embrace, crowding Aiyana to touch as much of him as she could. She sensed the camera's flash going off, but wouldn't let go of the man she loved. Come hell or high water, he was just going to have to accept that he was hers. He might smolder and they might make love—they *would* make love—but he had to also understand that he could trust her when she said she would never leave him again.

Mika jumped onto Salem's back. He pretended to stagger under her weight.

Aiyana released him. "Are you hungry, Dad?"

"Yes, starving, but more for your company than for food. I should eat at some point, though."

They agreed, but no one stopped hugging him, as though terrified he would disappear from their lives again if they didn't hold him tightly enough. Emily certainly didn't want to break contact, not after all the time Salem had been out of her reach and under Sheriff White's miserable watchful eye.

Salem kissed his daughters' foreheads. "I missed you so much."

Reaching for Emily, he embraced her and whispered, "Later."

What he meant by that, Emily wasn't sure, but she was open to anything, *everything,* with this man. She had her own plans for later, and Salem was just going to have to fall in line.

He looked different. Emily wasn't sure how, but the experience had changed him.

He frowned. "Why is it so quiet in here? Where's that machine Emily bought?"

She moved away and fussed with the karaoke machine.

"Put in the '50s CD." Salem hovered near her shoulder.

She did.

"Do you want us to sing? Come on, girls."

"No!" he shouted then continued at a lower volume. "Sit down. All of you on the sofa. I have something to share with you."

He hit a button and Elvis Presley's signature drum opening of "Jailhouse Rock" erupted. Emily and the girls exchanged puzzled glances. Their dad was going to sing Elvis?

Then he broke into song and their mouths dropped open.

Salem sang with authority and a sexy rasp, and…
holy relics…could he move his hips!

They screamed and jumped up to join him, bop-
ping about like maniacs while Salem killed the song.
Absolutely *killed* it.

When he finished, Mika and Aiyana flung themselves at him.

"You never told us you could sing."

"How could you keep this from us?"

"More, Dad."

"Sing something else."

He ran through a repertoire of '50s and '60s rock.
Feeling high and happier than she'd ever been, Emily
was the only one who heard the front door open and
saw Mr. Pearce enter the house, expression solemn.

CHAPTER TWELVE

THE MUSIC STOPPED abruptly and they came to a halt, their dancing interrupted by the sudden silence.

Mr. Pearce stood beside the karaoke machine. He'd turned off the music. A movement at the doorway to the hall alerted Emily to the presence of two men she didn't recognize.

"Grandpa, you're home." Mika threw her arms around her grandfather, oblivious to the other two men in the room, and the tension emanating from her father, the happy ease of the past twenty minutes dissipating like steam.

Emily, on the other hand, along with Salem, knew something big was going on. One of the men was tall and confident. Despite jeans, a cowboy shirt and cowboy boots, this man meant business. He might resemble a good old boy with his mustache and cowboy hat pushed to the back of his head, but he was dead serious about something. Her father's private investigator, Emily guessed.

The other man, quiet and at least a foot shorter, had lived many years. His shoulders hunched forward and his gnarled hands curled in on themselves, the arthritic knuckles swollen and misshapen. The bones of his Native American heritage lurked beneath a dried apple face.

Emily knew. "It's him, isn't it?"

"Yes." That one word came out of Salem with difficulty, the admission dragged out of him like a deep-rooted molar unwilling to give up the fight.

Good, Emily thought. "It's time to put an end to this misunderstanding."

Salem didn't respond.

"Who is he?" Emily asked, because everyone was waiting for Salem to move on this and he wasn't. Emily wanted him absolved now.

"Annie's father." Salem stepped toward the old man.

"He looks more like her grandfather."

"She was the late child of his second wife."

Mika and Aiyana had been standing silently, but approached their maternal grandfather. The sense Emily was picking up was that they didn't know him as well, but the affection was there. They moved easily into his arms.

"Hello, granddaughters. Have you been good girls?"

Mr. Pearce introduced both men to Emily and the P.I. to Salem. "Do you know why I brought them here, Salem?"

"I can guess, Dad."

"You can't take responsibility for a crime you didn't commit."

"But we can't send Ansel to jail."

Emily moved to stand in front of him. "Salem, if he committed the crime, he needs to face the consequences."

"Listen to your woman." The man's voice was as thin and creaky as his body. "This is right. Your father came to me at the reservation. He told me they arrested you. That is wrong."

"But—"

"Salem, Annie was my child. It was my responsibility to teach her to protect herself. To make the right decisions in life. I failed her. Getting rid of that pestilence, Caleb, was the only way to avenge my daughter's dignity. He killed my child. I killed him. Now I will go to the police."

The pain on Salem's face became Emily's. He loved this old man. Further, it was obvious he respected him, even knowing that he'd committed murder.

"Stop protecting me, Salem." Ansel rested his ancient hands on his son-in-law's shoulders. "Stop feeling guilty. Annie's death was not your fault. I saw how you treated my daughter with respect. I saw how you raised her daughters with love. I honor you."

To the private investigator, he said, "Let's go. I'm tired. I need to get to that jail cell to lie down."

Before he left, he turned to Salem. "Make peace with your woman here. She wants only what's best for you. She is right. You don't belong in jail. I do." He included the rest of the room in his next statement. "I have lived a good life, long and happy. I'm near the end. This will not hurt me. Nothing can hurt me more than Annie's death. Be at peace. I am. I will see her soon with my two wives."

At the front door, he turned back to Salem. "Tomorrow morning, you come to the jail and bring me those cinnamon buns you always brought to the reservation. That will make me happy."

"Yes, I can do that." Salem's voice trembled, but he managed to smile.

After the private investigator drove off with Ansel, presumably heading to the sheriff's office, Mr. Pearce said, "This is a bittersweet moment. I'm sorry Ansel will end his life in this way, but he committed a serious crime. We heard what he said and we must respect it. He is at peace."

He gestured to Aiyana. "Give me your phone, eh? We're ordering pizza. Tonight, we celebrate."

Salem stared out of the window long after Emily knew the car was gone. "Dad, I don't know if I can celebrate right now."

"I had many discussions with Ansel. Don't worry on his account. He is at peace." He stood beside his son. "Take it from me. He won't suffer long in that jail. I don't think he'll last until any court dates they set."

"I sensed something. What is it? Cancer?"

"Yes. He's eighty-nine. He's in pain. He's happy to go. We'll celebrate his life, eh?"

"WHERE DID YOU learn all of those songs?" Emily asked as she walked to her car beside Salem. He finally had her alone and wrapped his arm around her. He'd been like this all evening, touching her at every opportunity, just to experience the pure pleasure of having the freedom to do so.

Aiyana and Mika had already gone to bed with smiles on their faces, happy to have him home again. His dad was right. Tonight was for celebration. Soon enough, they would grieve at a funeral.

"That music was decades before our time," Emily said.

"My mom loved it. She used to play it and dance around the house while she was supposed to be doing laundry or cooking dinner. I guess I absorbed it by osmosis."

The night around them shimmered with moonlight, and Salem was free for good. The air smelled sweeter, the stars shone more brightly than he remembered. He thought about Emily's fiercely whispered promise when he was in jail. *I'm never leaving you again. How's that for a commitment?*

He held her close in his strong grip, and all was right in his world.

"While I lay in that jail cell, I thought of my mother a lot." Salem's voice carried on the quiet air. "I had time for thinking. I wondered if her marriage felt like a prison to her, if motherhood made her feel trapped. Maybe that was why she left."

"She did? I never knew that. Tell me about her."

"She was so many things," he said, dredging up memories that might have been better left buried, but he'd learned that nothing good came of hiding things.

"You know how sometimes you're not crazy about a person, you think you have every right to really dislike them, and then they do something so sweet it takes your breath away?"

She nodded.

"That was my mom. She wasn't like other mothers. Most days I wished she was." He leaned back against the Jeep and shifted her into his arms, pulling her back against his chest. "She was complicated, but what she was the *most* was unpredictable. Quicksilver. Some days there would be no dinner on the table because she'd felt like dancing to music all day.

"Then there were all the times she missed my school events—musicals, parent-teacher meetings, assemblies—because she forgot or didn't feel like it or just had something better to do. The other kids would have their mothers there with them, but not me. Dad would come to the evening things, but often Mom would miss those, too."

"I had no idea."

"Why would you know any of this? She died when I was twelve, long before you came to town, but she left us even before that."

"How did she die?"

"Car accident. She was driving. It was her fault. Thank God she was the only victim." He cleared clogged emotions from his throat, ancient resentment and anger blocking his development like phlegm. It was time to get rid of it, to acknowledge the bad memories and then move on to revel in the good. "She wasn't drunk or anything bad. She wasn't like that. She was probably just not paying attention, just lost in her own world."

Emily sighed.

"I don't think I've ever forgiven her for dying so carelessly, even if life was more peaceful with her out of the picture. With just Dad."

Emily rested her head back against his shoulder. He kissed the curve of her neck, dragging out these moments of discovery. Before they moved further into the relationship he planned to start tonight, he needed her to understand him.

"I don't like strong emotions, Emily. I like control."

"I know," she said, her tone filled with dry humor. "Trust me, Salem. I know."

He chuckled, but knew it sounded strained. "Mom's emotions were all over the place. She was larger than life. Laughed harder than others. Cried harder. *Felt* harder."

His lips touched her hair in a featherlight caress. He loved the way she smelled. He'd had a lot of time to think. He'd learned that every moment of life is meant to be grasped with both hands, that every speck of love needed to be acknowledged. Each second appreciated for the wonderful *now* that it was.

He needed Emily in his life. He needed her in his bed, but first…

"When I lose my temper," he whispered against her hair, "it reminds me of her and I wonder if I'm even human."

"You're human, Salem. Not a madman. You had a right to be angry with Justin. You had a right to be angry with Caleb. The things they did were appalling."

"They were, weren't they?"

"Yes." She was emphatic. "I like hearing about you. Tell me more about your mother."

"I was the wrong kind of kid for her. She didn't understand why I liked to read so much. She was the wrong kind of mother for me. I didn't understand why she had to be so busy all the time, but never with stuff that I needed. Never giving me clean clothes, or regular mealtimes."

"She must have thought you were a changeling or something, or that someone had switched babies at the hospital."

"Except I looked too much like her."

Emily lifted her head away from his shoulder and smiled. "Then she must have been a handsome woman."

He smiled. "Yes, she was. I remember that clearly. Aiyana looks a lot like her."

"Are you always angry with her, or do you ever miss her?"

"I miss the times when she did sweet things. Sometimes when I slept I would have dreams of her making sure I was tucked in and of her kissing my forehead. I know now that I have my own children that it was real. They weren't dreams."

"What other kinds of good things did she do?"

"She played a lot of music."

"I like that." He heard a smile in her voice. Of course she would like that his mother loved music.

"What else?" she asked.

"She made the best Halloween costumes. One year, she bought this huge piece of thin foam and cut out two enormous hands. She sewed them together with red yarn using a big blanket stitch, leaving the bottom open so I could pull it over myself.

"She was so proud of her creativity. She laughed and said it was the one and only time she had ever used that stitch since my grandmother taught her how to edge blankets." The memory used to make him sad. Now it filled him with joy.

"She cut a hole in the front for my face and two slits for my arms. On the back, she wrote Gimme Five. All the kids smacked my back all night long, but it was worth it. It was the most original costume in town."

For a long, quiet time he stared into the night.

"She left? Without warning?"

"That part is painful for me. I felt bad for a long, long time after that—thinking that maybe I'd pushed her away." Emily made a sound to object, but he kept talking. "I really pulled inside myself and books. But I think I understand her better now. She was a free spirit, Emily. She should never have married, should never have had a child. I saw so much in that jail cell. I wonder if she felt as trapped by us as I felt by those bars."

An owl hooted nearby. Salem breathed deeply of the peace of the night, celebrating the freedom of being able to do so. "I remembered wonderful things. Every night when I thought about my daughters, I also thought about her, and remembered what was good about her, all that I had forgotten in my bitterness about her leaving."

"Did your mother ever come back home to visit?"

"No. She went to Las Vegas. I can see her there in all of the lights, with all of that noise and music and laughter. She would have loved every gaudy bit of it. About a month after she left, we got word that she'd died."

"So, you really lost her twice."

"I've never thought of it that way before." She'd surprised him with her perception. "Maybe that's why it hit me so hard. For years, I was obsessed with keeping those around me safe. If my mom hadn't left home, she would still be alive."

"But…"

"But only physically. Her spirit would have died, and that would have been a shame."

"Was that what happened to you in jail? This big change? Before, you were annoyed that I'd bought the girls a karaoke machine."

"The jail cell was too quiet, like living with sensory deprivation. All of my life, I've wanted peace and order, but when I could no longer be with my girls, when I was forced away from them, I missed them so badly, and their spirits and laughter and messiness."

He tightened his arms around Emily. "I missed their crazy emotions and their quirks."

He whispered against her hair, "I missed you, too. I want life, Emily. All of it. I want you."

He turned her around to face him, and then kissed her for long, slow heady moments, as though absorbing her essence, the very heart of Emily Jordan.

"I want to sleep with you tonight, but not in this house while we aren't married."

Her breath hitched. "Are you asking me to marry you?" He heard her hesitation, the fear of believing something that might not be true.

"Yes, Emily, I am."

"Yes, oh yes. A thousand times yes, Salem."

"This isn't very romantic, is it?"

"It's the most romantic proposal I've ever heard."

His heart soared to the heavens, where it kissed the moon and all the stars. If it weren't so late at night, he would hoot and holler.

What could possibly be more romantic than the realization of a dream that had started so many years ago?

SOMETIMES THE LARGE moments could be felt in quiet joy, Emily thought.

She held Salem in her arms, touching his shoulders, breathing in his scent, absorbing his heat. Salem. She kissed him. Couldn't stop. When she came up for air, they were both trembling and breathing hard.

"The girls are young and impressionable," he said, his voice unsteady. "It wouldn't be right to sleep together down the hall."

She'd slept with him in his bed before, the night she

came home with malaria, but tonight Salem wasn't talking about *sleeping*.

"We could go to the B and B, but the town would have a field day with the gossip." He sounded frustrated.

He opened her car door. He was sending her home?

"Salem Pearce, if you think I'm not sleeping with you tonight, somewhere, *anywhere,* you need a lobotomy." Her hands shuddered with the effort not to tear off his clothes.

"My hands are shaking." He held one up. *Shaking* put it mildly. "I want you so badly."

There was no way on earth Emily was *not* spending this night with Salem. "Are you up for an adventure?"

"After the one I just went through, I'm up for *good* adventure."

"Get in the car."

Five minutes later, Emily pulled into her dad's driveway.

They ran around to the back of the house, giggling like children, high on freedom and drunk on love.

She led him to the backyard.

"We can't go in the front door," Emily whispered. "Well, I can, but you can't."

"What can we do? We're not going to make love in the garden shed or the garage."

She squeezed his hand. "No, we aren't." She pointed to the tree outside her back window. "You're going to climb that. I'll go in the front door and go on up to bed."

Salem studied the big, old tree. "It looks sturdy."

"It is. Remember the night I came to see you at the Cathedral when I was sick?"

"Of course."

"Dad's party was on and I didn't want them to catch me sneaking out, so I climbed down the tree."

Salem's hand touched his chest above his heart. "While you were sick? You could have fallen and broken your neck."

Emily grinned. "I didn't."

"You and your reckless ways." The words were critical, his tone was not. In fact, the subtle note in his voice sounded like admiration.

"Think you can climb it?" Emily asked.

"With you up in that bedroom, I'd climb a thread if it would get me to you." He grasped the back of her neck and kissed her long and hard then lingered before pulling away. Oh, he did that well. The temperature of the night soared. "Get yourself into the house and that bedroom."

She laughed.

"I've waited a long time for this, Emily." She couldn't see his face clearly, but the way his body swayed toward her told her everything she needed to know.

She sobered. "Oh, Salem, so have I. Years."

"Go," he whispered. "Hurry."

He grasped the bottom branch of the tree and pulled himself up.

Emily hurried around to the front of the house and let herself in.

"That you, Cody?" her father called from the living room. Thank goodness they hadn't tried to sneak in the front door. They would have been caught.

"Nope. It's me, Dad." Her voice sounded thin and breathy. Would he notice?

"Congratulations on getting Salem out."

"Thanks. I'm bushed. I'm heading up to bed. See you in the morning."

She climbed the first flight slowly then took the second two steps at a time, making sure she closed her door firmly behind her.

Salem was already waiting on the tiny balcony. Emily opened the French doors and he entered, taking her into his arms and squeezing the breath out of her.

They tore at each other's clothes, hot and impatient, eager and horny, like a pair of adolescents. They'd known each other for so long. If the age difference hadn't been so great, they should have been together as teenagers. They should have dated, and had their first kisses and their first sexual encounters with each other.

"Let's make this our first." She meant not just with each other, but their first time with any partner. The only thing that mattered was now.

"Yes," Salem said, as though he'd been reading her mind. Maybe he had. They'd always had that strange connection, as though their souls had known each other in another life. Tonight, they would connect physically. "It's the first of our whole lives together."

Emily heard buttons pinging onto the floor as Salem

tore her blouse from her body. She grasped his head to angle for a deeper kiss and he let her, all while he grappled with the zipper of her pants. She did the same with his, the action slower, more careful, because he was large and full and ready.

After what seemed an eternity, she had him in her hand, the weight of him delicious, and solemn and sturdy like the man.

He grasped her and held her tightly. "Shh. Let me hold you. Give me a second to celebrate this blessing."

Holding her in his strong, quiet way, she absorbed the intensity, the depth of his emotions. Still waters.

Then he moved, backing her up to the bed. She was naked. Somehow, Salem had done that. She was too slow getting his clothes off and shoved his shirt from his shoulders, her hands on his warm skin, her fingers learning the textures of his light dusting of hair, his smooth clavicle, his hard nipples.

He stood and shucked off his pants then came down on top of her, his weight welcome and right.

She opened her legs and he lay between them, where he belonged.

"Salem," she whispered seriously, because she'd come to a terrible realization. "I don't have birth control."

For a moment, he rested his head on her breast then smiled against her skin. "We don't need it."

Caught between panic and joy, she stilled. "Do you mean it?"

"I mean it. I want children with you." He raised

himself onto his hands, arms straight so he could look down on her in the meager moonlight spilling through the window. "I did a lot of thinking in that jail cell. We never had our chance, Emily. Never."

He touched his lips to her forehead. "Our chance—" he ran his lips down the side of her neck "—is—" he took her nipple into his mouth and her back arched off the bed "—now." He entered her and she'd never felt anything more sublime.

Now. Their time was now. At last.

Before now, Emily had had only two partners, a boy in college and Jean-Marc; she'd never made love without a condom, had never experienced skin to skin. To do so with Salem was an honor that left her speechless. The possibility that this loving act might produce a baby was miraculous.

She took her time exploring his body—the Zen of loving Salem, of noting every little detail. The ripple of muscle under skin. The way the hair on his legs rasped the soft flesh of her inner thighs. The silken glide of him inside her. The way their bodies belonged together as much as their hearts did.

Her hand cupped his face while he touched her with respect, and with pent-up longing. The man was a thinker...and made love like one. Slowly. Peacefully. Adoringly.

The wonder of love with Salem flooded her.

The beauty of his body, the strength of his affection, the tenderness of his touch...and then the passion of his lovemaking...took Emily's breath away.

She'd come home thinking she didn't deserve love, affection or family. She'd been wrong. She loved and gave to others with a generosity that should be acknowledged. She deserved this.

The tenderness of Salem's touch washed away ugly memories of the things she'd done to hold on to a man who hadn't been worth it. Jean-Marc hadn't deserved her. Salem did. With Salem, tawdriness faded and all was beauty, sweetness and then the glorious light of consummation.

They murmured endearments, learned the landscapes of each other's bodies with questing hands. Throughout the night, Emily found peace, self-forgiveness. Happiness.

Toward dawn, she fell asleep in Salem's arms.

"EMILY-Y-Y-Y-Y?"

Emily rolled over and murmured sleepily, snuggling close to the deliciously warm body in bed with her.

What? Who?

"Emily-y-y-y-y."

Yikes. Laura!

She had Salem in her bed, both of them as naked as the day they were born.

Salem shot up and so did she with a finger to her lips. *Don't make a sound.* Sunlight shone through the windows, her alarm clock said it was eight in the morning, and Laura was calling her from the bottom of her stairs.

The panic shooting through Salem's dark eyes was

the same one that raced through her. Oh, crap. Maybe Laura wouldn't come up. But if Emily told her not to, she would know for sure something was up and might even guess Salem was here.

Emily held her tongue and prayed Laura would stay downstairs. Maybe if she just didn't answer, Laura would leave. She lay down and dragged the bedsheet up to cover her head. The situation was just too absurd. She started to laugh.

Salem pulled the sheet down so he could see her face. "This isn't funny," he hissed in her ear.

She covered both of them with the sheet and poked his ribs. "It's hilarious," she whispered.

"No, it isn't. I value your father's good opinion. I respect him. I can't be caught in bed with his daughter."

"His daughter is thirty-one years old and has a mind of her own, thank you very much."

"This is still his house. We're under his ro—"

"Emily," Laura called. "Can you hear me?"

"Yes." The one word was full of banked laughter.

"I have eggs and bacon for breakfast," Laura said. "Come on down while everything's hot. Bring Salem with you."

Laura's throaty, infectious laugh rang up the stairs before she closed the door. Emily's jaw dropped. How did she *know?* Emily laughed harder.

Salem groaned. "How does she know I'm here?"

"I don't have a clue." It was too funny, and embarrassing, to be caught like a pair of kids.

"I feel like a teenager doing something wrong."

"The only thing wrong, Salem, is that I don't have my own apartment to bring you to. Besides, you don't look like a teenager."

He looked all man, with the bedsheet crumpled around his waist. Sunlight toasted his skin to golden honey and highlighted his broad shoulders and chest. If not for Laura, and probably her father, knowing that Salem was here, Emily would be feasting on the man, would be running her palms over him with her own brand of sunlight. Oh, he was beautiful. Prettier than anything she'd seen during all of her travels.

Nothing and no one compared to Salem. "I love you."

He gave her one of his smoldering looks and Emily had to get out of bed before she ravished him.

She threw back the bedclothes and said, "Let's shower."

Salem perked up. "Together?"

"Yes, but no funny business. Not with my parents downstairs."

"I want more of you, Emily. I want forever."

His earnest expression nearly brought her to tears. "Me, too," she whispered. Nothing more needed to be said.

After their shower, they joined the family at the kitchen table.

Her father stood and shook Salem's hand. "Congratulations, Salem."

Salem's startled gaze shot to Emily and she could

see the wheels spinning. *He's congratulating me for sleeping with his daughter?*

Laughter sparkled in her dad's eyes. "I *mean* I'm glad they found the right man and that you're off the hook for murder. Sit down."

Salem moved to stand behind one of the chairs. "I want you to know, sir, my intentions toward your daughter are honorable."

"I never assumed they weren't. Emily's a grown woman and can make her own decisions, but I appreciate your concern. Now sit. And relax."

Salem did as he was told and Emily sat beside him. As a father of two daughters, this had to be hard for him. As for Emily, she was too high on love and happiness to care what anyone thought. This had been a long time coming. She and Salem deserved their chance together.

"Thank you for the lawyer and the private investigator." Salem sounded stiff and formal. "I'll pay back every penny."

Her dad waved that away. "Nope. I wanted to do it. You're our friend, Salem. Practically a member of the family."

He raised his eyebrows at Emily and she nodded.

Her father's satisfied smile spoke volumes. "It's about time."

She noticed Pearl's gaze resting on her. A gentle smile curved her lips. She brought her hand up to give Emily a thumbs-up and they laughed together. Okay, she had the family's approval. No hurdles to jump over here. But what about Salem's daughters? It was one thing to hang around and teach them music, but would they want her as a stepmother?

Cody helped Laura pass around bacon and eggs then sat on Salem's other side.

"Hey, man, really good news you got out of jail yesterday. Listen, how would you feel about me asking your daughter out?"

"On a date?"

"Yes, he means on a date." Emily bit back a *duh*. Salem was brand-new to this business. He was probably scared to death of the whole process.

"I'll take care of her, Salem. I'm nothing like Justin."

"Aw, I know that, Cody. It's just…I can't believe my girls are old enough to date. If I trust anyone, it's you. If she wants to go out with you, it's okay with me."

Cody wolfed down his breakfast then excused himself from the table. Emily heard him trot upstairs. A few minutes later, he came back downstairs ready for school with a satisfied grin on his face.

"Couldn't wait until you got to school to ask her, could you?" Emily asked.

"Didn't want to take the chance I'd miss her. She said yes. We're going out tonight."

I never doubted you, Cody, Emily thought.

Laura clapped her hands. "So…any good news you'd like to share, E-mi-ly?"

"Yes, Lau-ra, Salem and I are getting married."

After all the hooting and high-fiving, Laura asked, "So, when can we start planning the wedding?"

"Just as soon as I get back from the Sudan," Emily said, spreading jam on her toast.

The startled hush around the table had her glancing up.

"What? Oh, I didn't tell you. I have to go back to take care of the prayer book."

"What prayer book?"

She finally felt free enough to tell the whole story. When she finished, Salem asked, "Why do you have to go back? Why can't Penny take care of it?"

The temperature in the room had dropped. She explained about the young PhD student, about her attempted suicide, about how Emily felt she had to finish this with Jean-Marc, to somehow make Jean-Marc accountable for his actions.

Salem stood and strode to the front door. She caught up to him just as he stepped outside.

"Salem, listen, please." She described how cathartic dealing with her old demons at school had been and how she needed to do the same here.

He didn't respond.

"You were right last year when you said I was running away. I'm not running this time. I'm finishing something."

She thought about his mother leaving him and never coming back. "I will be back, Salem." She grasped his arms. "Look at me."

When he did, she said, "I'm asking you to trust me.

I have so much to come back to now. I'm finishing an ugly chapter of my life and coming back to the best thing that has ever happened to me. You."

He stared into her eyes for a moment, and then took her into his arms, pressing her heart against his.

"Trust me," she whispered.

"Yes."

SALEM STEPPED INTO his house with Emily, still unsettled by her news. He didn't want her to go back, not because he didn't trust her, but because he never wanted to let her go again. What if her plane crashed? What if war broke out while she was there? What if she never came back to him?

Mika and Aiyana entered the foyer, ready for school.

"Hey, guys. Where were you?" Mika slung a knapsack over her shoulders.

Oh, boy, Salem thought, how does a father answer that question when the answer is *I was with this lovely woman beside me, and we weren't playing cards.* He'd tried to set a good example for his daughters in every area. It was beyond surreal that Emily's family had taken the situation in stride, but they were all older than his girls.

"Mika," Aiyana said, her face a study in older-sister patience, "they were with each other."

"I can see that. I meant where were they? Did you guys go out for breakfast? Didn't you bring back any of Laura's cinnamon buns?"

Aiyana nudged her out the door. "Mika, you and I need to have a serious talk about the birds and the bees."

"Oh, they were doing *that?* Why didn't they just say so?"

Salem's mouth dropped open. His younger daughter was okay with her dad doing *that* with a woman who wasn't her mother, and to whom he wasn't married?

Aiyana sent him a smile and a tiny thumbs-up before turning onto the sidewalk to head to school. Well, that was two thumbs-up. First Pearl and now Aiyana, and not a single objection from anyone.

"Does all of this seem really strange?" Salem scratched his head.

"Sort of like a magnetic flip of the earth? As though everything you knew to be real is all new and different? Yeah."

"Is the world crazy, or is it just me?"

"Everyone's happy for us, Salem. I guess they all saw it coming. That's why they aren't shocked."

"But do teenagers really see sex so casually these days?"

Emily raised her eyebrows.

"Was it casual sex?" At the voice behind him, Salem spun around.

"Dad." Salem expelled a sharp breath and his dad grinned at his exasperation. "You aren't supposed to be listening in on private conversations."

"Then don't have them in the hallway of the house I live in." The exaggerated circumflex of his father's eyebrows mocked Salem. He held used dish towels and dishcloths. "Everybody is happy, eh?" His chuckle followed him to the laundry room at the back of the house.

"Life is strange, Salem. Let's just accept all of the goodwill and move on." The tone of Emily's voice changed, became speculative. "Are you working today?"

"I don't have to. No."

"We can't go back to my place, not with Pearl and Laura, and maybe my dad, there."

Oh. He knew what she meant. Making love. He wanted more, too. Desperately.

Salem's father came out of the laundry room at the back of the hallway and marched to the front door. "Just remembered I was supposed to meet a bunch of the guys at the bakery for coffee. I'll be gone for hours."

Wily old coot was giving them privacy. "How did you hear that all the way down there when most of the time you don't catch a word I say?"

His dad sat on the bench beside the door to tie his shoelaces. "Don't always want to hear you. This time I did." He opened the front door. "I'll bring Ansel those cinnamon buns he wanted."

As though he could see Salem's guilt kick in, he said, "He's my friend, Salem. I want to take care of him." He winked at them. "Have fun."

"Well," Emily said when the door closed behind him, "I guess we have as much encouragement as we're ever going to need. Race you to your room."

Salem won, but only because he lifted Emily into his arms while she squealed, and carried her up the stairs. Once in his room, he tossed her onto the bed. On his pillow, her hair burst into rays of sunshine and shadow around her face.

He undressed slowly, taking his time because he liked the way she smiled as she watched him.

They made love in the morning sunlight streaming through the window and long past lunchtime, their only hunger their desires for each other.

In time, they showered and dressed and prepared to greet the girls when they came home from school. They found his father sleeping in the armchair downstairs, the footrest out and an afghan across his chest.

He snorted and awoke, then shook himself. His spine popped.

"You awake, old man?" Salem asked with deep satisfaction in his voice.

"Am now." He tossed off the blanket and flipped the lever to put the chair upright. "Couldn't take my nap upstairs. Too noisy."

Emily gasped and her cheeks turned pink. *Gotcha,* Salem thought, *now you know how I felt this morning with your family.*

A smile lurked in his dad's eyes.

"He's pulling your leg, Emily. This is his favorite chair. He sleeps here every evening. Not usually in the afternoon, though. You okay?"

"Yep. Didn't sleep as well at the res as usual. Too worried. All is good now."

Salem didn't think he would ever be able to relax completely where those he loved were concerned. Maybe he was destined to be a worrier.

Aiyana and Mika came home and joined them in the living room.

"Hey, girls, sit down." He waited until they were settled on the sofa. "How would you feel if Emily and I got married?"

His dad nodded, a sage old Indian seer. He'd probably seen the whole thing coming. Heck, he'd encouraged it, hadn't he?

She's *fun* trouble, he'd said, and he was so right. Emily brought color and music and life into his world.

Mika squealed, because that's what Mika always did when she got excited. Aiyana's reaction was more subdued, but no less gratifying. In her smile, Salem saw approval, love and hope.

They'd both weathered their storms. They couldn't have done it without the woman by his side.

AIYANA DRESSED WITH the same care she might use had the president invited her to the White House. Cody had called before school to ask her out on a date. A real one. He was taking her to dinner to celebrate her dad's exoneration.

The dress Dad bought her fit perfectly. She slipped into her black ballet flats. The diamond necklace he'd also bought her sparkled on her dresser. Dad was right. It was probably the smallest diamond on earth, but she loved it. After she put it on and finished applying makeup, a light touch of mascara and pink lip gloss, she studied herself in the mirror.

Never again would she put on more makeup than she liked just because she thought a boy might want it, or because it was fashionable. Justin might be a boy she would always remember with distaste, but he'd taught her a lot without meaning to. He'd taught her to be herself and to not dress for others. If a boy couldn't accept her for who she was then he wasn't worthy of her.

She dusted the tiniest bit of blush on her high cheekbones, the ones she'd inherited from her father. There. Done. She looked good, but still like herself. No more pretending. No more striving to be someone she wasn't.

The doorbell rang and her pulse fluttered in her throat. She might have more confidence since that debacle with Justin, but come on, she was going out on a date with Cody Jordan. She sighed, because it was hard not to. Cody. Never in her wildest dreams...

When he saw her coming downstairs, Cody's face lit up.

"Wow. You look gorgeous."

It warmed her heart. Yes, she had more self-confidence, and yes, she was sure of who she was and that she was worthy of *any* boy, but Cody's smile made her feel amazing.

Handsome in a plain white dress shirt and dark jeans, Cody escorted her to the car and opened her door.

"I mean it, Aiyana. You look incredible."

"Thanks. My dad got me this dress and the necklace for my birthday. It's the first really grown-up things he's ever bought me. He says the diamond's too small, but I love it." She was babbling. Why, oh why, did she have to be so lame? Despite the confidence, let's face it, she was still a nerd.

"Aiyana?"

"Yes?"

"Relax. There's no pressure with me. We're just having a nice dinner together. Okay?"

The tension in her shoulders eased. "Okay. This is my first real date. I don't count that disaster with Justin. It's lame that I'm so nervous, isn't it?"

"Everyone has a first date sometime in their lives."

"I can't believe you were ever nervous on a date."

"Are you kidding? My first date was with a girl a year older than me who I had the hots for like crazy, and I was terrified."

"Even you?" She giggled. "You mean you didn't come out of your mother's womb full of self-confidence and swagger?"

Oh, she liked the way his lips looked when he grinned. "I had my awkward phase."

"No way. I grew up in this town and watched you growing up. You've never been awkward. You've always been gorgeous." She clapped a hand to her mouth.

Cody laughed. "Hey, thanks, Aiyana."

She was horrified. "I can't believe I said that out loud."

"You've been watching me, eh?" His voice took on

a speculative note beneath the humor. "I noticed you, too, once you started to grow up. I like how unique you are."

Unique. Yeah, she liked that. Aiyana Pearce was unique, and there was nothing wrong with that.

At the restaurant, Cody behaved like a perfect gentleman. He even pulled out her chair before she sat down. She felt like a grown-up.

"What do you think of your dad and my sister hooking up?"

"I like it. It's more than a hookup. They're getting married."

"It's awesome, huh? They belong together. I think they'll be good for each other. You don't have to answer if you don't want to, but how do you feel about Emily as a stepmother?"

"I think she's amazing. I love her already. I think she'll make a great mother."

"And if they have more children you won't be jealous?"

"No. I'm too old for that. Besides, I had Dad's love for a lot of years. I don't think he would love another baby more than he loves me and Mika. It will be really cool to see him happy again."

They talked about what happened with Justin, and about how Emily had helped her to see it had nothing to do with her heritage.

"I'm surprised you thought it did."

"I've always been embarrassed about how different I look from, you know, the Brittanys and Madisons of the world."

"I'll tell you a secret. Brittany and Madison at school?"

She nodded.

"Dead boring to date. They think the sun rises and sets on them. All they talk about is themselves and gossip. It's a relief to go out with someone who isn't totally self-centered."

"They're older than me. I don't know them well."

"Trust me. You're easier to spend time with. You should celebrate who you are and try not to envy other girls. You're pretty and smart."

They toasted with their sodas.

Aiyana reached into her purse and took out the leather band she'd bought for Cody. "I wanted to get you something for helping me at school. I don't know if you'll like it."

He opened the box. "Hey. Cool. This is great." He put it on right away. It looked really good on his wrist, totally masculine.

"I didn't know if I should give you jewelry. Even saying the word *jewelry* when it's a gift for boy is strange, but I really liked it and—"

"Aiyana?"

"Yes?"

He squeezed her hand. "It's great. Thank you."

When Cody drove her home, he said, "Do you want to hang out this summer? I'll be going away in the fall, and you're only sixteen, so it's not like we can get all serious, but I like spending time with you."

"I'd like that, Cody. I honestly don't want to have sex with any guy. I realized with Justin I'm really not ready. I want to wait until I'm positive that's what I want to do." That she could even utter the word *sex* in a conversation with Cody said a lot about what a good job he'd done to help her relax this evening. The big thing, though, was realizing how true it was. She wasn't ready for sex and wasn't ready to settle for just any guy. She would know when both the time and the boy were right. She was sure of it.

Cody nodded. "Good. Glad to hear it. In the meantime, let's hang out."

He walked her to the door, gave her a chaste kiss on her cheek then said good-night.

She watched him drive away.

He'd given her a gift.

Celebrate who you are.

What a crazy beginning to her summer, from the lowest low to the highest high. There wasn't going to be a big romance with Cody—and that was okay—but he had confirmed what she was only just beginning to learn about herself. She was going to hang out with him all summer, with the coolest guy around, and not have to worry about impressing him—he already liked her the way she was—and not have to worry about him pressuring her to have sex. What could be better?

That night, she slept without a single concern. Her dad was back home with his family where he belonged, and she felt good about herself and her heritage. Her last thought before falling asleep was, *It's okay to be me.*

CHAPTER THIRTEEN

SALEM STOOD IN the sheriff's office with Emily beside him, and stared at Matt Breslin with his mouth open, having trouble taking in what the deputy had just said. Not deputy anymore, though. Sheriff.

"I'm serious." Matt leaned back in the chair and responded to Salem's disbelief. "I'm sheriff. Both White and his son were arrested first thing this morning, White on charges of assault and Justin for rape. It's good to get him off the streets."

Despite Matt's self-satisfied smile at being promoted, his sentiment was sincere. They'd had some good talks while Salem was incarcerated. Matt was an honest man. He liked to see justice done.

"What about Brent? He stood and watched White beat me without lifting a finger."

Matt leaned forward, dropping the front feet of the chair to the floor. "He's been charged as an accessory."

Good. As it should be. Their laws had been invented to keep civilized people...civilized. What had happened to Salem had been anything but.

He held up the box of pastries from the bakery. "I brought these for Ansel. May we see him?"

Matt's expression became compassionate. "'Fraid

not. He isn't here. We had him transferred to the hospital in Denver during the night. He was in bad shape. He isn't long for this world, Salem."

So, it was that close. A heaviness settled over him. The man had been like a second father to him. Yes, he was old. Yes, except for his daughter's tragic death, his life had been long and good.

Even so, his imminent passing filled Salem with sadness.

He handed the pastries to Matt. "Enjoy these and congratulations on the promotion."

"I might not stay on as sheriff. There will have to be an election."

"You'll win. You're a good guy and everyone likes you. I'll vote for you. You'll do a good job here, Matt."

"Thanks, Salem."

Out on the sidewalk, Emily took his hand. "I'm so sorry, Salem."

"I'm going to visit him in the hospital."

"Do you want me to come?"

"I think I'll take my dad with me. Can you get yourself home?"

"Of course."

A little over an hour later, Salem entered Ansel's room with his father by his side.

Ansel barely made a dent in the covers of the bed. His body was wasting away rapidly.

Salem stood on one side and his dad on the other.

"How are you doing, Ansel?"

He opened his eyes and smiled when he saw them. "Happy now. Kathy came to me last night."

Kathy, his first wife, dead at least forty years.

"She told me it's time to join her. She looked beautiful, just like when I married her."

Salem's hand convulsed on the blanket. He wasn't good with people leaving.

"You will be happy to see her, eh?" Good old Dad, always looking for the positive side.

"Yes. It won't be long." His clawed hand took Salem's. "Tell me about Annie. Tell me your memories."

Salem did, for hours, only the good memories. His father shared his memories, too. When they left late in the afternoon, Ansel had a smile on his face.

In the morning, Emily left for the Sudan.

That afternoon, Ansel died.

DESPITE SWEATING HANDS and a thunderous heartbeat at the airport in Khartoum, Emily made it into the Sudan without incident, which said volumes about Jean-Marc. He'd slandered her all over the internet, and to everyone within the archeological community, but he hadn't reported her to the authorities. What was he hiding that he didn't want the authorities to know about?

All of that mad worry for nothing.

The doors of the airport opened and belched her into the heat and dust of Khartoum. In her few short weeks at home in the cooler summer weather of Colorado, she'd forgotten about the climate here. Already she could feel her sinuses drying out. The incessant distant noise, the hum of five million people in a flat, spread-out city landscape that encompassed Khartoum proper, Khartoum North and Omdurman, bombarded her.

The airport had originally been built south of Khartoum, but population growth and development had swallowed it and currently it sat in the city center.

She took a taxi to her former apartment building, not because there was a place there for her to stay, but because Penelope lived there. And Jean-Marc.

As the driver navigated the streets, Emily remembered every place she'd visited in the city—the Souq al-Arabi with its pervasive scent of exotic spices, and the al-Mograri—the Confluence—where the Blue and White Nile rivers meet. At the University of Khartoum, she and Jean-Marc had once given a lecture to students thirsty for knowledge.

Yes, there was something to be said for all the experiences she'd had abroad, as interesting as they were, and she would treasure these memories always, but already she missed home and Salem, Aiyana and Mika, and her family.

Penelope greeted her at the door of her apartment.

Emily stepped into her friend's welcoming arms. "Oh, it's good to see you, Pen. I've missed you."

She hugged Les, too. "You, too. I missed you both. Tell me all the latest news. What work have you been doing?"

"The dig is closed, Emily. We've been packing. We're going home. The political instability in the region is too dangerous." Penelope led her to their small living room. "I'll make tea and we'll have a chat. Les, get Emily the prayer book, would you?"

When he returned from the bedroom, he handed her the relic wrapped in tissue paper.

"Oh, it survived beautifully," Emily exclaimed.

From the kitchen, Penny called, "Considering how much tape I had to cut through, it's no small wonder."

Emily had missed Penny's laugh, loud and horsey, yes, but from the heart.

Penny carried out a pot of tea and three small cups from the kitchen. "Mint tea okay?"

"Yes. I haven't had a cup since I left."

After the tea had been poured, Penelope leaned against Les's arm laid across the back of the sofa. "So? What's the plan? How are you going to handle this? Does it go straight to the museum or what?"

"I still have a key to Jean-Marc's apartment."

"So?" Les liked his tea boiling hot and had already finished one cup.

"So," Penny said, "she's going to put the book in his apartment." Good old Pen. She got it right away.

"Yes. I formulated the plan during the flight here. After I've planted the relic, I'm going to call the authorities with an anonymous tip that they should search his place."

"Clever, my dear."

"Any idea what his schedule is like these days?"

"When he isn't closing down the dig or doing an

inventory of everything that was collected, he spends his time with Adriana, his latest tart."

Les snorted a laugh and some of his tea back into his cup. "Pen, dear, look what you've made me do." There was laughter in his voice.

Penny got Les a clean cup and filled it with fresh tea. "Let us know if there's anything we can do."

When Emily left amid adjurations to *for God's sake, keep in touch,* she took the elevator to Jean-Marc's apartment on the fourth floor.

Using her key, she cracked the door open, listened and heard nothing. Good. The apartment was empty. She slipped inside. She'd spent many hours here and yet felt no sense of attachment. All she felt for the place and the man now were distaste.

She knew exactly where she wanted to hide the prayer book. Jean-Marc owned an old-fashioned foot-locker. She found it under the bed and pulled it out by one of its leather handles. In remarkably good shape, it was an old officer's locker, with metal stripping along all of the edges.

The lock was large and heavy, but Emily knew he never locked it simply because he had no key. She opened it, and gasped, unwilling to believe at first that she was actually seeing what was there.

Jean-Marc was a thief.

He had pieces in here that should be in the museum with all of the catalogued pieces they'd found in the dig. He'd been squirreling away some of the finds they had all entrusted to him as their leader to submit to the proper authorities. He had abused their trust, and the trust of the host country.

There was no doubt in her mind, *none,* that he planned to spirit these out of the country and sell them. Otherwise, why would they be here in his apartment, illegally? If the authorities found out, he would be thrown into jail. Even if he could talk his way out of charges, his reputation would be ruined. And so…this was the perfect spot for the prayer book.

She slipped it in, closed the lid and eased the box back under the bed. As she did so, the door to the apartment opened and she heard a feminine giggle in the living room along with Jean-Marc's deep laugh.

Balls. Caught. What was she going to do? If Jean-Marc caught her, he would dump the artifacts before she could get the authorities in here to discover them in his possession. She wouldn't let that happen. After what he'd done to her and the many other women, and his shoddy ethics in stealing rare artifacts, he deserved to be punished. Unfortunately, the front door was the only way out of here.

Wait. She glanced at the window. Not the *only* way.

The window was open, letting in the heat of the day. Jean-Marc loved heat, loved having sex that made him sweat. The hotter, the better.

She climbed out onto the small ledge that ran along the side of the building and stood with her back against the stone.

Don't, for the love of God, look down.

The sidewalk, four floors down, wouldn't welcome

her with a nice soft landing. Cripes, she'd hadn't thought when she'd left home that her life might be in danger. She'd thought she might face a jail sentence, but death or disfigurement? No.

Thank goodness Salem couldn't see her now. When she got home, she was *never* taking another risk.

In the distance, the White Nile shone like a jewel. She couldn't appreciate its beauty, or that of the sun glinting from the windows of the modern high-rises along its shores, not when she imagined her body broken on the pavement below.

Her breath came in shallow bursts.

She hated heights. Didn't mind the depths of the earth, or the sea. Would gladly go down in a submarine, or into an underground cave, but she hated heights. Disliked bridges. Had never gone to the top of the Eiffel Tower when she'd visited her mother in Paris.

She sidled away from the window because she could hear them in the bedroom.

"Come on, baby. Screw me good."

How many times had she heard that? He'd left her feeling dirty. Judging by Adriana's breathy moans, the woman had no problem getting down and dirty.

She thought of Salem and the beauty of his lovemaking. As soon as she got home, she was going to grab him and never let go.

Emily continued to sidle away from the window. No sense going to her old apartment. It would have been rented out to someone else immediately after she'd left.

Besides, it was on the far side of the window. Farther along this way, though, was Maria's apartment. If she could make it that far, surely they would let her in.

Tamping down the nausea rising in her throat, she continued to sidle along the ledge. The rough stone beneath her hands abraded her palms. On the street four stories below, someone hailed a cab. Time stretched.

How freaking far was Maria's window? Too far. She wouldn't make it.

She stepped in front of a window and heard a little squeal and then, "Mama, there's a woman in my window."

Maria! Emily had made it.

"It's me. It's me," she whispered frantically. "Maria..."

Emily heard her mother's cry of alarm. "Daniela, it's me. Emily. I need to come inside."

"Mama, it's Emily. She came back."

She felt Daniela's strong fingers grab her legs. "Are you crazy, Emily? What are you doing? Come in. Come in, quickly, before you splatter on the sidewalk below."

Terrible image. A little bile rose into her throat.

She managed to scramble inside, fall in more like, but made it safely. Daniela stood with her hands on her ample hips. "You had better have a good explanation for this."

Emily smiled weakly because she was still trying to control her unruly heartbeat. "May I have a cup of your Egyptian coffee? I need to sit. My knees are shaking. They won't hold me much longer."

"Of course. Come to the living room."

She collapsed onto a pile of colorful cushions on a velvet-covered divan. Maria sat beside her and patted the back of her hand. "You are very brave. I would never go out on a window ledge so high off the ground."

"No. Not brave, Maria. Just desperate." She reached into her bag and took out the postcard with the bear on it she'd carried all the way from Ingram's Pharmacy in Colorado.

Maria took it with a happy little smile.

Daniela returned from the kitchen with two Egyptian coffees for Emily and herself, and fruit juice for her daughter. "Tell me everything."

"Remember you told me that I could do better for myself than Jean-Marc?"

Daniela made a flicking motion with her fingers. "Phht."

"Well, I have." She told her about Salem first, and everything that had happened since she returned to Accord because, despite Daniela's practical nature, she adored a good love story. Then Emily told her about the prayer book and what she had just done with it. "I need to notify the authorities."

Daniela picked up her phone and handed it to Emily. "Screw the bastard."

Maria gasped. "Mama, that's a bad word."

"Yes, it is, and you will never use it. Neither will you tell your father I used it."

A sly grin formed on Maria's otherwise innocent

face. "Remember that doll I saw at the souk? You wouldn't buy it for me yesterday."

"All right, my little blackmailer. Tomorrow we will go out and get it."

Emily phoned the authorities. She stressed they should come immediately, along with a representative from the museum, because the dig had been completed and the crew had booked flights to leave. They said they would come right away.

Grinning, Emily held out her cup. "Another one, please? Do you mind if I wait here for the police to come? I don't want to miss it."

"Yes. I won't miss it, either. Do you know he made a pass at me one day?"

Emily watched Daniela's hips sway as she returned to the kitchen to put on the water to boil. Of course he had. She was a woman, she was beautiful and she was breathing. All attributes Jean-Marc admired greatly.

They heard the fireworks about an hour later, starting with Adriana's screeches. They opened Daniela's apartment door and peeked out. The young student stood in the hallway in her underwear pulling on her clothes while a couple of cops stood and watched, doing nothing to either help her or to avert their gazes.

Then they heard Jean-Marc's bellow.

"He cries like a stuck pig." Daniela characterized it perfectly. "It sounds good on him."

The big, bad bully sounded like a toddler having a tantrum. Like a big baby.

A pair of the local policemen hauled him out of

the apartment with his hands cuffed behind his back. Two more carried out the footlocker. The curator of the museum came out next. Emily and he had always enjoyed a mutual respect. He saw her watching. She winked at him. He understood right away that it had been she who had turned him in. He smiled. There was something to be said for spreading goodwill rather than lording your arrogance over others, as Jean-Marc had done.

At that moment, the man in question spotted her. His face became even redder. "It was her! That woman did this to me. She set me up."

The look that Emily gave the police said, isn't it a shame that he is so crazed that he would blame a lowly woman like me?

The curator smiled behind his hand. He knew who had handled all of the artifacts. He knew who was supposed to have been responsible for bringing every single one to him. There was no chance Jean-Marc had been set up by her or anyone else. He had withheld artifacts illegally.

Just before he followed everyone to the elevator, the curator winked at her.

EMILY COULDN'T WAIT to get home. It had been an exceedingly successful trip. No ties to her old life lingered, no age-old mummy wrapping choked her, not a single regret clouded her judgment, and Jean-Marc was getting his well-deserved comeuppance.

She was free and clear.

She'd brought home a local paper, had stayed around Khartoum long enough for the news to break, to show Salem that she'd destroyed the man who'd hurt her for so many years.

She had vanquished her last bully.

She'd never felt stronger. She had thumbed her nose at all of the bullies of the world and had triumphed. She would never allow it to happen to her again.

Her traveling days were over. She wanted Salem and Aiyana and Mika. She wanted her family. And Salem. She wanted her music students. And most of all, Salem.

Pulling her pashmina out of her knapsack, she wrapped it around her shoulders and settled in for a nap.

She couldn't settle, though, because of images of Salem, beautiful visions of lying with him and holding him.

Out of those wonderful memories came another—of Salem sharing how his mother had left him and his fears that still lingered.

It made sense that he worried about abandonment. To be fair, Emily had come and gone so many times since she'd become an adult. He was still expecting her to go, to leave not only the town, but also him, permanently. The most basic relationship in his life, his first with his mother, had ended in abandonment.

She had seen the fear when she'd told him she was returning to the Sudan. And yet he'd given her the incomparable gift of his trust.

I'm coming home, Salem.
Wait for me.

SALEM WAITED AT the airport holding one single red rose.

While Emily had been gone, Salem had managed, bolstered by her words of love and his memories of their stellar lovemaking, to blast to smithereens his old fears of abandonment and his neurotic need to keep his loved ones close and safe. He had managed to quell doubts and trust that Emily Jordan would come home to him.

He had trusted her, with all of his heart.

Now here she was, coming through customs and then noticing him. Her face lit up with the same love he felt brimming inside him. She was home. Safe.

He drank in the sight of her, her hair and eyes and the tiny freckles on her nose dear and familiar to him, but it was the clear freedom in those eyes that called to him. She'd succeeded. No more strings. No more bullies.

She was free.

He rushed to her and took her into his arms.

"Salem, I—"

"Shh, don't speak." He trembled with his need for her.

"But I need to show you—"

"Quiet. Shh."

"But I have a newspaper."

The woman just wouldn't stop talking. He would

have to shut her up. He kissed her, pouring everything he had into her, every scrap of love, every grain of insecurity, every bit of loneliness he'd felt while she'd been gone—only eight days, but it had been an eternity.

He kissed her until they ran out of air, and then he kissed her some more. Other passengers exiting customs jostled them. Still, they kissed.

Finally, he felt a pair of firm hands on his shoulders. "Dad. Please. You're drawing attention."

He pulled away from Emily, drinking in her flushed cheeks, bright eyes, swollen lips, pretty mouth curled into a satisfied smile.

"Hello, you," she whispered, still in his arms.

"Hello, you." He stepped away from her, but held her hand. Now that she was home, he couldn't *not* touch her. How could he ever release this woman again?

"I missed you." He heard the pain in his voice, as though he'd said, *I was dead while you were gone.* And indeed, part of him had been.

Aiyana jerked Emily away from him. "Cripes, Dad, give the rest of us a chance with her." She hugged Emily and then handed her off to Mika and then to his dad.

Next, Nick, Laura and Emily's siblings took her into the warm embrace of the Jordan family. Salem had been so focused on Emily, and showing her his love, he'd forgotten about everyone else who'd come to see the woman he loved.

THE PEARCES AND JORDANS had two celebrations that summer. Salem graduated, and his family and Emily attended.

In that moment, Salem's life became complete. He'd managed, during his career at the Heritage Center, to bring awareness of his culture to people in general, and pride in the culture to everyone on surrounding reservations.

Now, he would embark on the new career he'd worked his fingers to the bone studying for over the years.

Aiyana held him after the ceremony and whispered, "All of the hard work was worth it. I'm so proud of you, Dad."

What better reward could there possibly be for a man than to hear that from his child?

He cherished his family, and the woman he'd loved for so many years would soon become part of that family.

IN AUGUST, THEY HELD a wedding celebration. Emily couldn't believe they'd managed to pull one together so quickly.

She stood in the huge party room of the resort. Aiyana, Mika and their friends, including some of the girls who'd confronted Sheriff White in his office that day, had decorated to perfection with white and periwinkle blue streamers, small white lights everywhere, and floral arrangements Audrey at The Last Dance had pulled out all of the stops to create.

The wedding cake Laura had made for Emily and Salem shone like a jewel at the head table.

Cody approached, handsome and oh so grown-up in a tux. A minute ago, he'd been dancing with Aiyana.

"Happy, sis?"

"On cloud nine. What are you doing with Aiyana? You two have been hanging around together a lot."

"I figured I wasn't going to start a serious relationship this summer, not with heading to college in the fall."

"So you thought you'd give Aiyana a good experience?"

"Yeah. She deserved a hell of a lot more than Justin for a first date. This way, she's with someone safe, but experiencing all the firsts that can make a shy girl really nervous."

"Firsts? You don't mean…"

"Get your mind out of the gutter. She's only sixteen. I *mean,* first date, first dance with a boy, first kiss. A very innocent, chaste kiss."

Emily hugged him. "Cody, I love you."

"You, too, sis. You've got a good man in Salem. You two have a good life, y'hear."

Emily looked around the room, to find Salem watching her. Her heart filled with joy. Oh, they would have a *very* good life.

SALEM WATCHED EMILY talk to her brother and then search for him at the end of their conversation. She homed in on him with little effort.

It had always been like this. When they were in the same room they had been aware of each other, had known exactly where the other was. For years, they'd been unable to act on their attraction. Their time had finally come.

Salem started across the dance floor toward her.

Everything receded but Emily gazing at him with loving eyes, a confection of white lace covering a body he now knew intimately, and whose every tiny molecule he had loved with care. It would take years to appease his hunger for her. The music faded, and even his daughters' caterwauling with the karaoke machine couldn't intrude when he stared into his wife's lovely eyes.

This had been a long time coming. Everything, his entire life, every moment since she'd walked into his life as a stubborn, feisty twelve-year-old, had been about Emily Jordan. His love had ever and only been, and would forever more be, always Emily.

* * * * *

LARGER-PRINT BOOKS!
GET 2 FREE LARGER-PRINT NOVELS PLUS
2 FREE GIFTS!

HARLEQUIN

super romance

More Story...More Romance

YES! Please send me 2 FREE LARGER-PRINT Harlequin® Superromance® novels and my 2 FREE gifts (gifts are worth about $10). After receiving them, if I don't wish to receive any more books, I can return the shipping statement marked "cancel." If I don't cancel, I will receive 6 brand-new novels every month and be billed just $5.69 per book in the U.S. or $5.99 per book in Canada. That's a savings of at least 16% off the cover price! It's quite a bargain! Shipping and handling is just 50¢ per book in the U.S. or 75¢ per book in Canada.* I understand that accepting the 2 free books and gifts places me under no obligation to buy anything. I can always return a shipment and cancel at any time. Even if I never buy another book, the two free books and gifts are mine to keep forever.

139/339 HDN F46Y

Name _____ (PLEASE PRINT) _____

Address _____ Apt. # _____

City _____ State/Prov. _____ Zip/Postal Code _____

Signature (if under 18, a parent or guardian must sign)

Mail to the **Harlequin® Reader Service:**
IN U.S.A.: P.O. Box 1867, Buffalo, NY 14240-1867
IN CANADA: P.O. Box 609, Fort Erie, Ontario L2A 5X3

Are you a current subscriber to Harlequin Superromance books and want to receive the larger-print edition?
Call 1-800-873-8635 today or visit www.ReaderService.com.

* Terms and prices subject to change without notice. Prices do not include applicable taxes. Sales tax applicable in N.Y. Canadian residents will be charged applicable taxes. Offer not valid in Quebec. This offer is limited to one order per household. Not valid for current subscribers to Harlequin Superromance Larger-Print books. All orders subject to credit approval. Credit or debit balances in a customer's account(s) may be offset by any other outstanding balance owed by or to the customer. Please allow 4 to 6 weeks for delivery. Offer available while quantities last.

Your Privacy—The Harlequin® Reader Service is committed to protecting your privacy. Our Privacy Policy is available online at www.ReaderService.com or upon request from the Harlequin Reader Service.

We make a portion of our mailing list available to reputable third parties that offer products we believe may interest you. If you prefer that we not exchange your name with third parties, or if you wish to clarify or modify your communication preferences, please visit us at www.ReaderService.com/consumerschoice or write to us at Harlequin Reader Service Preference Service, P.O. Box 9062, Buffalo, NY 14269. Include your complete name and address.

HSRLP13R

LARGER-PRINT
BOOKS!

 **HARLEQUIN** *Presents*

PASSION GUARANTEED SEDUCTION

GET 2 FREE LARGER-PRINT
NOVELS PLUS 2 FREE GIFTS!

YES! Please send me 2 FREE LARGER-PRINT Harlequin Presents® novels and my 2 FREE gifts (gifts are worth about $10). After receiving them, if I don't wish to receive any more books, I can return the shipping statement marked "cancel." If I don't cancel, I will receive 6 brand-new novels every month and be billed just $5.05 per book in the U.S. or $5.49 per book in Canada. That's a saving of at least 16% off the cover price! It's quite a bargain! Shipping and handling is just 50¢ per book in the U.S. and 75¢ per book in Canada.* I understand that accepting the 2 free books and gifts places me under no obligation to buy anything. I can always return a shipment and cancel at any time. Even if I never buy another book, the two free books and gifts are mine to keep forever.

176/376 HDN F43N

Name	(PLEASE PRINT)

Address	Apt. #

City	State/Prov.	Zip/Postal Code

Signature (if under 18, a parent or guardian must sign)

Mail to the **Harlequin® Reader Service:**
IN U.S.A.: P.O. Box 1867, Buffalo, NY 14240-1867
IN CANADA: P.O. Box 609, Fort Erie, Ontario L2A 5X3

Are you a subscriber to Harlequin Presents books
and want to receive the larger-print edition?
Call 1-800-873-8635 today or visit us at www.ReaderService.com.

* Terms and prices subject to change without notice. Prices do not include applicable taxes. Sales tax applicable in N.Y. Canadian residents will be charged applicable taxes. Offer not valid in Quebec. This offer is limited to one order per household. Not valid for current subscribers to Harlequin Presents Larger-Print books. All orders subject to credit approval. Credit or debit balances in a customer's account(s) may be offset by any other outstanding balance owed by or to the customer. Please allow 4 to 6 weeks for delivery. Offer available while quantities last.

Your Privacy—The Harlequin® Reader Service is committed to protecting your privacy. Our Privacy Policy is available online at www.ReaderService.com or upon request from the Harlequin Reader Service.

We make a portion of our mailing list available to reputable third parties that offer products we believe may interest you. If you prefer that we not exchange your name with third parties, or if you wish to clarify or modify your communication preferences, please visit us at www.ReaderService.com/consumerschoice or write to us at Harlequin Reader Service Preference Service, P.O. Box 9062, Buffalo, NY 14269. Include your complete name and address.

HPLP13R

ReaderService.com

Manage your account online!

- Review your order history
- Manage your payments
- Update your address

> **We've designed
> the Harlequin® Reader Service
> website just for you.**

Enjoy all the features!

- Reader excerpts from any series
- Respond to mailings and
  special monthly offers
- Discover new series available to you
- Browse the Bonus Bucks catalog
- Share your feedback

Visit us at:

ReaderService.com